R3turnings

Kelly K. Doyle

R3turnings

ISBN: 979-8-9900172-0-7

TABLE OF CONTENTS

ACKNOWLEDGMENTS

Where to begin to thank everyone who has supported me in bringing this book to fruition?

Taking the advice of the King of Hearts (*Alice's Adventures in Wonderland*), I shall "Begin at the beginning, and go on till you come to the end: then stop."

It begins with my siblings, when one night over a family dinner I mentioned that I had always had an idea that I wanted to tell a story uniting these childhood heroines in an adventure. I did not have the vaguest notion of what the plot would be, but the idea was well received, and I was encouraged to give it a try. So here's thanks to my brother John, his wife Eileen, and my sisters, Janet, Maureen and Linda, who have been with me every step of the way since that night with encouragement and advice.

I noodled around for a while, writing fragments, but got nowhere until my old friend, Craig Patrick Browne, who was also working on a writing project, made a pact that we would send each other weekly drafts, sequentially, like an old-time serial. Thanks to you, Craig, my White Knight, I got my first draft done in a year.

I stumbled through a second draft and got some much-needed editing help from my cousin, Amy Stewart, who really helped especially in punching up the chapter headings as well as turning a critical eye on the writing.

Double thanks to my sister Maureen, who introduced me to Deb Peoples writing group. Week after week, chapter by chapter, they listened, critiqued, and got me to what I believed was my final draft.

Thinking I was ready to try and publish, I queried agents and investigated self-publishing options. In formatting the book for submissions, I found even more small corrections or edits.

And now a big thanks to Claire Doyle Ragin, my lifelong friend, who did the final editing pass, and has used her graphic skills to create the beautiful front cover and format the copy.

And to Bruce Goren, my life partner, who spent a year eating casseroles during the first draft writing, as I would come home from work each night with my head full of ideas, throw something on a pan and write for the 45 minutes it took to cook. Bruce gets thanks also for his patient coaching and editing of the audiobook recording.

Thanks to my children, Greg and Sabrina, for supporting me all through this process.

And I have to give a very special thanks to my parents, Jack and Eileen Kramer, who allowed me to sleep with the window open a crack, even in the dead of winter, just in case Peter decided to come for me.

AUTHOR'S NOTE

I am the oldest of five children; with ten years separating me from my youngest sibling, I naturally helped out, especially with the baby. I often read to Linda, becoming quite talented at giving "voices" to characters. I would make up tales. Here began my love of storytelling. The story I am proudest of from my youth is not written down, as I created an oral urban legend.

There was an old graveyard behind our house. One particular grave has a bust of a lovely young woman, looking to the sky. I told the younger children she had been buried alive! If you put your ear to her neck, you could hear her faint call. Imagine my delight, twenty years later when one of my nieces, with full sincerity, repeated this very same legend to me!

My book has been in my heart since childhood. Now is my time to tell it.

CHARACTERS AND PLACES

Most of the people you will meet here appear in one or more of the original stories which inspired this book. For those who may not have read them, here is a cast list.

Wonderland: A strange and sometimes confusing place, accessed via a rabbit hole. There is a strict royal hierarchy, and social structure based on the suits of playing cards. One must be very careful about what one consumes. Size is flexible here.

- Alice Liddell: A curious and impulsive little girl, who often finds herself in trouble after giving in to one or another of these traits
- White Rabbit: A rather well dressed and somewhat pompous bunny, overly concerned with punctuality
- Caterpillar: A hookah-smoking mycologist, generous with advice
- Cheshire Cat: A helpful feline, apt to appear just when he is needed, and to disappear when done
- Duchess: A friendly, though somewhat scatterbrained person, always willing to welcome a stranger
- Cook: Companion to the Duchess, an excellent chef, occasionally prone to overseasoning and tossing the crockery
- Pig Boy: Child of the Duchess, who seems to morph between pig and child, depending on the amount of pepper used in a dish
- Mary Ann: Housemaid to the White Rabbit, who bears no resemblance to Alice
- Playing Cards (suits): Royal guards and inept gardeners
- Playing Cards (royalty): Kings and Queens, rulers of Wonderland, fond of holding trials, croquet matches and occasional executions

Looking Glass: Next door to Wonderland, and laid out like a chessboard, with movement somewhat restricted. Chess pieces make up the governing body. Writing poetry and its interpretation are the national pastimes.

- Alice Liddell, again: The same curious child who steps through a mirror onto a chessboard who begins as a pawn, and successfully crosses to become a queen
- Talking Flowers: Silly, vain things, who talk much, but are often argumentative
- White Knight: A very helpful chess piece
- Humpty Dumpty: Like the nursery rhyme says, a large and intelligent egg

OZ: Magical land where animals talk, magic is real and almost anything can be alive, including scarecrows, glass cats and other normally inanimate objects. Currently in a state of turmoil due to an attempted coup.

- Dorothy Gale: Brave Kansas farm girl, who has made several visits to Oz, eventually settling there. (Appears in *The Wonderful Wizard of Oz, Ozma of Oz, Dorothy and the Wizard in Oz, The Road to Oz, The Emerald City of Oz, Tik-Tok of Oz, The Tin Woodman of Oz, The Lost Princess of Oz, The Magic of Oz,* and *Glinda of Oz*)
- Ozma: Fairy Princess and the true ruler of Oz. Missing for many years, during which the Wizard ruled Oz, she was rescued and assumed the throne. Dorothy is one of her dearest friends, and so she made her a princess as well. (Appears in *The Marvelous Land of Oz, Ozma of Oz, Dorothy and the Wizard in Oz, The Road to Oz, The Emerald City of Oz, The Patchwork Girl of Oz, Tik-Tok of Oz, The Tin Woodman of Oz, The Lost Princess of Oz, The Magic of Oz, The Lost Princess of Oz,* and *Glinda of Oz*)
- Gnome King: Ruggedo, also known as Roquat the Red, would-be king of Oz, who lives underground and rules the Gnomes. He is terrified of eggs, but little else, and continually tries to take over Oz. (Appears in *Ozma of Oz, The Emerald City of Oz, Tik-Tok of Oz,* and *The Magic of Oz*)
- Cowardly Lion: Early companion of Dorothy, a courageous creature, who acts bravely despite his very real fears. (Appears

in *The Wonderful Wizard of Oz, Ozma of Oz, The Road to Oz,* and *Glinda of Oz*)

- The Wizard: Oscar Zoroaster, a circus magician who came to Oz in a hot air balloon. Using his tricks, he was able to rule in Ozma's absence, but gave up the throne and unsuccessfully attempted to return Omaha. He eventually settled in Oz. (Appears in *The Wonderful Wizard of Oz, Dorothy and the Wizard in Oz, The Road to Oz, The Emerald City of Oz, The Lost Princess of Oz,* and *The Magic of Oz*)

- Scarecrow: First companion of Dorothy, famed for his incredible intelligence (once the Wizard made him so sharp) (Appears in *The Wonderful Wizard of Oz, Dorothy and the Wizard in Oz, The Road to Oz, The Marvelous Land of Oz, The Emerald City of Oz, The Scarecrow of Oz* and *Glinda of Oz*)

- Tin Man: Nick Chopper, a human woodsman who suffered multiple accidental amputations due to an evil witch enchanting his axe, until his body was entirely replaced by tin prosthetics. At first lacking a heart, once he acquired one, he became the most sentimental and caring being in Oz. (Appears in *The Wonderful Wizard of Oz, Dorothy and the Wizard in Oz, The Patchwork Girl of Oz, The Marvelous Land of Oz, Ozma of Oz,* and *The Tin Woodman of Oz*)

- Glinda: A powerful Sorceress, known as Glinda the Good, or the Good Witch of the South, she protects all of Oz's people. It was she who first created the Water of Forgetfulness, used to make the enemies of Oz forget their bad intentions. (Appears in *The Wonderful Wizard of Oz, The Marvelous Land of Oz, The Emerald City of Oz, The Road to Oz, The Lost Princess of Oz* and *Glinda of Oz*)

- Jellia Jam: A servant girl in the palace of the ruler of the Emerald City, she is kind and cheerful, and a great favorite of Ozma. (Appears in *The Wonderful Wizard of Oz, The Marvelous Land of Oz, Dorothy and the Wizard in Oz,* and *The Road to Oz*)

- Eureka the Kitten: Brought to Oz by Dorothy, Eureka chose to remain in Oz as it was so much fun to talk. Originally white, she now looks pink due to Oz's magic. (Appears in *Dorothy and the Wizard in Oz* and *Glinda of Oz*)

- Glass Cat: Originally a glass figurine, she was brought to life by the Magician Dr. Pipt to test a magic powder. She is proud

of her brains, which can be seen whirling about like pink marbles through her glass head, and can be quite vain and contrary (Appears/created in *The Patchwork Girl of Oz*)
- Soldier with the Green Whiskers: Guardian of the Gates of Oz, He appears as a minor character in many of the Oz books, always on guard at the gates of the Emerald City

Neverland: An ever-changing island, which usually only comes to children when they are asleep, and it holds whatever adventure they are dreaming of, and home to the fairies.
- Wendy Darling Winthrop: Eldest daughter of the Darling family, a loving yet practical girl, who enjoys storytelling
- John Darling: Second child of the Darling family, the eldest boy, inclined to be a bit pompous and bossy at times
- Michael Darling: Youngest child of the Darling family, a sweet and sensitive child
- Margaret Winthrop: Granddaughter of Wendy, daughter of a Lost Boy and Wendy's daughter Jane
- Tinker Bell: A fairy who mends pot and pans. Friend to Peter Pan, she can be kind and helpful, but also jealous and mean, as such tiny creatures can usually only hold one thought or feeling at a time.
- Lost Boys: Boys who are so foolish as to fall out of their carriages or get lost in some other way, they are picked up and taken by Peter Pan to the Neverland. This never seems to happen to girls.
- Mr. Smee: An oddly loveable and gentle pirate, once part of the notorious Captain's Hook's crew, he is loved by children and is the only pirate who does not seem to frighten them.
- Tiger Lily: Princess of the native people of Neverland, she is a proud yet cold warrior, a loyal friend once you have won her trust, who keeps her feelings well hidden
- Peter Pan: A brave yet careless boy who has never grown up. A friend to fairies, enemy of pirates and leader of the Lost Boys

PROLOGUE

You know these women. At least, you think you do. The truth is, when you knew them, they were girls, and you are likely looking back at them through the misty eyes of nostalgia, coupled with some forgetfulness of the details of actual, and truly dangerous, adventures these three women had as children.

And don't forget, when all those things happened, the oldest of them was likely no more than ten. All three returned safe, and seemingly undamaged. But were they, really?

Imagine, a girl of ten or less, faced with the possibility of beheading. Or another, becoming a surrogate mother to a ragtag troupe of boys, on a dangerous island made from the fantasies and nightmares of sleeping children. Imagine a girl, orphaned, and once having found a new family, is then swept away from her uncle and aunt to a strange and beautiful place, where she finds friends, but also finds fearsome enemies. Imagine that this girl, (no more than ten, I remind you) has to become a heroine and save her friends, not once, but many times over.

Imagine magic is everywhere. (It is, you know.)

Now imagine what it must have been like to return home. Are you believed? Was it real? How do you go back to school, to chores, to dull, dull real life? You find a way, but it is not a perfect way. There is guilt, regret and sometimes, a longing to return.

You think these stories have ended. You think you know the endings. The stories of Wendy, Alice and Dorothy are not over. Here is what happens next.

CHAPTER ONE

WENDY AT THE WINDOW

Standing in the darkened room, a few feet from the nursery window, Wendy looked out at the clear, cold night. The cloudless sky was filled with stars, with even the faintest ones twinkling clearly, no moon to dim their shine. She searched the expanse for the right one.

You never forget how to fly, or the feeling of flying. You never could, she thought. Even with her arms around herself, she was chilled, although the embers of the dying fire in the hearth still warmed the room.

Just think, wonderful, lovely thoughts, and up you go, she said to herself, desperately hoping that it would still work.

But there are no lovely thoughts for Wendy now, for she is long past the age when she might have reasonably had a chance to fly once more. Worse, she is wracked with fear, worry and an overwhelming sense of urgency. And yet…could she fly again? She had to fly. She must fly.

Wendy shook her head and tried to clear her mind of all the stray thoughts…her overwhelming anxiety, her suffocating fear, and she fixed all her attention on her granddaughter. That might be the one lovely thought that would get her there.

"Margaret," she had whispered. Fixing the child's smile in her mind, she centered her concentration on the image of Margaret, dancing Margaret, laughing Margaret, Margaret eating an ice cream cone, Margaret kissing her cheek.

Wendy took a deep breath and closed her eyes and advanced toward the window. Shuffling her bare feet forward, not looking down, she blindly moved forward until she felt the window's edge with the toes of her right foot. She moved the other foot forward till she was right up against the glass of the French windows.

She found the latch with her fingers and opened her eyes. She did not look down, but gazed steadfast at the night sky, looking for one very particular star. This star was part of no constellation ever recorded by any civilization, nor recorded on any astronomical map. It is mostly invisible to adults, but every child can find it easily.

Wendy had searched the sky, until tears began to cloud her vision. She started to wipe them away with the hem of her nightgown, but then reached into the pocket of her robe for a handkerchief. In the pocket she found one of Margaret's hair ribbons and dabbed at the tears with it instead. She looked up once more, and suddenly she fixed on it, alone in its quadrant save for a companion star, faint, but still visible, just to the right.

She hesitated for just a moment, but then she pulled open the windows. The cold blast of air which slapped her face, mixed with the dampness of low fog kissing her cheeks, momentarily caused her to take a step backwards. Was she crazy?

"No, I am not," she had said out loud, sounding braver than she felt, and stepped onto the ledge.

The soft grey fog had begun to creep up past the window while she had hesitated and obscured the fainter stars. Frantically, she waved her arm as if to clear away the mist, trying in vain to see the second star on the right once again through the insistent haze. There it was!

She placed one bare foot on the ledge, and then the other. Then, just as suddenly as the cold had slapped her face a few minutes before, strong, gentle hands pulled her back. She cried, she fought, but at sixty years old, she was not strong enough to break free, and now the pure image she had been holding in her mind of Margaret was muddied, muted with the unexpected attack. It slipped away from her.

She collapsed, sobbing, sinking into waiting arms, and then she seemed to lose consciousness, or at least her will to continue. She lay limp in her captor's grasp and closed her eyes.

CHAPTER TWO

WENDY IN THE HOSPITAL

Wendy awoke, groggy and achy. She looked around, and saw that she was in a strange place, a strange bed. There was an antiseptic smell, and a ticking noise, but not like a clock, something different. She had something taped to the back of her hand, and it stung a bit. Then it came to her. This was a hospital room. But how had she gotten here? What had happened? It was hard to think, her head felt so heavy, and she was scared. She fought against the rising panic, for she knew she had something important to do. What was it?

And then, Wendy remembered…

Wendy knew she had been brought here because they had assumed she was crazy, suicidal…who wouldn't? She had been found standing at an open window in her nightgown, apparently ready to jump.

She wanted to try and explain, ask for help, but she could no longer fight the effects of the sedatives. She heard the voices of two women but could not follow their words as she drifted off.

When she woke a few minutes later the voices were still talking. Her head was a little clearer, and although her lids felt enormously heavy, she was able to lift them enough to see what was happening. Something told her to be cautious.

Two women were in the room. Wendy studied them through lidded eyes, so they might not realize that she was awake just yet.

The first was a young woman with long dark braids, holding a clipboard. She was wearing some sort of a pinafore-style yellow dress. The other woman, with short, choppy hair, was wearing a white coat. Both stood in sharp contrast to the sage green wall.

There was something, a positive energy perhaps, about the young woman with the braids, which Wendy was attracted to. She considered letting her know that she was awake, but then Wendy shifted her gaze to the other woman in the room.

The second woman was a complete contrast to the first. She wore a plain white blouse, khaki pants, partially covered by a lab coat with some remnant of a yellowish stain around one pocket, as if something had leaked in there. A stethoscope hung around her neck. The woman had a large satchel of some sort slung over one shoulder, which looked to be in danger of slipping off at any moment.

This one was studying a clipboard, making notes, and humming tunelessly. She wore no make-up and sported a severe and choppy short haircut, which almost looked as if she had done it herself. She must be the doctor.

The woman with the severe haircut came over to Wendy's bed and began taking her vital signs. Wendy sighed and sank deeper into the bed. As she did not want to risk being further sedated, she closed her eyes completely, so the women would not realize she was already awake. She wasn't ready to talk to anyone yet. Wendy listened as the two discussed her situation.

"Wendy Moira Angela Darling Winthrop, beloved philanthropist and special friend to lost children," said the doctor, not unkindly. "What has brought you to this place?"

The question floated through Wendy's fuzzy consciousness, and she knew the answer. In her desperation to find Margaret, she had tried to fly to Neverland. She knew now that would not work. She had to find another way. But first, she had to get out of this hospital.

"Will she be awake soon?," the younger woman said.

"I'd say not, with 10 mg of Diazepam and 10 of Librium she'll be out till tomorrow morning," replied the other.

"Wow, that's a heavy dose, enough to knock out a cow," said the first.

"Listen, Dorothy Gale, maybe back in Kansas, you can take your chances, but around here we take seriously the ones who try to jump out of windows, most especially women like her."

"Oh, I am not questioning your medical judgement," replied the woman Wendy now knew was called Dorothy.

The doctor had taken hold of her wrist and was taking her pulse. Wendy risked a small peek. Her vision was clearing slightly, and she strained to read the nametag on the doctor's white coat.

Dr. A. Liddell, she read. Wendy hoped the women would not realize she was awake and listening. She did not want any more medication.

The doctor said, "Strong sedation was required. She was hysterical when she was brought in, claiming her granddaughter was lost, and she had to fly and rescue her. She had been standing at an open three-story window, in just her nightgown, about to jump. Her brother happened into the room just in time to pull her back."

"The child is actually missing, as it turns out," Dorothy replied. "Margaret hasn't been to school in weeks, yet Mrs. Winthrop made no report of any kind. Could it be a kidnapping? Was she threatened about going to the police?"

Dr. Liddell turned to Dorothy. "Perhaps," she replied. "But that doesn't explain her ravings at the window. I believe that Mrs. Winthrop's apparent suicide attempt and her suppression of what happened to her granddaughter is a result of her childhood trauma.

She herself, along with her brothers were also victims of a kidnapper."

"Yes," replied Dorothy. "As a child, she and her brothers disappeared one night. A sort of locked room mystery; there seemed to be no way the children could have left the house, for they had not passed through the downstairs, or the maid would have seen them. The only other exit had been a high window, too high for children to jump from, and no footprints or any evidence of their passing was found in the snow below."

"The very same high window," replied the doctor, "from which our Ms. Winthrop was about to jump."

Dorothy continued, "The children were gone for many weeks, and then, just as they had disappeared in a most mysterious and unexplained fashion, they returned, bringing with them a number of boys, most of whom had been missing for quite a long time, some for as long as ten years. Yet, these boys did not seem to have aged since their disappearances."

Dr. Liddell mused, "I don't think that is possible. Stunted growth from ill-treatment, perhaps."

She continued, "When questioned, however, the children denied any kidnapping or imprisonment, and all told a similar story of having been on a beautiful yet treacherous island, protected by a charismatic and feral boy, where they face all sorts of dangers.

"But despite the dangers, all seemed to have relished the excitement and treated the experience as the adventure of a lifetime. The consistency of their stories, including such details as the description of their underground home were remarkable, but not remarkable enough to lend even a shred of credence to the fantastic tale. This is not an uncommon reaction to trauma for a child, but it is unusual that all should have developed the same fantasy to cope."

Wendy listened to this compete misunderstanding of her experience and was glad she had resisted the urge to try and explain herself to these two.

"I remember this!" said Ms. Gale. "The Darlings, Wendy's parents, declared their intentions of raising all the boys as their own, despite the very limited financial resources available to them."

"Right," replied the doctor. "But the publicity surrounding the return not only of the Darling children, but of the six other boys, led to the reappearance of the parents and relatives of the long missing boys. One by one, parents reclaimed their lost children."

Dr. Liddell concluded, "As time wore on, most of these children gave up the story of this 'Peter Pan' and the Neverland—for that is what they called the island, and their supposed leader."

"But once it was all over, Mrs. Winthrop appeared to live a charmed life, with no real long-term effects," exclaimed Ms. Gale.

Dr. Liddell replied, "There are always after-effects. That is why I am here."

Wendy risked another peek at the women, and gave a small, bitter laugh at the notion that her life had been "charmed".

Ms. Gale looked puzzled. "Of course, her life was charmed. Well, yes, she did lose her husband at a young age, but she went on to found orphanages, with facilities far surpassing those of the finest boarding schools. She started a center for runaway children, first to give them a safe place, and then to explore what it might take to either reunite them with their parents or to find a nurturing home if the parents were not suitable or able to provide one. Her life's work was the care and protection of lost children. Whenever she was asked about why she devoted herself and her wealth to this cause, she would gently remind the questioner that she and her brothers had once been lost."

Dr. Liddell snorted, "As if the loss of her husband had not been enough sorrow for this great lady, a second tragedy had touched this woman just six years ago. Her only daughter, Jane, along with her husband, was killed in an automobile accident, leaving Mrs. Winthrop as the sole guardian of her newborn granddaughter, Margaret. I don't call that charmed. You are such an unrealistic optimist, Dorothy Gale."

While the two conversed, with no understanding of her true history, Wendy listened, and watched through half-closed eyes.

Wendy sees it now. She knows there must be a clue as to what had happened to Margaret in her memories, if only she could find it.

Wendy sighs and seems to settle deeper into sleep. She is trying now to ignore the chatter, but her mind is racing as she forces herself to remember it all.

CHAPTER THREE

REMEMBERING PETER

Wendy can still clearly recall the inevitable and painful decision to return to her parents. Her motivations and reasons back then were those of a child, and yet, even as a child, she always knew for certain what she had to do, for herself, her brothers, and the Lost Boys. Now she was rethinking all those decisions. She had been so sure at that time.

But I had to bring the Lost Boys back, all of them, of course. Peter had not been happy about that.

Her parents, thrilled to have their children back home, and eagerly willing to adopt all the boys, seemed at first to believe her story. What other explanation could there be? How else could good parents have lost their children?

Once the initial relief of their children's return wore off, their parents discouraged all talk of this Neverland. At first, they discouraged it gently, then sternly, and finally forcefully.

As the news spread of the remarkable reappearance of the Darling children, along with the lost ones, the parents of other children came hopefully forward to claim them. One by one, the Lost Boys were reunited with their biological parents or some other relative.

Wendy had been heartbroken. These were her children. She had raised them in Neverland. But no one believed her.

Sweet Michael, being the youngest, soon forgot almost all the details of their time with Peter, although he believed for almost as long as Wendy did in Peter.

John, on the other hand, rather quickly came to believe (as the authorities also concluded, and firmly insisted, when the children said otherwise) that they had all been kidnapped and drugged, and he cared not to think on what might really have happened to them.

Wendy did not give up her certainty in what she knew had truly occurred, but, wise in her years, knowing how the world worked, she eventually went along with John, at least in public.

Nevertheless, she had faith, for Peter had said that he would come every year to take her back for spring cleaning. And so, he did come, at least for the first year. He missed the next, and when he finally came again the following year, he didn't even seem to realize he had missed a whole year.

He came once more, and then not again until she was quite grown.

CHAPTER FOUR

PETER AND JANE

Wendy sighed, as she usually did when she thought about Peter. Reluctantly, she turned her thoughts back to the first time she saw Peter after she had become a grown-up woman. This was never easy to think about.

Wendy had been sitting in the nursery one night when Jane was nine, darning socks by the fire. For some reason, she knew she should not be far from her child that night. It was a silly thing, really, to be darning socks, for they could easily afford new socks. Still, the nostalgia of the motion, slowly moving the needle in and out, comforted Wendy. Tonight, she felt a great unease and a chill ran through her whole body, despite the cheery and crackling fire.

A wind blew through the nursery through a tiny crack in the unlocked windows., rustling the curtains and lifting the shawl Wendy had thrown across her lap. A cold hand seemed to pass over her heart.

Then, one by one, as they had many, many years ago, the nightlights had gone out. Wendy had been alarmed, still not suspecting Peter at all. It had been so very long since Peter had visited. She was sure something else, something sinister, must be happening.

Wrapping the shawl tightly around her, she rose to look out the window. Just as she stood up, the window blew open, the shutters clattering, and gusts of snowflakes swirled into the room. Wendy stepped backwards, standing behind Jane's bed. She put one hand on her child, and with the other, picked up the fire poker.

Peter flew in, just as he had years before. She gasped, and quickly stepped back further into the shadows, and draped the shawl over her head, so he might not see that she was taller than he.

Wendy knew immediately that this night would be almost unbearably sad. She could not bear for Peter to see her now, a grown-up woman, knowing that Peter would still be the same thoughtless, arrogant boy, and would not understand.

He landed on the carpet in the center of the room, and casually surveyed his surroundings. She could see his cockiness at once. Peter never changed.

Wendy knew, of course, that Peter had come looking for her, looking for the girl she had been so many years ago. He stood proudly in the center of the room, hands on his hips, and let forth with a lusty crow. Jane stirred but did not awaken.

When there was no immediate reaction to his crow, Peter looked around uncertainly. Wendy took a small step forward, not far enough to bring her into the light, but enough to attract his attention. She spoke to him from the shadows, hiding beneath her shawl.

"Peter…" she said quietly.

"Hullo, Wendy!" he replied. Wendy tried at first to make conversation, asking after old friends and enemies. As is typical with Peter, he did not care to discuss anything more than a day or two past.

Finally, she asked, "Do you remember nothing of our time together? Our children? Why are you here, Thoughtless Boy?"

"Spring cleaning," he replied, as if that should be obvious, and walked over to Jane's bed and peered curiously at the sleeping child.

Yes, Peter had forgotten about her for some time, although far too late he had finally remembered her. He was here to take her back to the Neverland for Spring cleaning. But he was not looking for the woman that Wendy had become, but for the girl Wendy had once been, and that girl was not here anymore.

"It has been quite a while," Wendy said quietly. "I don't think you know quite how long." She stepped out of the shadows, and broke Peter's heart.

He realized at once what had happened, and he began to cry. Wendy, unable to bear it at last, fled the nursery.

She returned a few minutes later, having composed herself as only a mother can, to find Jane was flying lazily about the nursery. Peter was crowing, all his sorrow seemingly forgotten.

In the end, he took Jane instead of her. It seemed a simple solution. Peter agreed, as he had once agreed with Wendy's mother, that he would return her after two weeks of Spring cleaning. He did not seem to notice the tears in Wendy's eyes as he grabbed Jane by the hand and flew out the window.

Wendy watched them go, tracking them as far as the second star. When she finally lost sight of them, she closed the window, and thought about how she would explain their daughter's disappearance to her husband. She fixed her thoughts firmly on her kind and loving husband and wiped the vestige of the tears she had foolishly shed for the callous boy.

Peter did return Jane, just as he had promised, and, for another year or two, Peter showed up in the nursery with surprising regularity, and Jane went with him for Spring cleaning.

After that first night, Wendy never came to the nursery when Peter was there. She would not let him see her again, so big, and so grown up. She never asked Jane about the Neverland, or how Peter was, and Jane did not tell her mother. Somehow, both Jane and Wendy knew it was not a good idea, yet Wendy could not help but sense that it was not the same for Jane as it had been for her.

Jane went with Peter two more times, and, then just as he had with Wendy, he stopped coming. Jane didn't seem to mind.

When Peter did not return, Wendy thought he had forgotten again. Or perhaps he had realized that Jane, like Wendy, had grown older, too old for Neverland. She did not think she would ever see the boy again. She was wrong.

CHAPTER FIVE

PETER TAKES MARGARET

Peter did return, as he always will. It was after Jane had died, and Margaret was six years old. This was when the trouble started.

Looking back at the week before Peter returned, Wendy knew she should have been more careful. There were warnings, but she did not take them seriously.

The first sign was the behavior of the night lights. They had been flickering, yet the electrician she called could find no short or fault in the system. One night, when she had gone in to check on Margaret, she found they had been out entirely, and she had been unable to make them relight. She had gone to bed, troubled, but in the morning, when she went to wake Margaret, they were burning as brightly as ever.

The following evening, she found the window latch was broken. But since the nursery was on the third floor, she was not overly worried, and she resolved to have it fixed later in the week. She had not noticed the tiny black and torn thread, of something like a shadow, caught in the hinge of the window, till much later.

Most troubling and alarming, the night before Peter showed again, the fairy Tinker Bell came to Wendy. If nothing else alarmed her, she should have known something was wrong when Tink appeared.

Wendy and the fairy had never gotten along, so she was very surprised to see Tinker Bell flitting about her room. Wendy had thought Tink was dead.

As a matter of fact, when Peter had come for her for her very first spring cleaning, he did not seem to remember Tink, and carelessly told her that fairies did not live very long, and that if he had ever known a fairy named Tinker Bell, she must be dead.

Wendy could not help but believe him, for she saw no sign of Tink, or any fairy for that matter, on her return to the Neverland for her first Spring cleaning. It saddened her that Peter did not seem to have grieved for the fairy, nor did he have any truly clear recollection of their previous time in Neverland. Peter was forgetful, she knew, or perhaps he only remembered those things that he wished to remember.

But now Tink was here, and clearly Peter had not been honest with her about the fairy. Unlike her first encounter as a child, when Tinker Bell flew round the room at almost lightning speed, this time the fairy passed slowly, languidly, tiredly through the air. She twittered at Wendy, trying to say something, but as always, all Wendy could hear were the tinkling tones, which are the fairy language.

The fairy landed on Margaret's bed, and spoke at some length, but still Wendy could not understand a word. Obviously agitated, Tinker Bell flew between Wendy and the child's bed, and gave a hard tug on Wendy's hair. This at least, was familiar, for Tink had always been jealous of Wendy's bond with Peter and would often pull her hair or pinch her.

The tiny creature tugged furiously at Wendy's hair, her bell-like voice deafening Wendy with its peals of rage and frustration. "Tinker Bell, what is it?" she asked. "What is wrong? Is Peter in danger?" At this, Tink's fairy voice rose to a cacophony, and she tugged even harder at Wendy's hair.

Without warning, the fairy loosened her grip and fell to the floor, and her light suddenly winked out. Wendy searched the nursery floor for hours, but she did not find her, nor even the slightest bit of fairy dust. This was troubling.

The next night, Peter came for Margaret.

Cuddling together by the fire, she was once again telling Margaret the old, favorite story, of how Peter had come to the nursery that first time to eavesdrop on the bedtime stories that their mother had been telling. Once again, she told Margaret how Peter had lost his shadow, and how she had sewn it back on for him.

She told this story every night, as she had once done every night for Jane until Peter had returned. Each night, another chapter of Neverland would unfold, until, at last, it ended with the children safe in their nursery once more. The adventures took several nights to tell, but once the story was done, she would begin it anew.

Margaret always asked if someday, Peter might come for her. "Perhaps," Wendy would murmur. "Someday he might. But he can be very forgetful, you know." Although in her heart, she did not believe that it would happen. Still…

Wendy continued her story, "Peter saw at once that I was a brave and useful girl, and so took me and my brothers to the Neverland. I never would have gone without them."

Wendy looked to the window. She had told this story so often that it came out automatically, like a song or a poem. She had not actually thought about the words for many years.

She had hesitated this night to tell it, as she was still troubled by Tinker Bell's visit. But she had been telling this story every night to Jane, and then to Margaret, for as long as they believed, and she could not stop now. It would seem odd.

Margaret was almost asleep, and Wendy was about to carry her to bed, when the lights went out. A sudden recognition of what was happening came to Wendy, with some surprise. It came to her all at once but also, too late, that Margaret was too young for the Neverland, but she had no time to think.

Wendy realized that Peter would be here momentarily, so she stood up and stepped back into a shadow in the corner of the room, cradling the child in her arms. Margaret awoke at once, and squirmed in Wendy's arms, but she held tight. Wendy drew her shawl around her head, to hide her face as much as possible, as she had years ago, and tried to hush Margaret.

The windows flew open without a sound, and in came Peter. He looked, as he always looks, and will always look, handsome and proud. His eyes searched the room, and he seemed not to see Wendy standing in the shadows. He smiled as he gazed around the room. Wendy knew that smile and realized that Peter had seen her. She felt round her neck and held onto the acorn, which she had worn on a chain since her childhood.

Peter let out a crow and made a sweeping bow, gesturing toward the open window. At this, Margaret leapt out of Wendy's arms, and jumped to a chair. She stood up in the chair and cried, "Peter!"

Wendy realized that she need not have bothered to hide herself, for Peter paid her no attention and flew over to Margaret. "Time for Spring cleaning," he cried, sprinkling her with fairy dust.

Wendy tried to steady her voice, to keep the quaver of age at bay and to sound at least as young as she had when she had first let Jane fly off to Neverland.

"Peter, this is Margaret," she began.

Peter answered her airily, without even a glance in her direction. "Yes, Wendy, I know," he replied. "Did you think I forgot? Did you think I was not paying attention? I know when it is time for Spring cleaning."

Peter took Margaret by the hands and swung her up and around, releasing her mid swing. Released from his grasp, she awkwardly flew towards the ceiling and then around the room, alighting on her bed.

Peter was at her side in an instant, and in a stage whisper, which he clearly meant for Wendy to hear, "Do you want to swim with mermaids, meet fairies and come away with me?" His eyes darted quickly to Wendy in the shadows, then back to the little girl.

Without looking at her again, eyes fixed on Margaret, Peter said seriously, "Wendy, I must take her with me. I'll take good care. You know I will."

Wendy was frightened, far more frightened than when Peter had come for Jane. And yet, she could not refuse him. She never could.

"Just for Spring cleaning, that's all. Two weeks, Peter, just two weeks," she said in a whisper.

"Yes, Wendy, of course," he replied, carelessly followed by a lusty crow. He gestured to the window, and Margaret ran over eagerly. Peter smiled, looking not at Wendy, but at the child, and both rose slowly from the floor and flew out the window into the chilly night.

In retrospect, she ought to have questioned her decision more. Margaret was so young, and Peter was so…Peter. But it had been so sudden, so unexpected. When Peter came, she had let Margaret go, as she had gone before and had let Jane go.

Jane had come back all right, and on time, although Jane had been reluctant to share her experiences with Wendy. That seemed right, but Jane had also seemed troubled upon her return. Without asking for detail, Wendy comforted her child. Wendy had comforted herself at the time as well, with the good memories she had of Neverland. She did not worry that Jane was reluctant to share her adventures. Wendy had not dared to tell her mother all that had happened in the Neverland, so of course, Jane might be the same.

But Margaret and Peter had flown away more than six weeks ago, and Spring cleaning should only last two weeks, three at most. Days passed into weeks, and Wendy's anxiety turned to panic. Now, Wendy was terrified. She was sure something dreadful had happened to Peter and Margaret. She had to find a way to save them, and there was only one way she could think of doing so.

Despite her age, and how difficult it was to think only happy thoughts when she was wracked with worry, and dressed only in her nightgown, she had walked towards the windows and opened the shutters. "Second star to the right and straight on till morning," she had whispered to herself.

Now, here she was. Lying helpless in a strange bed, with no way to save Peter and Margaret from whatever had befallen them. She suppressed a small sob, unnoticed by the women in her room.

CHAPTER SIX

DR. ALICE

D r. Liddell placed her hand gently on the patient's forehead and brushed aside a few stray hairs. The touch was one of deep tenderness and intimacy, and her hand lingered for a moment longer than might be considered professional. The doctor looked down at the sleeping woman, wondering.

She was not normally a sentimental woman, and her unanticipated feelings for this patient were uncomfortable and odd for her. She could not explain them to herself with any satisfaction. She was suddenly aware of the scrutiny of the other occupant of the room, and, self-conscious, she took her hand away from the woman's forehead, turned abruptly, and left the patient's room, leaving Ms. Gale behind.

Alice Liddell was abnormally agitated by this patient. It was not her regular sort of case, and yet, somehow, it was. She marched in her angry clump down the hall and bit her lip thoughtfully. This situation required some careful consideration. Children were her specialty, not addled older women, no matter how rich or famous they might be, or even if they owned the hospital she worked at. This should not be her case!

She continued stomping down the hall, towards her office door, muttering vague protestations against the office politics that had assigned her this case. She took a moment outside the door to remind herself of who she was and her important place in the world of psychiatry.

She considered calling her department head, to complain but she could already hear his voice in her head.

Dr. Liddell you are considered to be the expert on childhood trauma, he would say in his always soft and condescending tone.

Your theory and practice are focused on those desperately tragic situations in which a child had been forced to cope with an extremely awful and frightening ordeal. Kidnappings, slavery, abuse, and other such crimes are your stock in trade, he would chuckle.

In these circumstances, according to your well-known theory, it is usual for the child to invent a fantasy world to mask the actual horror of their all-too-real experience. And this may very well be what has happened to our dear benefactor. I had to assign the best, he would finish, a*nd that is you, my dear Alice.*

There was no point in making the actual call, and reluctantly, she had to admit he would be right. Alice's research and work were intensely important to her, for they were founded on her own childhood delusion. When she was seven (or eight, really, it was so hard to remember), she had been kidnapped. And not just once, but twice! Each time, she had no recollection of where she had been, nor what had happened. Instead, try as she might, she could only recall a mad fantasy world of impossible creatures and terrible danger.

The experiences had sharpened her already preternatural curiosity, so as an adult she had devoted herself to finding an explanation for her strange memories. The only logical one was that she had gone a little bit mad, to cope with a terrible and traumatizing situation. Who had taken her? How had she escaped?

These questions were not important, it was only important that she had escaped. But escaping the fantasy hell had only led to real and documentable horrors. Psychiatry is not always kind or gentle in treating the delusional. Best not to dwell.

And now, Dr. Alice Liddell has been called to treat this woman. A woman, like herself, who had been kidnapped and subjected to things no sane person could imagine. A woman who had had a lifetime to come to terms with what must have been a terrible and frightening time in her young life…kidnapped along with her brothers, forced to act as mother to not only her own siblings, but also six other kidnapped boys, who, from all reports, had been raised in an almost feral state, in a constant atmosphere of perceived danger.

She tried to recall the details. Wasn't there one boy, from all accounts, still missing to this day? The missing boy seemed to have been of a particular significance to the patient.

She unlocked the door to her office and seated herself at her desk. She took a cigarette out of her pocket, almost lit it, then tore it to pieces and threw it in the trash. *Damn, filthy habit!* She looked longingly at the remains of the tattered cigarette, then vigorously shook her head. She substitutes a pencil, chewing slowly on the eraser. It tasted terrible.

Dr. Liddell pulled the file from her desk and began to read. Alice frowned as she read the files. Despite the sensationalism surrounding the Darling children's mysterious disappearance and miraculous return, it seems no treatment had been sought for any of the victims, nor had there been any real investigation. Perhaps, in those times, it was thought to be for the best.

She sighed. Wendy Darling had been lucky, in fact. No treatment was better than destructive treatment. Dr. Liddell's experience after her two disappearances had not been gentle. She gazed again at the cigarette tatters, against her will recalling her own story.

When young Alice returned from her imprisonment (from God knows where), she had been faced with disbelief from her family, followed shortly by veiled threats of hospitalization, and finally, when she did not recant, actual hospitalization. She shuddered.

The hospital was a hellish nightmare for the child. With no proof and only her own memories, desperate to return to a normal, safe existence, she came to realize that she must have invented the mad world she remembered in such heartbreaking detail. Yet it seemed so very real!

I must have been trying to avoid remembering something else, something so awful, so terrible, so much worse than what I thought I remembered, or why else would I have invented such things?, Alice mused.

This is the question that has haunted her through her troubled childhood, awkward adolescence, and somewhat lonely early adulthood and that led her to the field of child psychiatry. Here she first discovered her unique talent. Her special gift was an ability to help those unfortunate children who had suffered such indescribable abuse, such unimaginable suffering, that they were unable to recall it, but instead, like herself, had substituted a belief in a fantasy world in place of those memories.

Such worlds, though frightening at times, always ended with the child as a hero, rescuing themselves from the dangers.

The conventional wisdom in dealing with buried trauma was that recall was essential to recovery. Alice's technique was radical: she believed that recall was not needed and that it could be as damaging as the initial triggering events.

By taking recall out of the process and helping the child to focus on the here and now instead, Alice Liddell had achieved extraordinary results in far less time than the usual therapies. She was able to help her patients move forward with their lives without having to take that painful look back.

This particular case was especially troubling for Dr. Liddell. Here was a woman, who had seemingly moved past her childhood issues, only to have them catch up in the frightening kidnapping of her grandchild fifty years later. Could the same person who kidnapped the Darling children still be alive? That was the theory of the police. And if he was, why wait so long to return?

This would be a very different sort of treatment, for now she would have to help Wendy Darling Winthrop move past the trauma of long ago, and yet recall the events leading to her granddaughter's abduction.

From what little she could make of Mrs. Winthrop's remarks before she was sedated, it seemed she had reverted back to her childhood delusion about flying away with a magical boy. She must bring her back to reality so the truth could be uncovered. But how could she do it without unearthing the original trauma? Time was of the essence, and there was not much time. The child had already been gone for six weeks.

Alice shook her head and thought about having a glass of brandy. Although the case would be painful on a personal level, raising her own ghosts, she resisted the temptation. She did not like to think back about her own childhood, but it was always necessary to do so if she was to help a troubled child. In this case, she must help a troubled old woman, but since the trouble came from childhood, the process was the same. Alice needed to return to the child she had been, the fear of beheading, the fear of flowers, and the painful walk she had taken back to sanity. She would need to lead Mrs. Winthrop down that path, so she must be sure of the way.

A few hairs swept across her forehead, momentarily distracting her from her thoughts. She glanced quickly, as quickly as she could, into a small mirror. (Alice did not like looking into mirrors. They seemed dangerous. That was one reason why she kept her hair short, wore no makeup, and did all her clothes shopping online. Still, as a professional, she had to keep herself looking presentable, hence the small compact with a very tiny mirror).

Alice knew that the mirror phobia was a bit of unfinished baggage from her past, but she had already unpacked enough bags, thank you very much, and if she managed her phobia without embarrassing herself, why go through the pain? "I've got it covered," she muttered to herself.

Dr. Liddell snapped the mirror shut. She said out loud, "So I don't like mirrors. Nothing wrong with that, really. A harmless phobia, occasionally inconvenient, but at least it has kept me from frivolous vanity." She felt a touch of embarrassment but brushed it away. "After all, what is the harm, really? It's not like it affects my work." She stuffed the compact as deep as she could into her bag.

Alice sighed. "I know I lead a fairly solitary life, which is how I like it."

Dr. Liddell has never married, dates only occasionally, and on those rare occasions when she actually does venture into the highly suspicious and uncertain waters of the dating pool, it is usually under pressure, set up by a well-meaning but clueless matchmaker.

There are no second dates. She has no friends, only colleagues and acquaintances. She does, however, have cats. Lots of cats. Sometimes she worries that she is, in fact, a "Cat Lady."

"Still, only five, that's not really a cat lady, now, is it?" she said out loud to herself. "Cat ladies have dozens of them and do not care for them well. Those poor kitties are neglected, are not fed regularly, and their litter is not cleaned often enough. I am a very good custodian of my pets."

It is true, she keeps herself, her cats, and her house clean. The cats are well fed, there have never been any more than five, really, except for that one time. *And those were special circumstances, after all,* she thinks.

Dr. Alice Liddell gets all the love, companionship, and affection she has ever needed or wanted from her cats. Besides, she has a well-paying and satisfying job, has been published multiple times, is considered an expert in her field, and is often sought out for consultations. So, what could be wrong about that? Her life is well ordered and just about perfect, isn't it?

Well, she does talk to herself. She considered, "But nothing wrong with that, now is there? Especially when the only other person to talk with today is that annoying Dorothy Gale."

Alice picked up the case file for her latest patient again. Wendy Moira Angela Darling Winthrop is sixty years old. Ms. Darling is the legal guardian of her granddaughter Margaret and became so after the death of Wendy's daughter Jane and her son-in-law Tootles. They had both died in an automobile accident shortly after Margaret's birth.

Tootles? That isn't any sort of a proper name for a man to have, thought Alice. She noted, in passing, that Tootles had been much older than Jane. He had, in fact, been one of the boys who came back with the Darling children after their abduction and escape.

She shook her head and rubbed her eyes, turning to the section documenting Ms. Winthrop's current situation. She pulled a pair of battered reading glasses from her pocket, pushed a few stray wisps of hair behind her ear, and put them on.

She removed the glasses as the hairs escaped, breathed on them to steam them, and wiped them on the hem of her lab coat, adding yet another scratch to the lenses. She fixed them on her face and bent her head to read. The glasses slipped down her nose and she pushed them back, along with those pesky wisps of hair. Neither the glasses nor the hair cooperated, and she removed the glasses, held the paper closer to her face, and began to read.

CHAPTER SEVEN

DR. LIDDELL EXAMINES THE EVIDENCE

Margaret, Mrs. Winthrop's granddaughter, is six years old. She attends a rather tony private school, founded by her grandmother. A full 50% of the students who are attending the academy benefit from a scholarship fund endowed by Mrs. Winthrop. So, when Margaret did not return to school after the spring holiday break, no great fuss was made. Mrs. Winthrop informed the school that they were taking an extended holiday, and Margaret would be back in another week or two.

But now, it seemed, it had been over six weeks since anyone has seen the child. The school had, reluctantly, discreetly, begun to ask questions.

And last night, Mrs. Winthrop had been caught standing at an open window in the upstairs nursery by her brother Michael, apparently about to jump. Clearly, Mrs. Winthrop had some frightful information about the situation, information so horrible that she had contemplated ending her life.

What made this case of interest to Dr. Liddell was Mrs. Winthrop's history. Certain remarks made by Mrs. Winthrop upon admittance to the hospital caused Alice to suspect that the key to unlocking the current riddle of Margaret's disappearance lay in unlocking the riddle of Wendy Darling Winthrop's childhood trauma.

She turned back to the file. As a child, Mrs. Winthrop and her two brothers, John and Michael Darling, had all vanished for several months. There were no clues, no ransom, nor any leads as to what had happened to the children. Then, just when the press was tiring of the story, just when the Darling parents had all but given up hope, they returned.

More astonishing, when they returned, they also brought back six boys, most of whom had been missing for years. The Darling children had been found in their beds, just as if they had never left. Once they were discovered there by their mother, they brought in the other boys. All told a similar story of living on a magic island, in an underground house with a strange and fantastic boy. They spoke of dangerous pirates and other wild and mysterious creatures. Their stories were remarkably consistent, and yet, obviously, they could not have been true. Alice shook her head to clear out the atrocities she imagined must have occurred, so that flying off to this Neverland place could actually seem a refuge of safety.

At first, the children were indulged, and later were challenged to tell the truth of what had really happened, for it was more than possible that a sadistic kidnapper was still at large. One by one, each gave up this unbelievable story, but had no alternate explanation for their missing time. Dr. Liddell rubbed her forehead. *Just like me. It is just too frightening to remember.*

But there are always clues in the fantasy for the keen analyst. This was Alice's great talent…decoding the clues. Just look at her last case…a boy who did not believe that he was really a human boy, but instead thought he was a magic puppet, brought to life and yet still made of jointed wood.

Alice deduced that this boy had been in a frightening situation in which he felt he had no control over himself. He had been enslaved, perhaps he had even been a sex slave for some deranged villain. Hence, the puppet persona had emerged.

The boy had also exhibited a pathological fear about telling a lie. He was absolutely convinced that if he told a lie, his face would become brutally deformed. His captor must have threatened mutilation of some sort for any trespass.

Finally, his own moral compass seemed to exist outside of himself. He had no internal sense of right or wrong but depended on a talking cricket (which only he could see or hear) for guidance.

It was obvious that his captor had psychologically stripped him of all power, his power to move independently, to decide right from wrong…and so he became a puppet in his mind. Alice had worked long and deeply with the boy. It took quite some time, but finally she was able to convince the child that he was a real boy, not a puppet.

She looked back at the file for the Darling children. All the children had been consistent in saying that they lived in an underground home. Undoubtedly, they had been held prisoners in a basement somewhere. This was the first clue, but Alice was sure she would find many others if she was diligent in studying the case. Although Mrs. Winthrop was no longer a child, it may very well be that unraveling the events of her childhood will yield the clue to finding and rescuing her granddaughter. The disappearance was of course the cause of the suicide attempt. What else could she deduce?

Alice sighed, looked about furtively, although there was no one in her office. Her earlier resolve to forgo the brandy had dissipated. She reached into her desk drawer and pulled out a thermos. There was a hand-written label on the thermos, which read, "Drink me." It always made her smile.

Alice poured some brandy into a coffee cup. She closed her eyes and tried to imagine the child Mrs. Winthrop had been so long ago. She did not notice, off in the corner of her mind, the child she had been so long ago standing at the edge of her thoughts, holding a white chess piece in her hand, and watching her expectantly.

CHAPTER EIGHT

DOROTHY GALE

Dorothy watched Dr. Liddell leave the room without surprise. She shook her head and smiled. Dr. Liddell wasted no time, and yet Dorothy had to admit that she could be remarkably effective with the right patient. Dorothy, while not so efficient, was nevertheless quite effective with a certain type of patient, and Mrs. Winthrop was not a patient who would be helped with Dr. Liddell's methods.

Dorothy took a few minutes to enjoy the moment. It was always pleasing to come across someone she could help, someone who needed her particular expertise, a patient she could actually save. She knew she could not save everyone. Dark memories of failure pushed forward, but Dorothy pushed them back. This time, she would make a difference. She would not fail. Past failures must be banished if she were to do some good, and she was determined to help this woman.

She sat down in a corner chair and pulled out her copy of the file of the patient's history, identical to the file Dr. Liddell was now reading. Dorothy, however, was seeing something quite different in the narrative.

It was very obvious to Dorothy that Wendy and the other children had truly been transported to a strange and sometimes dangerous place, but that these children had emerged as heroes. It was especially obvious to Dorothy, for she had experienced something quite like this when she was a child. She leaned back in the stiff and uncomfortable chair and closed her eyes.

Memories of the fearful tornado that had taken her to Oz seemed tame now, compared to what had transpired since that first frightening event. Oz had been a transformative place. All her experiences as a child growing up in Kansas would never have prepared her for the work she did now. Oz had changed her forever.

In Oz, Dorothy had never faced such fears, nor known such love, as most ordinary people could ever imagine. A deep homesickness for Oz overwhelmed her for a moment. A tear teased at the corner of her eye but did not fall. Yet, here she sat, a voluntary exile from Oz, fleeing…best not to think of that now. She had work to do. Dorothy gathered her wits and leaned forward, gazing at the sleeping woman.

The persistent thought that she was an exile from Oz, would not be dismissed. She had failed. *No,* she thought. *I cannot think of that. I have work to do here.*

Since her departure from her magical place, Dorothy had devoted her life to helping those who had also made a journey. Dorothy knew she was not unique in her experiences.

There are many, many people in this world, mostly children, who have been to far away and fantastic places. These children, when they come back, are often not doing very well. Not well at all. Some of them are considered mad, and some are hospitalized. Some are in complete denial of their experiences and pretend that nothing has happened. Most actually come to believe that nothing has happened.

In any case, they are not able to be comfortable in the world to which they have returned and in which they must now live. They need help. Traditional psychiatry is not able to provide what they need. Dorothy knows this.

As one who has been there, she is in a unique position to help these people. This has been her cause, her redemption, and her penance. But, how to find them, and how to be in a place where she could effect change for them?

The solution was simple. She became a patient advocate at a prestigious hospital, with a world-famous pediatric unit. Here, she was most likely to find those needing her unique brand of therapy. She could bring them validation, acceptance, and peace with the life they must now live.

The work was good, the work was needed, and the work gave Dorothy's life meaning and purpose along with an imperfect truce with her past. But the question lingers, why would Dorothy leave Oz, a place where she was a heroine, happy, surrounded by friends, and (let us not forget) a princess by appointment?

This work does seem to provide Dorothy a valid reason for leaving Oz, even at a time when Oz was in a place of great peril. Dorothy has work here. She helps children. This is a good reason to explain her return to this duller, less magical place.

This case was different for Dorothy. Generally, a person (usually a child) in crisis after a trip to one of the other places would need her help to ground themselves again in our world.

But after her adventure, Wendy had adjusted, it seemed, and had gone on to have a very full and meaningful life, happy in most ways, yet not without its sorrows. She had married, an apparently happy marriage, until her husband's death at a relatively young age. She had never remarried and had raised her only child on her own.

Her daughter, Jane, had married late, but she and her husband also had one daughter, Margaret. Sadly, both parents had died in a car accident, leaving Wendy as the guardian of their baby girl. (She tried to correct herself and think of the woman as "Mrs. Winthrop," but Dorothy could not think of the woman lying on the bed that way. Despite her years, there was still something essentially girlish about Wendy. She was Wendy.)

One item in the file attracted Dorothy's attention. Dorothy noted that Wendy had chosen to live her entire life in her childhood home. Her husband had been extremely well-to-do, and yet they lived in the modest house that her parents had lived in when she was a child. Somehow, her connection to her otherworld was fixed there, and she could not close that door...or window?

Now, it seems likely that her other world may have caught up with her...for where was her granddaughter?

Dorothy flipped back and forth, reading a passage here and a passage there, flipping through the pages randomly. She noticed that there were references to a few short disappearances for both Wendy and her daughter in the years following Wendy's first disappearance and Jane's first absence from school, but these were always explained as an extended holiday—just as Margaret's present disappearance had been initially explained.

But now, too much time had passed, and it was clear that the child was missing. Wendy had been at the window hoping to find her granddaughter, but what had she been looking for? What did she think she was going to do?

Dorothy turned to the statements from the other children who had returned with the Darlings. Perhaps a clue could be found there.

She became so absorbed in reading the initial statements from the "lost" boys, and then comparing them with later interviews, that she did not hear the door open until the well-dressed man entered the room.

CHAPTER NINE

MICHAEL

He looked to be in his late forties or early fifties, tall and broad-shouldered, with a shock of sandy brown hair, which he nervously smoothed back as he entered the room. *A bit plump, perhaps,* Dorothy thought, *but not unattractively so.* His suit was well-tailored and made of a subtly expensive fabric. It was the sort of suit that a well-trained eye could see belonged to a man of wealth, who cared more for comfort than show.

Contrasting with the elegance of his suit, under his arm, he carried a small, well-worn teddy bear. The bear had lost an eye, and the brown fur was matted, as if it had been through too many cycles in a washing machine. But he carried it as if it were the most precious thing on earth.

He walked over to the old woman's bedside. He placed the bear on the pillow near her face, stood for a moment looking down at the woman. His face seemed to crumple with sorrow. He stood a few minutes and at last took the bear back for a moment, and then rearranged it so it was nestled in her arms. He leaned forward and kissed her on the forehead. "Oh, Wendy, you know you can't fly anymore," he said.

Dorothy realized that he was not aware of her presence, and so she cleared her throat. The man turned, and Dorothy could see that he was older than she had thought at first. She stood up, held out her hand to him and introduced herself. "I'm Dorothy Gale, Patient Advocate for Mrs. Winthrop." She gestured to her name badge.

"I'm Wendy's brother, Michael Darling. How is she?" Michael was looking at Dorothy with a look of utter despair. Although his eyes were dry, his voice was hoarse with tears.

Dorothy thought quickly and made a risky decision. No time to wait. She took a chance and asked, "Were you once able to fly? Is that what she was trying to do?" She held her breath as she waited for the answer.

Michael turned to his sister. His shoulders slumped, and it was a few minutes before he spoke. "We thought we could, or at least we imagined we could," he finally replied. He walked to the window and looked off into the night sky. He made a noise. Dorothy could not tell if it was a laugh, a cough, or a sob.

Michael Darling continued, looking out the window, his back towards Dorothy. "Wendy and I believed far longer than any of the others. John was the first to give up the notion. I was so young when it happened, I hardly remember anything. The Boys, once they separated us and placed them back with their own families, well, they gave it up too. Had to, I suppose. Wendy eventually said she did too, but I don't think she ever really gave up the idea. Peter was so important to her, you know."

Michael Darling turned from the window, and Dorothy could see that he had been crying, but he had stopped. He walked back to Wendy's side and lifted the necklace his sister wore. It was a simple silver chain, with an acorn as the pendant. He rolled the acorn around in his hand, and finally held it out so Dorothy could see it. It was just an ordinary acorn, pierced with a ring, and hung on the chain.

Dorothy could see now that he has begun tearing up again, but just a little bit. A tear lingered in the corner of his left eye, and he did not wipe it away.

"He gave her this, I think. She called it a 'kiss.' Has worn it all her life." Michael looked at Dorothy with the heartbreak in his eyes.

"What will happen to my sister? Is she crazy? And what has happened to Margaret?"

Dorothy struggled in her mind how to answer his questions. Best to just be straightforward. She finally replied, "I don't know how to tell you this, really, other than to say it plainly."

She pulled open the file to the relevant page, and tried to look as professional and sane as she could.

"Your sister's original statements, as a child, say that this Peter will come every year to take her back to this place you went... Neverland? For spring cleaning? The records show your sister did disappear for a week or two in the spring a year after your adventure, and it looks like your niece Jane did have a few 'extended holidays' as well. I think that this Peter did come for each of them, he was just not terribly consistent. There are long gaps in the timeline. Now your grandniece Margaret is missing. I believe that this Peter Pan has taken her, as he did your sister and niece. Something has happened to prevent Margaret's timely return. You and I both know full well that your sister was not trying to jump from that window but was trying to fly to Neverland."

Dorothy looked at Michael Darling with a triumphant expression, but he looked back with disbelief.

"Are you really a patient advocate or are you just a patient? You sound a little bit crazy," he replied, turning back to his sister again.

"Perhaps I am or perhaps I'm not," she said. "But humor me anyway, and tell me about your sister, this Peter, and Neverland."

Michael Darling turned and looked at the young woman who so clearly was giving credence to the childhood fantasy that he and his sister had once shared. He shook his head and with a weary look back at his sister, he sank down into a chair, burying his face in his hands.

Dorothy continued. "You know it is real. If it makes you happier, or at least more comfortable to pretend that it isn't, that's fine. So, humor the madwoman...and tell me everything you can remember."

Michael Darling lifted his head, and shook it slowly, as if clearing the cobwebs from an old memory. "I always did know, deep inside, that it was all true. And I will tell you, at least what I can remember."

"I was very young, and I don't really remember very much at all. We were kidnapped, I am told, but Wendy told me we had been to a magical island, called...yes, called Neverland. I do remember for certain that Wendy took care of me, of all of us, and Peter too. You can never forget Peter." When he spoke the name, "Peter," a look of pure and intense love crossed his face. Dorothy had never seen anything like it.

"There was a terrible man, a man with a hook instead of a hand, and he was going to kill us all. He was a pirate, and he had a terrible and frightening crew. We were going to have to walk the plank. Peter saved us and brought us home, but he would not stay. Wendy asked him to, of course, but he would not. Wendy was very sad, and cried and cried, but our mother told us Peter would come back and Wendy would go with him, but only for a very little while.

"I waited up with her the first spring to see if Peter would really come, for by then, almost everyone else had stopped believing. He did come and I saw her fly out the window with him, but of course they told me that cannot have been true. Under the present circumstances, I suppose it must have been true. I've spent so long trying to believe it was not true.

"Next year, he never came, and John told me it could not have been true. But the year after that, Wendy was gone for two whole weeks, and Mother never said a word, but that 'Wendy was off doing spring cleaning'.

"When my sister came back after that time, she cried for a day. She wouldn't say why. Next year, my sister waited at the window every night for weeks and weeks, but Peter never came. So I moved on with growing up and stopped believing."

Michael looked again at his sister, gently brushing his hand on her cheek. He re-adjusted the toy bear in her arms, and again touched her forehead. "But you never stopped, did you, Wendy? You just pretended to stop. It was true, then, wasn't it? Wendy, what can we do? Can Peter save Margaret?"

Dorothy's heart ached for the Darling children and a resolve rose in her heart. Dorothy walked over to Michael Darling and threw her arms around him. She held him, and he sank into her arms, allowing all his doubt and grief and fear to wash over her.

"It was all true," she said to him gently. "And you and your siblings are not the only ones. I have been to other lands, like you, came home, and was not believed. I can help you, and I will help your sister, and I will save your grandniece."

Dorothy spoke confidently, but within, she wondered, *Can I?*

Michael Darling looked at Dorothy. Now, a full torrent of tears was streaming down his face. "Real?" he said, his voice catching, "You are telling me it was all real? If Peter Pan is Margaret's only hope, we have no hope."

There was a sudden noise, and both Michael and Dorothy turned towards the bed where Wendy had been sleeping. Wendy sat up in bed. She looked at Dorothy with clear, wild, open eyes for a full minute without speaking. Then, turning to Michael, the flames, which had lit her eyes as she looked at Dorothy, mellowed and became loving warmth.

"Michael," she said, reaching out to touch his cheek. She looked down at the stuffed bear which he had placed in her arms, and closed her eyes, almost about to cry. "I'm all right. I won't try to fly again. And Margaret will be alright. It is all true, and we both know it."

He reached out and held both her hands. The teddy bear dropped to the floor. His sister looked at him, holding his gaze, saying nothing. Wendy waited, looking into her brother's eyes beseechingly. She held his gaze and would not let it go.

Finally, Michael Darling shook his head again, this time saying, "Yes, I think I always knew it was true. So this person," he gestured to Dorothy, "this is Margaret's only chance?"

Wendy reached out and drew her brother close and kissed him. "Yes, she is," she murmured. They stayed, locked together for a few minutes. Dorothy did not wish to intrude on the family moment, but eventually she cleared her throat. Wendy reluctantly broke the embrace with her brother and turned to Dorothy.

Despite the nightgown, despite her position in a hospital bed, despite the IV in her arm, Wendy Winthrop was all steel and strength now. Gently, firmly, she commanded, "Michael, let me have a few private words with this young woman."

Michael nodded, and without another word, left the room. "Now", said Wendy, sitting up straighter and with an air of absolute authority, "You seem to know my story. Tell me, what is yours?"

CHAPTER TEN

MICHAEL AND ALICE

D r. Liddell tilted her chair back as far as it could go and lay back, chewing on the end of the pencil still, wishing to God it was a cigarette. She gazed regretfully at the torn remains of the cigarette in the trash. She rooted around in her bag for a stick of nicotine gum, and finally came up with a rather squashed piece, wrapper half torn off, with a bit of lint clinging to it. She held it up, considered it momentarily, but finally tossed it away. She unlocked the bottom drawer of her desk and pulled out the thermos again.

She poured herself a small teacup of brandy from the thermos, lay back in her chair again, and tried to make sense of Mrs. Winthrop's case. *Alice*, she said to herself, *What can it all mean?*

Nine children, each with a remarkably consistent delusion, even to seemingly meaningless details…the color and decorations on the pirate's captain's coat, the number of mermaids in the lagoon, the wild beasts that roamed the imaginary island, all consistent down to the last leaf of the strange garb of their "leader", Peter Pan.

"Kidnapper, more likely, or at least the henchman of this so-called pirate Hook," Alice said aloud. Each of the children, at least initially, had told the same story.

According to the reports, it had been very difficult to convince the children to give up this story, until at last, John Darling, Wendy's brother, began to show some inconsistencies in his narrative, claiming, for example that it was he and not this Peter who had defeated the Hookman.

Once a crack in the story appeared, it was only a matter of time until the whole thing fell apart. That is how it goes, one by one, the children admitted that there was no "Neverland." Wendy Winthrop, it seems, had been the last to give up the delusion.

Alice was suddenly sure that this had not been a suicide attempt. Michael Darling had reported that his sister had been crying that she must get to this "Neverland" when he pulled her from the ledge. She was trying to fly, Alice realized.

Alice forced herself back along her own difficult past to better understand her patient. She herself had never been able to recall the actual events that led to her creation of the horrible and ironically named "Wonderland" she once thought she had visited. "Rude Land, is what they ought to call it," she said. "Imagine all that nonsense about chivalry and knights, and the White Knight just goes off and leaves me with nothing but Silly Poetry…although, of course, I did become a Queen." She smiled. There was a moment of satisfaction in that memory, at least.

She sat up suddenly and shook her head. "But of course, it wasn't true," she said. "Something terrible happened to me, and I made up these outlandish tales to cope. Now, I see that. It doesn't matter what happened to me. I survived, I came home, and I am an extremely proper and celebrated psychologist, who has been published and…Oh, hello, Ruby."

A small reddish-orange kitten had come out from under her chair, nuzzling about her ankle. A warm and safe feeling washed over her as she scooped up Ruby. Her desire for a cigarette gone, she settled the kitten in her lap. *Nothing that can't be solved if you have a cat on your lap*, she said to herself. She went back to the case file.

"Curiouser and curiouser," she mused. "It seems that there have been some further unexplained disappearances of Darling-Winthrop children through the years, yet they all returned safely.

There was no serious investigation." She continued to flip through the pages, skimming for relevant data.

She considered Mrs. Winthrop's "supposed" suicide attempt, and the reported "Neverland" remarks. Something must still remain of Wendy's childhood horror, and in there would be a clue to the missing child's whereabouts.

She was deep into the file when she was startled by a soft knock. Quickly, she tucked the kitten and thermos into her handbag, tossed the teacup in the trash, and went to the door.

Alice opened the door and looked at the visitor. There stood a man, perhaps fifty years old, with an absurd shock of straw-colored hair crowning his balding head. His hands were held open in front of his chest, as if he was expecting a gift of some kind. He was ever so slightly plump, reminding Alice of a teddy bear, and his ocean blue eyes brimmed with tears. He smiled shyly at her. Alice had never seen a sweeter or a sadder man.

"Hello," he said, wiping quickly at his eyes with a linen handkerchief. "I'm Michael Darling, Wendy Winthrop's brother. You are her doctor?" He looked eagerly into her eyes.

"Yes," Alice replied, putting on her most professional face, hoping she did not smell of brandy. Thank God she had resisted the cigarette!

"I'm Dr. Liddell. I've been assigned to your sister because of my expertise in childhood trauma." At these words, a look of confusion crossed his face.

"I know your sister is no child, but you and all your siblings did experience…'something' in childhood, and I believe this 'something' is the key to your sister's seeming suicide attempt and your grandniece's disappearance."

She plunged forward, confident in her diagnosis. "Mr. Darling," she said. "I cannot help but notice that there have been intermittent instances through the years when a child…at first your sister, then your niece Jane, and now your grandniece Margaret, have disappeared for weeks at a time. The only family member who was concerned about these happenings has been your brother John. The initial kidnapping case, the kidnapping of yourself, your siblings, and other lost children, was never solved. Not one of you can recall any details of what really happened."

"I am going out on a limb here," she said, "But I think that the same person who took you all, had in turn taken your sister again when she was a child, then your niece, and now your grandniece. For some reason, your sister seems to have been an accomplice in these disappearances and so far, the chosen child has been returned on a pre-arranged schedule. But something has gone awry this time, and we must now at last uncover what happened to you and the other children so very long ago." Alice took a deep breath and smiled inwardly at her own brilliance.

Michael smiled again the same sweet shy smile. "Well, you know," said Michael, ducking his head and giving her a sidelong glance, "No one can refuse Peter. Wendy certainly could not."

Alice was horrified, but she maintained her professional demeanor. She ushered the man to a chair and sat down in another next to him. Steadying her voice to a soothing and appropriately professional cadence, she said, "You are speaking as though you still believe in your trauma-induced delusion."

Looking at his soft, dreaming face, she put her hand under her chin and leaned forward, with a quizzical look, which she hoped did not betray her agitation at his remark.

She did not immediately speak but waited for Michael Darling to continue. It had been her experience, that subjected to a smoldering stare and a prolonged, heavy silence, a patient would feel compelled to speak, and what that patient then spoke, would be the truth.

"I did think it was delusion, yes," he finally said after a withering minute under her rather intense gaze. "We all did, I guess, but truth be told, I never thought that Wendy had stopped believing. I never was sure. But I think my sister finally figured out that it was better to say she didn't believe any more."

"But now…" he paused and buried his face in his hands. "But now…with what has happened to Margaret…" He lifted his head, wiped again at the trace of tears, composed himself, and continued excitedly, "But now, that your colleague has confirmed that, in fact, it was no delusion and everything, EVERYTHING, was all true, what are we to do?" He gazed at her, a look of idiot hope and desperation on his face.

Alice was now far beyond merely horrified. She was enraged. She felt her cheeks grow red and flushed, and her fingers twitched involuntarily, so she put her hand down into the bag to touch the kitten (sleeping, thankfully) and with the greatest of efforts, she spoke calmly.

"My colleague, Ms. Gale, do you mean? She confirmed your childhood story?" she asked, stroking the kitten in an effort to maintain some semblance of professionalism, despite the overwhelming urge to scream out loud. She didn't really think she was succeeding, but Mr. Darling did not seem to notice her agitation, he was so caught in his renewed fantasy.

"Yes," Mr. Darling replied. "It was such a great relief to my sister and me, to have the story validated at last, and to know that we have a lead as to what might have happened to Margaret."

Alice furiously stroked the kitten until it wriggled away and buried itself deeper into the bag, and with all the self-control left to her, she said, "Thank you, Mr. Darling. Rest assured that your sister will receive the utmost care and the most modern and appropriate therapies. We will work kindly and thoughtfully with her to uncover the buried knowledge that will lead us to Margaret's kidnapper. Now if you will excuse me…"

She rose abruptly, slinging the bag with the kitten and brandy over her shoulder, and stalked down the hallway towards Mrs. Winthrop's room, leaving Michael Darling sitting puzzled and alone in his chair. He shook his head and remarked to himself, "Maybe I am crazy, crazy as my sister." He shook his head again. "Or, maybe I am not".

CHAPTER ELEVEN

DOROTHY GALE HAS REALLY DONE IT NOW

Alice Liddell stormed down the hall. "Now she's really done it," she said, her voice seething with indignation. "How totally unprofessional, how unorthodox, how, how, how... INAPPROPRIATE!"

Yes, Dorothy Gale really had done it now, encouraging the patient in her fantasies. "And not just Mrs. Winthrop, but speaking that way to her brother, re-awaking his own delusions!" she exclaimed, continuing her thunderstorm down the hall, oblivious to the knowing looks and winking nods from the other staff as she passed.

Dr. Liddell arrived at the door of Mrs. Winthrop's room, and took a moment to pull herself together, flattening down her hair and straightening her lab coat. *Must be professional,* she told herself. *Take the higher ground.* Then she opened the door without knocking.

Mrs. Winthrop was sitting on the side of her bed, the IV removed from her arm. Dorothy Gale sat next to her. Alice listened incredulously to their conversation.

Dorothy was saying, "I was just a little girl when I went away for the first time", she said. "My parents died in a terrible fire. I went to live with my Aunty Em and Uncle Henry on their farm in Kansas. They were so good to me, so very good…"

The two women were so wrapped up in their conversation, they had not noticed Alice's entrance. Alice stood silently at the door and watched, pursing her lips, and folding her arms across her chest.

This should be good, she thought. Inspired, she uncrossed her arms to reach into her lab coat and turned on her pocket recorder. She recrossed her arms and leaned back to watch the show.

"One day there was a terrible tornado, and I didn't make it into the cellar in time. So my dog Toto and I, and our whole house, were swept up in it and landed in a magic place called Oz."

"I had some adventures, let me tell you," Dorothy laughed. "But I wanted to go home because Aunty Em and Uncle Henry would be so worried. But I made lots of good friends—really wonderful and true friends, the best friends a girl could ever have, and then even after I got home, I went back there many times. There were dangers and some truly evil creatures, but some wonderful creatures too. Finally, Aunty Em and Uncle Henry moved there and I became a Princess of Oz." Dorothy smiled with pride, and touched her head, as if adjusting a crown.

Dorothy continued. "Ozma, the Fairy Queen of Oz, still looks in on me from time to time in her magic mirror. If I am ever in real trouble, she will help me."

"So why are you here?" Wendy asked. "Why aren't you in Oz?"

Dorothy shifted uncomfortably and looked at the floor. "There was a problem," she said, looking away. "For a number of reasons, I needed to leave Oz. Now I am here, and I try to help those who have also been to another place, another world."

Alice took a step back into the hall. This was far more egregious than she had thought. She was torn between stopping this crazy conversation immediately or waiting to see where the clearly disturbed Ms. Gale would go with it. She stepped quietly back to the door, still unnoticed and continued to listen and record.

"You almost never get there the same way twice," Dorothy was saying. "So flying back out your window, of course it didn't work."

"Almost never..." Wendy sighed. "But I don't know how else to get there. And I did get there several times that way, so it isn't actually 'never', now is it?"

Wendy put her face in her hands and shook her head. Then she sat up, composed herself as best she could, and said ruefully, "I thought it was worth a try."

Dorothy smiled, patted her on the arm, and continued breathlessly, "I've gotten back to Oz in oh so many different ways... tornado at first, also an earthquake, shipwreck, and of course, Ozma's Magic Belt...but we must find a way back to *your* Neverland. I don't know if Ozma will be able to help. It's a different place, and in all my time in Oz I never heard of it."

"There must be other ways to get there," mused Wendy. "Peter brought the children, but there were adult pirates and natives there. I wonder how they came to the Neverland."

Standing at the door, her fingers twitching and drumming silently on her crossed arms, Alice could contain herself no longer. She cleared her throat loudly and artificially.

"Ms. Gale," she said, in as even a voice as she could muster, "Ms. Gale, you really have gone too far this time. Indulging the patient's fantasies to such a degree is shocking! Why, if you were a doctor, you would have your license revoked."

She took the recorder out of her pocket and held it up triumphantly. "You may not have a license to lose, but I can assure you that I will have you fired!"

Dorothy Gale turned and looked at Dr. Liddell without speaking. A queer look crossed her face. She seemed to be pondering her next words very carefully. "Dr. Liddell," she said. She hesitated, then, in a tender voice, "Alice."

Dorothy hesitated again. *How to say this?* It was something she had been thinking about talking to Dr. Liddell about for some time, but until this crisis, there had been no hurry. *Better to wait for the right moment*, she had thought. The right moment would come, it always did. But now, there would be no right moment, only this crisis situation.

Dorothy spoke slowly and deliberately. "You and I have had our differences, certainly. But both of us want to help those children, those people who have been to a different place. They are real, you know, those other worlds. I know you have been to one. I have. You have. Wendy Winthrop has. We have all been there…someplace else, some place magical and dangerous and beautiful and strange."

Dorothy was looking right into Alice's eyes, with a clear and caring gaze. "When a child returns from any different place, it can be disorienting, scary, and worst of all, no one believes you. It's traumatic. These people, mostly children, need help! So there are two ways to help…your way, which is to make the different place not real, something they imagined, so that only this is real. It works, and it helps some people. Truly it does. You've done great work. They can live in this world, and never look back."

"But my way…my way is to let them know that they are not crazy, and that there really are other places, but that now that they are home, they need to put the other place away, as a memory, or a story for their children, and be happy here, or else they need to find a way to return and never come back. Either way, whatever happened in that other world must be dealt with."

Dorothy paused. "You went someplace," she said. "I can see that. Because you are so brilliant, no one at the hospital minds all your peculiarities…no mirrors, kittens everywhere, or that you forbid your patients from having playing cards…"

Alice Liddell was furious. She thrust her hand into the bag and felt for the sleeping kitten, but it had buried itself too deep for her to reach.

"Nonsense," she exclaimed. "I had terrible childhood traumas, and I invented this bizarre and dangerous land to protect myself from what really happened and where I really was. Kidnapped, tortured perhaps, who knows? But I escaped, and it doesn't matter if I covered it with false memories, or even what really happened. What matters is that I live in the here and now, and I am just fine." She gazed back at Dorothy with a stern and withering look. In her head, she repeated, *Just fine.*

Dorothy gazed at Dr. Liddell with an expression that could only be described as amusement.

Dr. Liddell huffed and said hotly, "If I have a few eccentricities, well that is to be expected, under the circumstances. Harmless eccentricities. But it does not in any way prove the existence of a 'wonderland' filled with odd and rude creatures, unwilling to help a lost child."

Unexpectedly, Alice's expression changed, looking soft and hurt for a moment. "Without even the decency to serve her a proper cup of tea."

Wendy Winthrop stepped in between the two women. She no longer seemed like an older, tired woman in a night gown, but instead had become a mythological heroine, an avenging angel, an earth mother, a goddess. Her eyes sparkled with purpose.

"I do not care about your differences," she said sternly. "I believe that I will require help from both of you to get me to Neverland and rescue Margaret." She placed a hand on each of their shoulders and looked from one to the other with a fierce intensity.

Alice was shaken out of her reverie, and she angrily declared, "There is no Neverland, no Oz, and certainly no Wonderland, or a world behind the mirror. Dorothy Gale, your time at this hospital is done!"

Dorothy stood for a moment, looking at Alice Liddell with a quizzical look. Wendy remained between the two, blazing, looking from one to the other.

"Stop it, you two," Wendy shouted, pushing them both back to arm's length, keeping her a hand on each one. "Don't you see I need *both* of you to help me?"

Dorothy seemed to be pondering something. Finally, she made up her mind and shook Wendy's hand from her shoulder. She stepped over to the closet and opened the door.

On the back of the door, was an unbreakable (for the patients' safety) full-length mirror. She turned to Alice Liddell and said, "So if there is no Wonderland, no Looking Glass land, you won't have any trouble looking into this mirror."

This was a bet on Dorothy's part. She knew if she lost this bet, her time here was truly done. Dorothy had no information about Dr. Liddell's actual experiences, but her many phobias, especially around mirrors, were legendary in the hospital, and she was gambling that this particular phobia had something to do with the passage to the other place.

Dr. Liddell hesitated. She did hate mirrors. Once again, she reached for the kitten and this time was able to touch the comforting fur and feel the gentle purr. She looked at Wendy in confusion.

Wendy Winthrop put on a bathrobe and went to Alice, and put an arm around her waist. "It's all right, dear," she said. "Dorothy and I will be right beside you."

Dorothy stepped to the other side of Wendy, who circled Dorothy with her other arm. All three stepped towards the mirror.

Dr. Alice Liddell steadied her nerves. She stiffened her spine and thrust her shoulders back, to appear taller and stronger. *Nothing will happen,* she thought. *Nothing at all.* She looked at the reflection of herself and the two women walking towards the mirror. "Nothing at all," she repeated aloud.

CHAPTER TWELVE

THROUGH THE LOOKING GLASS

The mirror reflected nothing but the three women, and the hospital room. There was Dr. Liddell, lab coat and bag, with an iron look on her face that barely concealed her fear. There was Dorothy Gale, smiling and expectant. Finally, there was Wendy, standing between the two women. Even in her bathrobe and slippered feet, shortest of the three, she was nevertheless the leader, possessed of calming power. Instinctively, she pulled them closer, as if she could protect them from whatever the mirror held.

At first, they saw only themselves. As they continued to gaze at the mirror, the reflection wavered, and the background began a slow yet subtle change. The reflected walls of the room were becoming transparent, but instead of the hospital grounds outside the walls, there was an incredible garden, with a riot of flowers. Dorothy held her breath, and Wendy pulled Alice closer as she felt the doctor shiver.

Slowly, Alice closed her eyes and turned her head to look behind, hoping that when she opened them again, she would see that she was actually in the plain but comfortingly real hospital room, that she was not back in the fantastic and all too familiar garden of her childhood.

She opened her eyes and groaned. The garden, with its riot of flowers was, indeed, behind them. Quickly she turned her head back to where the mirror ought to be. Instead of the mirror, there just was more of the garden, stretching out for acres with winding paths.

Dorothy looked around in delight and clapped her hands. "What a beautiful place! Look at all the amazing flowers."

At first glance, it was a typical English garden with well-tended beds of flowers and herbs, and paths of crushed gravel. A second look, however, revealed some peculiarities.

The flowers, on closer inspection, had features more than coincidentally like actual faces, and they moved in directions not dictated by the wind, but twisted and turned as if under their own power.

All the flowers turned to face our travelers. A hum, not of bees but of voices, grew loud and filled the air, although no people were to be seen.

A Tiger Lily, which had been preening its orange and black speckled petals, turned to Dorothy, and clearly said, "Why, thank you, my dear."

Dorothy heard a small titter of laughter, or something like laughter. She looked down to see a small patch of violets by her feet blush from a rosy pink-purple color to indigo.

The Tiger Lily was clearly in charge, or at least she thought she was. "Nice to see you again," said the Tiger Lily, turning to Alice. "But I'd advise you and your friends to move on. The gardener is coming soon, and you are looking a little weedy and overgrown. Wouldn't want you to be pulled out or dead-headed."

Alice was looking about frantically, and moaning, "No, no, no!" She did not appear to have heard the Tiger Lily at all.

"Thank you for the advice," Dorothy politely replied. Her experience in Oz had long ago taught her that it always pays to be polite, no matter how strange a person or thing you are speaking with. She turned to her companions. Wendy did not seem at all fazed by the sudden change in their environment, and was looking towards the distant horizon, where the outline of a castle could be seen through a silver fog that was rising from a nearby bog. Alice, on the other hand...

Alice was now sitting on a nearby stone bench, her eyes closed and her hands at her temples, shaking her head. "Real, real, real..." she muttered. "Should not be, but real, damn it all."

Wendy seemed content to stare at the castle, and Alice was clearly not dealing well with the situation. Dorothy knew, however, that they could not remain in the garden for long.

"Come on," said Dorothy urgently, "We must get out of here before the gardener arrives. Deadheading sounds dangerous. We should try and find your friends here."

She touched Alice on the shoulder, but Alice did not respond. She just sat there, head in hands repeating her mantra over and over.

Now Dorothy put a hand on each shoulder and shook her roughly, thrusting her face close to Alice's and studying her intently. "Your friends?" she repeated. "Where can we find your friends?"

Alice closed her eyes and took a moment. *Alright,* she thought. *So, it was real. IS real.*

She was shaken and felt unsteady. Her entire belief system had been pulled out from under her. Then, angry acceptance came over her. It had been real, and it had been awful.

Dorothy's insistent questioning finally broke through her internal dialog. Alice opened her eyes, dropped her hands to her lap and gave a short, harsh laugh. "Friends? I have no friends here. This is a terrible place, full of strange and incredibly rude creatures. You would not want to be friends with anyone or anything here."

Wendy had been searching the landscape for some clue to Margaret, but when she caught the pain in Alice's voice, she turned and ran to her, knelt down, and held her hands, and gently asked, "What happened to you here?"

Alice laughed again, but it was not a very pleasant laugh. She looked about and spotted a gate. "At least we were dropped at the perimeter. Let's get out of this garden. It is a long story…it is actually two stories, but I can tell you as we walk."

The women headed to the garden gate, which opened to a dirt path, which led into some woods. As they walked towards the gate, each of the flowers seemed to have something to say for itself. They were all talking at once, so it was hard to sort out what each was saying. The Daisies kept hinting that they had a secret. The Irises told them to keep their eyes open, and the Snapdragons just kept snapping at their ankles.

The Tiger Lily, always in charge, called to Alice as they approached the gate. "Now dear, do be careful and don't make the same mistakes twice. Make new ones!" Alice shook her head and sighed.

As they opened the gate and headed toward the woods, Dorothy waved thanks to the flowers, while Alice scowled and kept her head down. Wendy put a tentative arm around her but pulled it back at the chill in her posture. With motherly concern, Wendy asked again, "What happened to you here?"

Surprisingly, Alice told them.

CHAPTER THIRTEEN
ALICE'S STORY

As they walked, Alice Liddell spoke. "The first time, I was bored, reading with my sister, and I saw a White Rabbit with a pocket watch, which made me quite curious. I was a very curious child. I had never seen a rabbit in clothes with a watch, and then he talked! So, naturally I followed him down a rabbit hole. I could not catch up to him for the longest time, but I tried anyway. I came to realize that I had fallen into a very peculiar place, where nothing ever seemed to have any logic. Along the way, every creature I met was extremely bizarre, as well as rude or insane, mostly both. I was a little girl, I was lost, and it was terrible. No one would help me, and I couldn't make sense of anything. And they were all so rude!"

As she spoke, Alice became more and more agitated. Her face was flushed, her voice got higher, and the words came faster and faster.

Dorothy weighed her next question carefully. "Are you sure they were being rude?" she asked. "Sometimes, when you are in a new country, and you don't understand the local customs, something may appear rude to you, but it may be considered proper and mannerly by the people who live there. Conversely, you may think you are being perfectly logical and polite, but to the native population, you may seem to be the rude or insane creature."

"Listen" said Alice, already far beyond vexed at the conversation, "Here is just one example. I went to this tea party…"

"Oh, a Tea Party! How nice to be invited to a Tea Party!" said Wendy. Then, a touch wistfully, "Peter and I would sometimes have tea together. Of course, it was not real tea, just water, and we did not eat real teacakes, just some bread…while I did my best, the kitchen facilities were not terribly modern, and baking anything fancy was just out of the question. I think there was a proper stove on the pirate ship…" Wendy seemed to be drifting back into her own memories.

Alice interrupted. "That's just it! I was not invited! There was this big table, all set for tea, with only the Hatter, the Hare, and the Dormouse, and they told me there was no room. I could see there was plenty of room, so I just sat myself down."

"Well," said Dorothy, "Right off, I can see how they might think *you* rude, sitting down without being invited. Suppose they were waiting on other guests and only had just enough chairs?"

"Well, there wasn't anyone else coming," Alice replied crossly. "At least, no one else showed up."

She looked doubtful for a moment, and then shook her head. "The Hatter's watch was broken because the Hare had put butter in it. Now tell me, is that not a loony way to try and repair a watch?"

"Was it good butter?" inquired Dorothy.

"It was the Best Butter, according to the Hare," Alice replied sourly.

"Well," said Dorothy, "I only asked because we oil our machines with mineral oil. Perhaps they use butter like we use oil. It could just be a different custom, and not crazy at all."

"Then," Alice continued, ignoring Dorothy, "the Dormouse, who, by the way, slept half of the time, with his head either on the table or in the food, recited the most nonsensical poem and told an extremely dreary story which I think he was making up as he went along. Then they asked a riddle with no answer. Everyone here is mad about reciting poetry, which makes no sense at all."

They had exited the garden and were now walking through a meadow, towards the woods. The plants here seemed to be ordinary plants, not capable or perhaps not interested in conversation. This was a disappointment to Dorothy.

Wendy said nostalgically, "It was the stories that first brought Peter to my window. He would listen, and then he would go and tell the Lost Boys. I cannot think it could be considered rude to tell a story, even if it was not exactly to your taste."

Dorothy said, "Yes, I am fairly sure that in reciting the Poem, and telling the Story, these people were doing their very best to be good hosts and to entertain you, even though you were an uninvited guest. And it is certainly very hard to learn to appreciate the arts of another culture or time. I know that I cannot listen to the old chants from church, which the monks used to sing, because they just make me sleepy. But I know that they are beautiful to some, and perhaps if I understood more, I might hear the beauty there."

A dark look had crossed Alice's face. Seeing trouble and hoping to break the tension, Wendy asked, "Can you remember any of these poems? Perhaps if Dorothy and I heard them, we would understand…"

Alice sighed. "There were so many I heard." She stopped and thought for a moment. "Well, just listen to this."

She stepped up onto a nearby rock, which served as her stage. She composed herself, standing straight and folding her hands together as if reciting at school.

> 'Twas brillig, and the slithy toves,
> Did gyre and gimble in the wabe;
> All mimsy were the borogoves,
> And the mome raths outgrabe.
>
> "Beware the Jabberwock, my son!
> The jaws that bite, the claws that catch!

Beware the Jubjub bird, and shun
The frumious Bandersnatch!"

It was a scary poem, and Dorothy had grown paler and paler with each verse. Before Alice could finish, Dorothy interrupted and cried, "What does it mean? Did you ever find out what it means?"

Alice, glad at least not to be the only one disturbed by their circumstances, replied, "A little bit of it, yes. I met Humpty Dumpty (another rude individual, I might add), who was able to explain some of the first verse. For instance, 'slithy' means lithe and slimy. Some of the words are combinations of other words. But some are creatures, which must be native to this place. He told me a rath is a sort of green pig."

"And you heard many more like this?" Dorothy asked urgently. "Yes, of course," said Alice, "I told you everyone here is mad about poetry, but I am not going to recite them all for you now."

Wendy seemed to have pulled out of her reverie. She looked at the two women who were, through fate or circumstance, destined to be her heroes on the rescue mission, and saw that both were in distress. She must rally her champions.

She said carefully to Alice, "I don't think that you were entirely friendless here. Humpty Dumpty kindly explained the words you did not understand in the poems. I think you must have had many more gestures of friendship and aid, although you may not have realized it at the time."

Wendy smiled and gently laid her hand on Alice's shoulder. "You were just a small child, after all. Think carefully...who helped you here, who gave you advice or direction, or had you as a guest?"

"Humpty Dumpty!" said Dorothy urgently. "We must find him!"

Wendy gestured to Dorothy to be quiet and kept her attention on Alice.

Alice ignored Dorothy and thought. "Well, let's see. I suppose the Cheshire Cat was friendly, and I am awfully fond of cats. And the White Knight rescued me from the Red Knight and escorted me across the chessboard so I could become a queen. And the Dodo bird, well, he did organize a Caucus race to help dry me and the mouse and the other small creatures after we had been flooded with my tears. And the Caterpillar helped with my size problem, and…"

They had now entered the woods. Dorothy, still agitated and impatient, but respecting Wendy's admonition to "hush," looked around at the forest.

The proportions seemed wrong. They had entered a wood with trees and ferns and wildflowers, on a path of fine soil and dead leaves. Now the ferns seemed to tower over their heads, the trees were like walls, and they were walking ankle deep though a pile of enormous leaves. Just then, they rounded a corner of the path, and there before them was an incredibly large mushroom, and on it sat an equally large blue Caterpillar, smoking a hookah.

All three stood looking up at the Caterpillar and the mushroom. The mushroom was about six feet tall, if they could judge by their own height, and they could just touch the edges if they stood up on tiptoe. They could see the gills underneath, pink and frilly, and a feathery ring encircling the stem. Dorothy and Wendy could not see the top from where they stood, but Alice knew that it would be red, with white splotches all about.

The Caterpillar himself was a deep rich blue, the color of a mountain lake. The fat segments on his body were divided by buttercup yellow joints. He was covered with a fine soft hair-like fur (or fur-like hair) of a lighter, sky-blue shade. He wore a pair of tinted (blue, of course) glasses, but no other garment. His short arms, or perhaps legs, held the ornate silver hookah, which seemed to have all his attention. He did not appear to notice his visitors.

Rolling her eyes, Alice noisily cleared her throat, and the Caterpillar slowly turned towards them. He blew a smoke ring, which drifted lazily over their heads, and watched it dreamily. When it finally dissipated, he settled his gaze on Alice, peering down at her.

"Hello, you," he said casually. Then, turning to Wendy and Dorothy, he blew another ring of smoke and asked, in a more formal tone, "Who are you?" The smoke rings floated lazily above their heads. Alice tried to fan them away without success.

Dorothy curtsied deeply, "I'm Dorothy Gale, from Kansas."

Wendy also curtsied, although not so low, due to her aging knees. "Wendy Moira Angela Darling Winthrop," she replied, her voice sinking ever so slightly on the "Winthrop."

This seemed to satisfy the Caterpillar, so he resumed puffing on his hookah and did not seem inclined to continue the conversation. Alice rolled her eyes. "Rude, I tell you," she muttered. "Everyone here is rude."

The Caterpillar turned to her, as quickly as a caterpillar might. "You think so?" he asked. He was now looking directly at Alice, and he coiled his body to hang out and just over the edge of the mushroom, his face quite close to hers.

She shifted from one foot to the other uncomfortably. "Perhaps," she said, with some difficulty, "perhaps I did not quite understand your intentions."

The Caterpillar looked at her with an unreadable expression, pulled himself back up and took another deep draw from the hookah. He let forth another smoke ring, which drifted up and over their heads, hanging in the air for several minutes along with Alice's words, before dissolving into wisps.

"Perhaps," he replied at last. "Perhaps you did not. I imagine the mushroom bits you took last time are either used or terribly dried. You may take some more if you like."

Wendy whispered to Alice, "It would be impolite not to take his gift." Alice nodded, and reached around the mushroom, as far as her hands would reach, and broke off a piece from each side. She put the piece from the left side in the left-hand pocket of her lab coat, and the piece from the right side in her right-hand pocket.

She nodded to the Caterpillar, who nodded back. He resumed smoking the hookah and paid them no more attention. It was clear he was done with the conversation. The women turned and walked on.

Wendy patted Alice's shoulder again. "You see, that was not so bad. It never hurts to be nice. I really think you do have friends here."

"Yes" said Dorothy impatiently. "Let's find this Humpty Dumpty. And do you remember any more of the verses?"

Alice had had more than enough of Dorothy Gale, and once again, Alice ignored her. "I suppose we'd better go find the White Rabbit. Now that I think of it, I wasn't very nice to him. He had mistaken me for his maid, Mary Ann, and instead of correcting him, I went to his house to collect his fan and did some damage there."

"No," Dorothy said emphatically. "We must go to Humpty Dumpty. I want to talk to him about these poems!"

"Why ever so, dear?" Wendy inquired. "As Dr. Liddell says, they are just nonsense."

"No…" Dorothy replied slowly. "There is something important in them—a clue, I think. I must use it to save my friend, and these poems have the answer."

CHAPTER FOURTEEN

THE WHITE KNIGHT

Before the other two could ask Dorothy to explain her startling statement, a deafening clattering of hooves and clinking of iron drowned out any further conversation. A sudden cloud of dust rolled across their path, and when it cleared, there before them stood a White Knight upon his horse. He looked rather old, and a little fragile, as if he had been riding for some time and was a bit worn out with it all. His armor (ill-fitting, as if intended for a larger man), his hair (which stuck out from his helmet in great spider web-like wisps), his weapons (hanging loosely about his armor without any sense of order), his horse (old, thin, and knobby-kneed), and all the horse's trappings (worn and threadbare) were white.

The clattering did not stop when the horse stopped, for the Knight trembled and shook with every move, as if he and the horse were not pieced together securely. The Knight raised his visor and revealed his face. Although not quite white, his skin was pale and wrinkled with age. Tufts of white hair wreathed his face. His nose was large, his lips thin, but his eyes were very blue and very kind, and his smile was sweet and sad.

Alice curtsied, automatically, and then stood up and looked around with a look that somehow combined her embarrassment and scorn. Wendy also curtsied, as much as her aged knees would allow, but instead of curtsying, Dorothy ran forward, clutched the Knight's hand, and asked, "Can you take us to Humpty Dumpty? It's terribly important! I think he is the only one who can save my friend!" Tears were streaming down her face, and the Knight reached down to brush the tear from her cheek, but in doing so, he fell off his horse with another great clatter.

Wendy, who could not bear to see someone in distress, was torn between helping the Knight, or Dorothy. The Knight waved her off, and so she went to Dorothy and wrapped her arms around her.

The Knight gathered himself together as well as he could and stood up. He looked at Alice briefly, and said, with great affection and kindness, "Oh, hello, your Majesty!"

He immediately turned his attention to Dorothy, the damsel in distress, and knelt before her. "Your quest is my quest, child. Of course, I will take you to Humpty Dumpty."

He then looked back at Alice with an affectionate look and asked, "So, doing alright since we last met?"

Alice replied stiffly, "Yes, I think so." She shifted uncomfortably and looked at Wendy before continuing. She coughed and finally said to the Knight, "I don't know that I ever properly thanked you for your help last time I passed this way."

"No, you did not," the Knight replied without rancor. "But that is no matter. A Knight does not serve for thanks, a Knight serves to serve." He tried to bow to Alice, but as Dorothy still held his hands, and Wendy was holding Dorothy in her arms, the best he could manage without tumbling over the lot of them was a nod of his head. This caused his visor to fall over his face, which he could not correct while Dorothy held his hands.

Wendy calmed Dorothy down and induced her to let go of the Knight, who then stood stiffly awaiting orders. Wendy continued to soothe Dorothy, while Alice, regaining some composure, studied the situation clinically.

Realizing that she did not have enough information to make a reasoned response, Alice looked at Dorothy and asked, "What is going on? Why are these poems important to you? They are nonsense!"

Dorothy looked at Alice with impatience. She shook her head and sighed, deeply. "You don't get it? Do you really still think you are the only child who has ever been taken to another land, another world? No, I am afraid not. There are hundreds, thousands of us. Some of us have had wonderful times, and some have had terrible times. Some come home, some do not. Some come home willingly, and some do not. You, Wendy, and I, we came home."

Dorothy's eyes were blazing, and as she spoke, she paced back and forth. She turned to Alice. " You want my story? Okay, here it is. My parents died before I could even remember them. I was an orphan, taken in by my very loving but dirt-poor aunt and uncle, to live on a farm in Kansas. A little dull, I admit, but I was loved, I had a dog, and even if I dreamed of more, it was home."

"One day a tornado struck. I couldn't get into the cellar in time, so I hid in the house. That was no good. The tornado ripped the house off its foundations and took me to a beautiful and dangerous land called Oz."

Dorothy stopped her pacing and hesitated before continuing. She took a moment to try and compose herself, with only mediocre success.

"There I found the best and truest friends any girl could have. They wanted me to stay, but I wasn't ready to stay, even though it was so exciting and magical compared to Kansas. But in Kansas, I had an Aunt Em and Uncle Henry who loved and needed me, and whom I loved, so I went back."

At this, Wendy nodded with understanding. Alice listened quietly, an unreadable expression on her face.

"But Oz kept calling me. I went back, time and again, for new adventures. Finally, I brought Aunt Em and Uncle Henry with me to live in that magical land. We should have stayed forever and been happy there, but I…I made a mistake, a bad one. A really bad one."

She swallowed and took a deep breath. In a deceptively calm voice, she said, "My dearest friend paid the consequence. I could not help him, so I left. I came back to the world we know. I came back and stayed for good."

Dorothy pushed her sleeve back, and from under the cuff, she pushed forward a bracelet. It looked to be woven from straw or twigs, in a rustic style. She caressed the bracelet for a moment, but then she abruptly pushed it back under her sleeve, out of sight.

She continued, "Since I didn't think I could help my friend, I stayed and grew up in our world, and after a time, I discovered that I was not the only one. Children, and even grownups, have these experiences all the time! Coming back and staying back is really hard."

She furiously wiped away the remnants of her tears, drew herself up proudly and declared, "So I have devoted myself to helping others who, like me, like you, have gone to another place and returned. I help them come to terms with the experience. I didn't know if this makes up for my mistake, but I had hoped so."

"And now," she finished, "Now, if I can understand these poems, I think I can help him."

With surprising speed, Wendy hugged Dorothy again. It seemed that Wendy would have held her forever, had not the Knight coughed significantly, and he and his horse began to amble down an overgrown path. The women followed.

The White Knight and his horse were quite old, so it was not difficult to keep up on foot. Wendy walked beside the Knight, full of questions about the land. Alice lagged behind, and Dorothy slowed her pace to walk beside Alice.

Dorothy looked across the path to Alice Liddell, and thought about how best to begin a conversation. She had known Dr. Liddell for quite some time, and mostly had considered her an eccentric, powerful pain in the ass. It was only recently that Dorothy had begun to suspect they might share a similar history.

Dorothy's time in Oz had had more than its share of frights, terror, and danger, but mostly, Dorothy had found friends, safety, and love. From what she had observed in the hospital, confirmed by their short time in this new land, it was clear that Alice had not found these things in her time here.

Looking Glass World/Wonderland did not seem all that terrible, but Dorothy had only just arrived. How much of Alice's unhappiness was truly of her experiences in this place, and how much was Alice's perception of it, was not clear to Dorothy.

As she walked along, following the Knight, head down, Alice kicked every stone she could see. Her mind was racing. Every theory she had, every paper she wrote, every patient she cured, was based on the premise that these other worlds were not real. Yet here she was, either crazy or completely wrong. Alice was breathing heavily, with a troubled look on her face.

The path they were on brought them to a small creek, a mere trickle, which they easily crossed with a small jump. Dorothy noted with surprise that the creek did not meander, as one would expect, but flowed in a perfectly straight channel as far as she could see in either direction.

After crossing the small stream, they emerged from the forest. Alice looked up from her stone kicking and surveyed the landscape. She recognized the lush green meadow, dotted with tiny, non-verbal white flowers, with butterflies floating about. She thought that they were near the home of the Tweedle brothers, but Alice had no desire to revisit those quarrelsome twins.

"Well," she said to Dorothy, composing herself and straightening her shoulders. She assumed her professional Dr. Liddell voice, attempting to retain at least some measure of dignity and self-worth. "Well, Ms. Gale, now that you have gotten us here, how shall we get back? I don't suppose we will find Mrs. Winthrop's granddaughter here?"

"Please, I think under these circumstances, you must call me Dorothy," she replied. "And may I call you Alice?"

"Alice, it is, then, but again, do you know how to get us out of here?"

"Yes, I think so," Dorothy replied, hesitantly. "My good friend, Ozma, the ruler of all Oz, has a magic picture, which will show her whatever she wants to see. She looks for me every week, on Friday, and if I make a certain sign, she will bring me to Oz, with the magic belt I took from the Gnome King."

As she spoke the words "Gnome King" her voice trembled, and Alice saw real fear in her face. "But I cannot do it just yet."

"Why ever not?" Alice exclaimed impatiently. She stopped walking and crossed her arms, glaring at Dorothy.

Dorothy replied slowly, "I think there may be something here that can help my friend. He's terribly, terribly hurt." Dorothy looked away.

Seeing Dorothy's distress, Alice asked in her kindest, practiced, and most therapeutic voice, "What happened to your friend? Is this why you left this incredibly wonderful place, where you were a princess in a kingdom full of family and friends, to come back to our dreary world?"

Dorothy's face fell. "I don't want to think about that right now," she replied. A small and somewhat mean part of Alice was glad that her skills of observation and intuition were still intact. A larger and better part of Alice felt great empathy with the young woman walking beside her. She remained silent.

They came to another stream, small and straight as the first, and hopped across. They continued, walking a short distance behind Wendy and the Knight. Alice was relieved to see that the Knight's horse was obviously experienced in the crossings, as there was no sign of an imminent tumbling so far.

They walked in silence through the meadow. Alice waited, knowing that sooner or later, Dorothy would speak.

"Here is the thing…" Dorothy said at last. "In Oz, no one actually dies or grows old, but sometimes, terrible things can happen. They may be imprisoned, chopped up, or transformed into something, or forget who they are…terrible things. She seemed to be looking at something far away, and her voice trailed off, repeating, "Terrible things…"

Dorothy broke out of her reverie when she realized that Alice was watching her intently. "Sorry," she said, "just remembering."

"Sounds to me like you have unfinished business," Alice said cautiously. "Maybe I do too. Why are these poems so important to you?"

Just as cautiously, Dorothy replied, "My friend has suffered a brain injury, and he has been reciting poems like these, including the one you recited. So, it seems to me that if the poems are from this place, then the injury is linked to this place, and the cure must be too."

Wendy walked ahead, talking with the Knight. At first, she chatted politely, asking him simple questions, such as how long he had had his horse, and how he came to be a Knight. As they walked, she looked about, and saw that despite the meadow wildflowers, the ground seemed laid out in some sort of checkerboard pattern, and they had just crossed some sort of line. She recalled the two straight creeks that they had recently crossed.

"The landscaping here is very beautiful, although a bit unusual," Wendy said.

"It's to mark your place," the Knight replied, looking at her kindly, "As a newcomer, you are a pawn and can only move forward a space or two. I, as a Knight can make quite a clever maneuver…

one step over and then two forward, or three steps forward and then one over. Miss Alice can move anywhere she pleases, since she is a Queen," he said, glancing over his shoulder.

"Alice was quite a little girl when she first came here. She has grown up marvelously, but I would know her anywhere," the knight said fondly.

"Do little girls appear here often?" Wendy asked hopefully. "Have any new little girls shown up recently?"

"Not often," the Knight replied. "Actually, I think Miss Alice was the last." The Knight paused. "I'm sure you must all be getting hungry. I know where to find a very good cook."

CHAPTER FIFTEEN

THE COOK AND THE DUCHESS

The Knight picked up his pace and turned down a narrow path, moving so swiftly that Wendy, Alice, and Dorothy had to run to keep up with him.

Up until now, there had been an orderliness to the terrain, straight streams or paths at regular intervals. Now the Knight lead them across a bridge, which crossed a small brook which meandered in the usual way. The path also took a few turns, and it was not easy to see what lay ahead.

"We have left the Board", the Knight said solemnly.

Suddenly they turned a corner and came upon a small house, looking much like any English country cottage. It was surrounded by a small kitchen garden, grown wild with herbs and vegetables.

From within the house, a tremendous clattering almost deafened them. Alice gasped. She knew this house. "The Duchess and the Cook live here!" she exclaimed.

Alice had stopped in here on her way to the Queen's croquet game and met the residents and their very peculiar baby. From the noise coming from within, it appeared little had changed.

Oh dear, Alice thought. *I wonder what could have happened to the baby*. The last time Alice had been here, the household had been so noisy, the air so filled with the smell of pepper and flying dishware that she had taken the Duchess's baby away for its own safety. Imagine her surprise when, once they were safely in the woods, it turned into a piglet in her arms. She had turned it loose and hoped for the best.

A moment of silence was followed by the clanging of iron and the sound of breaking glass. Wendy and Dorothy stopped in alarm. Alice shrugged off the memory, as her hunger was growing stronger than her curiosity, for once.

"Oh, that will be the Cook," Alice explained. "She throws things while cooking. But she is an excellent chef, as long as she doesn't overdo the seasoning. Be careful, now."

The three women, led by the Knight, walked up to the door. The Knight knocked politely. But of course, with the din of flying crockery within, they were not heard. Impatiently, Alice strode forward and opened the door.

Inside, there was the old Duchess, wearing a royal blue dress and a white wimple, which was far too large for her and kept slipping down over her eyes.

Also within, there was a handsome young man sitting at the table, who ducked his head shyly and looked at Alice through his long, lowered eyelashes.

And there was the Cook, with her chef's hat pinned to her hair so it would not come loose while she continued throwing the spices and crockery all about.

"Will you stop flinging things about?" Alice shouted.

Immediately, the Cook stopped. "All you had to do was ask," she replied, and stirred the soup, which was bubbling on the stove, in a most peaceful manner.

The smell was tantalizing, with the scent of sweet, caramelized onions and some herbs that Wendy could not place. She was suddenly very hungry.

The Duchess rushed forward and embraced Alice, squeezing her so tightly she could scarcely breathe. Alice struggled to break free, but the Duchess continued to embrace her and showed no signs of letting go.

"My dear, how lovely to see you again! It has been so long...or has it? How are you? And who are your friends? Have you seen my child? Of course, you have, I remember. It was very naughty of you to release him in the woods, but you were just a child and had no notion of how to handle babies. Who are your friends? Introduce me!"

The Duchess, still clinging to Alice, peeked over Alice's shoulder at the other women with an eager smile.

The Duchess, Alice recalled, had actually been quite friendly to Alice, overly friendly, in fact. It seems this, also, had not changed. She slowly managed to extricate herself from the Duchess's embrace.

"This is Dorothy Gale," she said, pointing to Dorothy, who bowed low and did a deep curtsy.

"Honored indeed, to meet you," Dorothy said.

Alice rolled her eyes, but fortunately, no one noticed. "And this is Mrs. Wendy Moira Angela Darling Winthrop," she said. "Oh, and the Knight, the White Knight... he's been awfully helpful."

"Pleased to meet you!" the Duchess exclaimed. "And here is Cook! Alice, you remember Cook!"

The Cook looked up briefly from the kettle and nodded to Alice. Alice was dismayed to see a large peppermill sitting by the stove, but for the moment, at least, the Cook was letting it be.

Then the Duchess gestured towards the young man, and with motherly pride exclaimed, "And here is my Boy!" There was something very familiar about the "Boy", but Alice could not quite put her finger on it.

Cook set the table in relative silence, not speaking until the bowls had been placed before the guests.

"Seasoning," said the Cook. "It's all about getting the seasoning right." She looked at Alice triumphantly. "Don't you think so? Too much of the wrong spice and one never knows how it might affect one, right child?" She patted the young man's head, and continued, "But a good cook can always make adjustments so it come out as it should in the end."

Alice replied cautiously, "I think last time I was here, you had a little bit of a heavy hand with the pepper, but this smells delicious." At this remark, the young man looked around nervously, then covered his face with his handkerchief.

Alice wanted to inquire more deeply about the young man, but suddenly the Duchess exclaimed, "Gossip! Such good gossip! Do you have any idea what has been happening since you left? Well, it seems that the White Rabbit's Mary Ann went on trial for destruction of property, and she is due to be executed at sunrise tomorrow!"

Alice gasped. "But that isn't right! She didn't do it. We must save her." Alice knew quite well that she, not Mary Ann, had been the agent of destruction of the White Rabbit's house.

"Who is this Mary Ann?" Wendy asked. "And how do you know she is innocent?"

Adult Alice had almost completely forgotten about Mary Ann and the White Rabbit's house. In fact, as she thought about it now, it had not been her proudest moment.

"There was this White Rabbit, you see", she said. "He had mistaken me for his maid Mary Ann and sent me to his house for gloves and fan. And maybe I ate something there that made me a little too big to get out."

She hesitated; a bit embarrassed. "So I guess I broke out through the roof. And maybe I kicked a lizard up the chimney who was trying to get in." She looked away. She couldn't tell what the others were thinking about her confession.

But it wasn't really my fault, she thought. *It's not right to leave shrinking and growing potions, which aren't even properly labeled regarding the side effects, within reach of a child.*

"I was the one who did all the damage, and maybe injured poor Bill the Lizard. We have to go and clear Mary Ann's name," Alice finished quietly.

"I suppose you must," said the Duchess, as if this were not an extraordinary development. "Of course, you must. But let me have Cook pack you a basket for the road."

Cook turned back to the oven and turned down the soup. She quickly packed a delicious lunch for the travelers: a large thermos of soup, some sweet cakes, and a bottle of lemonade.

"Soup, soup, beautiful soup," Cook sang softly as she assembled the basket, adding in napkins, plates, spoons, a large salt mill and an equally large pepper shaker.

"So important to get the seasoning just right," she said. "As I don't know your tastes, I'm including these and a few other special things to make sure you have just what you need." She worked quickly, stuffing the basket with an assortment of items.

Alice and Dorothy thanked the Duchess and the Cook. Alice gathered the basket and looked back at the young man. It came to her all at once, and she almost laughed, but stifled it for politeness.

"Weren't you a pig, the last time I saw you?" she asked.

The young man blushed, and Cook said, "Yes, of course he was. Improper seasoning. Too much pepper, you remember. But with the proper ingredients, now he's right as rain."

CHAPTER SIXTEEN

THE QUEST

And now to Humpty Dumpty!" Dorothy shouted as they left the house.

"No!" said Wendy. "It's clear from my conversation with the Knight that Margaret is not here. We must find a way to Neverland."

"No," said Alice. "There has been a great injustice done to Mary Ann, and we must right it."

All three stubbornly stopped and folded their arms, resolutely refusing to take a further step. When it was clear that no one would budge from her conviction, all three women turned to the Knight.

Dorothy pleaded, "You must take us to Humpty Dumpty!"

Wendy beseeched, "My granddaughter is not here. You must get us out of this land."

Alice, calmer than the other two, and recalling at last how to manage in this strange place, bowed low before the Knight and said, "A great injustice has been done. An innocent's life is in danger. You must help me to vindicate Mary Ann."

The Knight paused and looked slowly and carefully at the three women. He spoke to Dorothy, answering the one who had pleaded with him first. "Is your friend in actual immediate physical danger?"

"I don't think so," Dorothy replied slowly. "But he has been terribly hurt and I think Humpty Dumpty can help."

He nodded, and turned to Wendy. "Your Granddaughter is missing, yes? But you do not know for certain that she is in mortal danger, do you?"

"No," Wendy replied. "But Peter would have brought her back on time unless something terrible had happened."

The Knight nodded again. He turned to Alice. "This innocent, Mary Ann—is she in mortal danger?"

"Yes," Alice replied emphatically. "When I was child, I did something foolish and caused some damage. And now, it appears that she will be executed for what I did!"

Alice stood still, her shoulders stooped, face fallen and head bent down, awaiting the Knight's judgment or reproach.

"Triage," said the Knight, murmuring to himself. "We must practice triage."

He closed his eyes and stroked his impressive mustache. After a few moments' thought, he said, "Mary Ann is in mortal danger, so we must rescue her first. Dorothy's friend is terribly hurt, so he must be next. Finally, Miss Wendy, as worrisome as it is not to know the fate of your granddaughter, we do not know that she is in any actual danger at all, so she must be our third priority."

The Knight closed his eyes and nodded. He seemed about to fall asleep. Just as Alice was thinking she ought to shake him or something, he opened his eyes.

"Haste!" the Knight shouted suddenly and put two fingers in his mouth and gave a loud whistle. From out of the forest came three other knights, one dressed in white, the other two in red. The White Knight conferred briefly with the other White Knight, and far longer with the two Red Knights, and finally approached the women.

"We will take you where you need to go," he said. "Fortunately, we are between matches and are on good terms. I will have to make some sacrifices in the next round," he sighed.

Alice climbed up behind her Knight, Dorothy behind the other White Knight, and Wendy behind one of the Reds. The other Red Knight scooped up their basket and belongings, and all four Knights proceeded down the road, with Alice's White Knight in the lead.

The Knights carried them swiftly, tacking left and right at random, until all three women were quite dizzy, and had no hope of finding their way back to where they had been.

They passed through towns and farms so quickly, it was not possible for any of them to describe with any accuracy what they had passed. Alice thought she had spied a familiar place or two, but with the speed of the Knights, she could not be certain.

They came abruptly upon a tall brick tower. Suddenly, as a gong sounded, the knights all stopped abruptly. All three women were thrown from their mounts, and the fourth Knight threw their belongings to the ground. "A Game!" they cried in unison. "To our Squares!"

The women watched the Knights dash off. The White Knight tried to turn back and bow, but he tumbled halfway off his horse. He was held on by his saddle strap, and so the horse rode onward, with the Knight dangling upside down, trying to right himself, until they were out of sight.

Alice sighed. "He was a good friend; I see that now. But, what to do about Mary Ann?" Alice sat on a nearby stone and rested her chin on the palms of her hands.

"Where are we? Wendy inquired. "Is this where we will find Mary Ann, or must we go farther on?"

"I don't think the Knights would just leave us without some direction. I think this is where we need to be," Dorothy replied. "They seem like very responsible fellows."

As they spoke, all three became aware of a sobbing, coming from a tower window far above.

CHAPTER SEVENTEEN

THE RESCUE OF MARY ANN

H ello, up there," Alice called. "Are you alright?"
"I am not alright," replied Mary Ann, leaning out of a
window at the top of the tower. (For indeed, it was Mary Ann, and
this was her prison.) "I'm locked up for something I did not do, and
I am to be executed tomorrow!"

The young woman, who was wearing an almost comical kitchen
maid's hat, burst into loud sobs.

Alice looked at the prison. The window was easily large enough
for Mary Ann to escape, it was just too high. "I know what to do,"
she said. She reached into her left pocket and pulled out a
mushroom bit, thinking this would help her reach the window.
Before she could do anything else, she heard a purring in her ear.

"Careful, my dear," the Cheshire Cat said between purrs. "That's
not exactly the same mushroom you had last time."

Alice looked at the mushroom bit. It did look different. There
was no Cat to be seen, but Alice felt his weight on her shoulder. His
purr dropped down to a whisper, and the Cat murmured some more
words into Alice's ear. Her eyes widened, and she put the mushroom
back in her pocket.

"Maybe I don't know what to do," she said.

"Should we try and find a ladder?" Dorothy asked.

Alice felt the Cheshire Cat again, this time weaving round her
ankles. As she looked down, he slowly appeared, first the grin, then
the tail and bit by bit all the parts in between. The sleek portly beast

was wearing a crown, although not on his head, for it would not have fit there. It was on his back.

Dorothy and Wendy had not noticed the cat, as Wendy was now speaking to Mary Ann, trying to assure her that rescue was imminent, while Dorothy looked about for a ladder or something to reach the window.

"You left this behind, last time," he purred. "Put it on. You are a Queen, and Queens can move in any direction."

"Why, so they can!" Alice exclaimed. She put on the crown, which she had won long ago when she had been a mere pawn on this chessboard. Her success in passing through the Looking Glass land had earned her this honor.

Just placing the crown on her head gave her an unexpected surge of confidence. Alice straightened her shoulders and assumed as regal a stance as she could muster. *I can move in any direction*, she thought. Then out loud, she shouted, "I am a Queen!"

Slowly Alice began to rise upwards, towards Mary Ann's window. Both Wendy and Dorothy turned at Alice's cry and watched with awe.

Once she had risen to the height of the window, Alice helped the girl to climb out, and held her in her arms (a bit awkwardly, as the girl was quite plump), and drifted regally back down.

I've done it! she thought. Wendy and Dorothy applauded.

But, once Alice set foot again on solid ground, and before she had a chance to recover her bearings, she was rudely grabbed by a pair of hands. She whirled around to face the Ace of Clubs.

They weren't in the Chessboard land now. They were in the land of the Playing Cards, and Alice was starting to be frightened, as the memory of her treatment last time she had been brought before the Queen of Hearts came rushing back.

She saw that Dorothy and Wendy were now held fast by the Ace of Diamonds and Ace of Hearts respectively. Mary Ann was seized by the Ace of Spades.

Dorothy was threatening to rip the Ace of Diamonds in half if he did not release her, while Wendy struggled vainly to break free of the Ace of Hearts.

The Ace laughed at Wendy's efforts, and she cried hotly, "You have no heart, heartless thing!" The Ace merely sneered and gripped her tighter.

The Aces were surprisingly strong, considering that they seemed to be made only of thick paper. From the front, they looked like ordinary soldiers, but sideways, they were no thicker than the playing cards they were named for.

"Aiding and abetting an escape attempt!" cried the Ace of Clubs. "It's off to the Queens with you lot!"

Alice looked about. The Cat, naturally, was nowhere to be seen. She was able to snatch up her bag and saw that Dorothy had managed to grab up the pack the Cook had given them. Wendy was still struggling in the arms of the Ace of Hearts.

Mary Ann was sobbing loudly in the grip of the Ace of Spades. "I'm innocent, I tell you, innocent!" she wailed.

"She is innocent," Alice declared. "And I am a Queen, and I demand that you release her!"

"You are a Chess Piece Queen, and we are Playing Cards," said the Ace of Clubs with disdain. "Perhaps that will earn you some professional courtesy from our Queens. But that is not for us to decide."

The Cards marched the four women around the prison tower to a wrought iron gate, with intricate filigree depicting all of the suits. A Flamingo was strolling across the lawn, but when it caught sight of Alice, it darted away.

No croquet for you today, she thought glumly.

As they were marched across the courtyard, Alice's attention was caught by a familiar voice.

"Oh, Mary Ann," said the White Rabbit, coming up to Alice. "Why were you so naughty? I never meant for you to be punished so severely!"

The Rabbit, the cause of all her troubles, had not changed a bit. He still wore his waistcoat, with the heavy watch chain hanging out of his pocket. His nose and ears twitched as he looked sorrowfully at Alice.

"But I wasn't naughty!" exclaimed Mary Ann. "It must have been someone else. I would never break your things and certainly never drink or eat anything I found in your house. I know better."

Mary Ann looked with suspicion at Alice. "Maybe it was her?"

At this outburst, the Rabbit turned to see the true Mary Ann. He looked at Alice, then at Mary Ann and back again in confusion. "Why, you two could be twins!" he exclaimed.

But before they could have any further conversation, the Aces hustled them off. The Rabbit called after them, "I would stay and act as a character witness, but I mustn't be late," and he hurried off.

Now it was Alice's turn to be confused. She looked at Mary Ann but could not understand how the Rabbit might think they were twins. There was no resemblance, not even a bit.

Shaking her head, she said to Wendy, "We look nothing alike. Never did. I told you this was a crazy place. Imagine that Rabbit mistaking me for her!"

Wendy looked over at Mary Ann, as the Cards continued to march them across the courtyard.

"Well," Wendy replied, "It's true you are much older now, but I do see a resemblance. Did you look like that when you were a girl, when you first came here? She looks to be about the age you said you were. And I remember that the first time Peter came back when

I was a grown-up woman, he did not see the grown-up woman. He only saw his Wendy."

Wendy sighed, and almost shed a tear, but when one is being hustled along by a Playing Card, tears are a luxury one cannot afford.

At last they reached the gates of the castle proper, and the White Rabbit, who had sprinted past them just in time to stand at the doors and blow a trumpet, and call out "Announcing the… prisoners!"

CHAPTER EIGHTEEN
THE QUEENS

This was not the throne room of the Queen of Hearts. "Thank goodness," muttered Alice. Instead of one, there were four thrones, with double seats, and on each sat the Kings and Queens of Hearts, Diamonds, Clubs, and Spades.

There was a distinct family resemblance among the Queens and Kings. All had long curling hair, heavy lidded eyes, thin mouths, and rounded faces. There were differences, as well. The Queen of Hearts' fiery orange hair was a wild corkscrew of curls, while the Queen of Diamonds' hair was a ruddy chestnut and curled softly around her face.

While the Black Queens each had long black hair, the Queen of Spades had a stern, set expression on her face, while the Queen of Clubs had a merry smile. Her eyes twinkled and Alice almost thought she saw some affection and camaraderie in her look.

The Kings, to a man (or card, perhaps), reflected the appearance of their respective Queens. All the Kings looked nervous.

The Queen of Hearts looked at Alice and hissed, "You again! Wasn't it off with her head for you?"

The Black Queens both stood up and shushed her, and the Queen of Diamonds looked embarrassed. "Forgive my sister," she said. "She is often a little impatient with justice."

"But justice will be done," the Queen of Spades declared. The Queen of Clubs asked Alice to step forward. The Queen of Clubs then bent down and removed the crown from Alice's head. She held it up and studied it carefully.

"You are a Queen, too?" The Queen of Clubs said thoughtfully. "A Chess Piece Queen, to be sure, but I think my sisters and I must take that into consideration in deciding your case."

The Kings had remained seated and silent during this conversation. Alice whispered to Dorothy, "That's how it is here. The Queens rule it all."

The four Queens all rose and walked together to an alcove off to one side of the thrones and bent their heads for a whispered discussion. The Kings shifted uneasily in their thrones, and the King of Hearts gave Alice a kindly wink and beckoned her to step forward. She did so, looking rather miserable in spite of his friendly gesture.

From the back of the room, Wendy and Dorothy could only catch small bits of the Queens' discussion, mostly owing to Mary Ann's incessant sobbing, which made eavesdropping next to impossible. Wendy looked as though she would stride forward and barge in on the Queens, but Dorothy held her back.

Finally, all four Queens returned to their thrones. The Queen of Hearts seemed especially out of sorts.

"We have decided," the Queen of Spades declared, "to grant professional courtesy to the Chess Piece Queen and her pawns. You three are free to go and will not be charged." She handed Alice back her crown. She looked sternly at Mary Ann. "You, however, must pay for your crimes."

At this Mary Ann moved from desperate sobbing to outright caterwauling. "I am innocent!" she cried.

Alice placed the crown on her head and stepped boldly forward. She crossed her arms and faced the Queens.

"What is she doing?" Wendy whispered to Dorothy. "Just let's watch," the other replied.

"She is innocent!" Alice declared. "It was I who drank the potion and became so big that I broke the White Rabbit's house. It was I who kicked Bill the Lizard through the chimney in my attempt to escape, and I alone who caused the damage."

Alice walked across the courtroom to stand next to the accused Mary Ann. She bent down and put her face next to Mary Ann's. Alice looked at the crowd of cards and waved her hand from her own face to that of the crying maid.

Met with a stunned silence and puzzled stares, she looked about impatiently, and at last said, "Don't you see the resemblance? Naturally, the White Rabbit mistook me for her. Release her and let me face my crimes." She rose, and stood protectively in front of Mary Ann, daring anyone to harm her.

The courtroom fell entirely silent. All the Card faces, along with Wendy, Dorothy, and Mary Ann, were looking at Alice, jaws slack, eyes wide. She straightened her shoulders, adjusted her crown, and straightened her shoulders again. "Well?" she asked.

Wendy was the first to break the silence. She broke free of the Ace's grip and rushed to Alice. "How brave and true you are!" she exclaimed. "I am so proud of you!"

Startled, Alice blushed. She felt like a child again, the child she might have been if Wonderland had not upset her world so terribly. Against her will, she glowed warmly in this mother-like praise. Then Wendy turned to face the Queens. Wendy no longer looked weak and frail to Alice but seemed to be made of steel.

With a cool and measured gaze, Wendy met the eyes of each of the Queens. She drew herself up, looking far more regal and powerful than any woman in a bathrobe should, and addressed the crowd.

"Alice has confessed, so Mary Ann must go free," Wendy began. "But I must remind the Court of several important facts in Alice Liddell's favor before you make any judgments against her."

She paused just long enough for the Queens to become uncomfortable under her gaze, and then continued.

"First, Alice Liddell has confessed freely, of her own volition, out of a desire to free the innocent, Mary Ann. Second, we are here not on one, but on two missions of mercy, to save the friend of this young woman," indicating Dorothy. Dorothy stepped forward and bowed low.

Wendy's voice cracked a bit, and a tear fought its way out of her eye, but she brushed it back. "As for our second mission, we are here to save my granddaughter, who is missing and no doubt in terrible danger."

The Queen of Hearts took a deep breath, clearly planning to interrupt her, but before the Queen could speak, Wendy continued.

"Third, Alice Liddell is a Queen here, a Chess Piece Queen, to be sure, but certainly that deserves some consideration. Fourth, and finally, Alice Liddell had no notions of your ways or customs when she arrived, and was no doubt confused and frightened. Whatever damage she may have caused was not from evil intent, but ignorance and impetuousness."

Wendy paused, and continued in a gentle voice, "She was, after all, only a child." Wendy stepped back and put her arm around Alice.

Alice looked around. Many of the faces had tears running down their cheeks. Others looked completely puzzled. She looked at Dorothy Gale and saw an expression she had never seen before. It took her a moment or two to identify it as admiration.

Alice stepped forward and spoke in a low voice, "I don't suppose it will make any difference to anyone to say that I am sorry," she began.

But the Rabbit (who had appeared after all) and Mary Ann, and along with several others, including the Duchess, the handsome boy, and a Lizard with a missing tail (*Bill?* she wondered) all began applauding. Alice looked around in confusion. Where had all these people come from and why were they applauding?

Alice continued, "But I do not wish to be excused just because I was a child. I work with children, and the notion that children should be excused by reason of their youth is a fallacy. I have met good children, brave children, evil children, selfish children, and many, many thoughtless and stupid children. I don't buy that 'just a child' nonsense." A pained look crossed Wendy's face, but she kept her arm around Alice.

"I am afraid that I was not a particularly good child when I was here. I think, looking back, that I was a bit rude and thoughtless. And I am truly, truly sorry." Alice looked down.

At this, the whole courtroom, with the exception of the Queen of Hearts, followed in the applause.

The Duchess stepped forward. "We all liked you so much!" she declared. "We always did! And you haven't changed a bit, except for the better."

Suddenly, the King of Hearts stood up. A hush fell over the court. "All are pardoned!" he declared and sat down again. The Queen of Hearts immediately began screaming and boxing his ears, but the rest of the courtroom was too busy cheering to take any notice.

Alice felt a Cat winding round her ankles. She looked down and saw the tail of the Cheshire Cat, tracing a figure eight. The tail moved from Alice to Dorothy, as more and more of the Cat began to appear. "You have places to go," it purred. "I've got a guide for you."

CHAPTER NINETEEN
HUMPTY DUMPTY?

The Cheshire Cat led them out of the courtroom without incident. By the time they made it back to the courtyard, the Cat had fully appeared, and looked up at Alice with its signature smile. He gestured to the right with his tail. There stood the White Knight.

"I thought you were in Play," Alice said.

"I was," the Knight replied. "But I was thoroughly trounced by a Bishop, of all things, so I am out of play and am free to continue to guide and assist you until the next match. A Bishop, can you imagine?" The Knight shook his head in disbelief. "I must check my notes."

He pulled out an enormously large roll of notepaper. "Poem, poem, poem," he muttered, trailing his finger down the sheet. "Very good poem, poem, poem, not so good poem…" He stopped, and tore a section out, and fed it to his horse. "Ah here we are," he said, "Triage! So, this Mary Ann is vindicated?"

"Yes," Alice replied.

"Then," the Knight declared, "it is off to Humpty Dumpty to save this young woman's friend!"

He bowed low to Dorothy, falling from his horse in the process. Dorothy ran forward to pick him up. Not wanting to embarrass the Knight, Alice turned her head away from the re-mounting, just in time to see the last of Cheshire Cat, a few whiskers and a smile. The cat had been slowly vanishing since first producing the Knight.

"Thank you," she called to the fading smile.

For a brief moment, the entire Cat flickered into view. "Thank you," he replied. "This has been the most interesting time I have had in quite some time. And…," the Cat added, "I liked you too. I can always recognize a cat person." The Cat winked out, as if a light switch had been flipped off.

Dorothy eagerly stepped up to the Knight. "Show us the way! How shall we get there?" she asked.

"I shall lead you, of course, and protect you," the Knight replied. "But my brother knights are still in play," he said, looking a trifle embarrassed, "so I cannot provide you with mounts. We must walk. It is not far."

The Knight led them back to the road they had been on and pointed west towards the afternoon sun. There were still many hours of daylight. They seemed to be leaving the city and heading towards a more rural, pastoral landscape. The buildings were few and farther apart, and the fields were not planted with flowers, but with crops. Just now, it seemed, there were stalks of wheat and corn everywhere. Dorothy did not like to see the fields of grain, and walked quickly ahead, trying to get past them as quickly as possible.

Alice and Wendy let Dorothy walk ahead. The two conversed quietly, as Alice removed her crown and placed it in the cook's basket. "Seems a bit much to be wearing all the time, and it is heavy for travel," she said.

"Tell me more about this Humpty Dumpty person," Wendy asked.

"He was a bit cocky," Alice replied. "But he did seem to know quite a bit about the local slang, or whatever you call it. I wonder why Dorothy is so keen on speaking to him about it."

As they walked, the Knight galloped up to Dorothy's side. "My child," he said, "you should tell me a little more about your quest.

The more I know, the more helpful I may be, and it will help me afterwards to compose the poem I will write about this adventure."

Dorothy hesitated. This wasn't something she liked to think about, much less talk about. She was not used to failure. She had, if she was honest with herself, pretty much given up on this quest. Now, after all this time, all these years, it seemed there was finally a chance she might be able to help the Scarecrow.

So Dorothy told him. She told him about going on her first trip to Oz, and how she returned home. She told him about the wonderful friends she made there. She told him about returning again and going home again, over and over, until finally, she had brought her Auntie and Uncle to Oz, and thought to live there happily ever after, knowing that this was where she was meant to be.

"But," Dorothy told the Knight, "Oz is a fairyland, and there is good magic and evil magic, and no one is more versed in evil magic than the Gnome King. My friends and I defeated him not once, but twice. And yet, he has risen again and has taken a terrible revenge on my friends. I am the one he wishes to hurt, but he has done so by harming my friends, not me. Oh, how I wish I could take their places!" She buried her face in her hands.

Gently, the Knight pulled her hands back and lifted her tear-stained face to look into his sad blue eyes.

"You cannot," the Knight replied slowly, "Unless you are a Rook, and can castle, and even then, I don't think it will do you much good."

"No, I don't think I can," Dorothy replied. "But my friend, who has suffered a grave injury to his brain, is reciting poetry that seems to come from this place. I never heard anything like it until I came here. We all thought it was nonsense, of course, but now I see that if I can figure out what the poems mean, maybe I can figure out how to help him. I think Humpty Dumpty can help."

"Poetry…" the Knight declared, "can often be a personal experience. Not everyone has the same interpretation. Are you sure this Poem is the right path to discover your friend's cure?" Dorothy nodded vigorously.

The Knight coughed. "Recite some of the poem your friend is spouting in his madness. I want to make sure it is not from one of mine."

Wendy and Alice still walked behind Dorothy and the Knight. They could hear the conversation quite clearly but did not intrude. For some time, they listened in silence. Finally, Wendy whispered to Alice, "I understand what the Knight is doing for Dorothy. You had to make right what went wrong when you were here last."

Alice muttered, "Was it just yesterday? Last week? I don't understand how time works here." She shook her head and said, "But you are right. This was something I had to do, and something I had to understand."

Wendy continued, with a catch in her voice, "Dorothy also has something she needs to make right. So as worried as I am about my granddaughter, I know we must help Dorothy's friend first. But we must always stay alert for clues about Margaret."

The trip was much shorter and swifter than any of them had anticipated. Within a few paces, they rounded a corner, and there, blocking the path before them, was a low, stone wall. It was a typical country-style, rough wall, made of mismatched boulders pieced together and yet somehow clearly solid.

On that wall, sat a pretty girl. Pretty, yes, but not a human girl. She was clearly an egg. She was round and white, shaped just like an egg, and midway down, she wore a frock of pink polka dots, and had a parasol in one hand, shading herself from the sun, and in the other, a fan, with which she was cooling herself. Above the frock, she had a pretty face, with blue eyes with incredibly long lashes, and blonde curls. Behind the wall, a flock of chickens scurried, with a magnificent rooster strutting about. The egg-shaped girl smiled as they approached.

"Why, she's an egg!" Dorothy exclaimed. At this, the Egg girl looked offended. "I mean," Dorothy said hastily, "you resemble an egg, but in the best possible way." The Egg girl seemed pleased with this remark and giggled.

Dorothy turned to Alice and whispered. "You didn't tell me Humpty Dumpty was an egg. This could be important."

Alice glared at Dorothy and replied, "I would have thought that was obvious, given the name. We all know the rhyme."

Wendy stepped forward, pushing the other two discreetly but firmly aside. "Hello, young lady," she said. "We are here looking for Humpty Dumpty. And we are also seeking any word of strangers who have passed this way, especially small girls." She curtsied to the Egg girl. "I am Wendy Darling," she said, forgetting to add all her other names. She gestured behind her. "And this is Dr. Alice Liddell and Dorothy Gale."

The girl nodded, looking pleased at Wendy's speech, batted her eyes and continued fanning herself. At last, she replied in a high, sweet voice, "Humpty Dumpty is my father, and he has hatched."

She nodded significantly towards the rooster. "I am Humpta Dumpta, his daughter, but perhaps I can help you?" She smiled kindly at Wendy, and leaned forward, almost tumbling off the wall, but catching herself in time.

Dorothy quickly stepped forward, moving Wendy aside. "Your father once explained some poems to Dr. Liddell."

Humpta Dumpta looked confused. "To Alice," Dorothy said, pointing to Alice Liddell.

She now seemed to understand, for she looked intently at Dorothy. Dorothy continued, "My friend has suffered a brain injury, and he is reciting some of the poetry Alice heard here, which your father kindly was able to explain. I am hoping your father can give us a clue to the cure."

Wendy stepped forward, and asked, "And have there been any strangers passing through here? Especially a small girl?"

Humpta answered Wendy first. "No small girls, I am afraid, but yes, strangers. A strange little man came by. He did not seem a very nice person on approach, and when he got close to me, he screamed and ran away! I was so sad. I did not think I was that frightening or ugly." She began to cry.

Wendy stepped forward and threw her arms around the Egg girl as far as they could reach, taking care not to crack her shell. "Oh no, you are quite a lovely creature!" she exclaimed. She paid no heed and continued sobbing.

Dorothy, at the mention of the strange little man, gasped.

"The Gnome King!" she cried. "The most evilist villain in all of Oz! He makes the Wicked Witch look like a saint! The Gnome King has been here, and this is where he must have found the evil enchantment which has transformed my friend from the smartest being in all of Oz to an…" she choked, finally sobbing, "an idiot, a madman!"

Humpta continued sobbing, and Dorothy was touched by her pain, and composed herself.

"No, no," she soothed. "You are quite beautiful. But the Gnome King is terrified of eggs, and so you frightened him. You may…" she mused, "actually have escaped great harm."

During this exchange, Wendy had remained by Humpta, dabbing at her tears with the ribbon from her bathrobe pocket.

Alice had wandered over to the fence, and was staring at the Rooster. The Rooster was staring back at her, with his head cocked and his eye fixed upon her. The Rooster crowed, clucked, and crowed again. He scratched furiously with his right foot. The marks in the ground seemed deliberate.

Humpta Dumpta very carefully and gently lowered herself from the wall. There was a scary moment when she teetered on the edge, but she righted herself and was able to set foot on solid ground without a crack. She walked over to the fence and looked at the Rooster. He let out a series of shrill clucks and crows, and Humpta Dumpta nodded.

"My father says that the ugly man has taken something from here that can transform," she translated. "The poetry he is speaking is but a side effect of using something from this land in another. What have you seen here that can transform?"

"Oh!" Alice snorted. "What doesn't? Cakes, drinks, mushrooms, pepper…wait a minute, pepper!" At the word "pepper," the Rooster crowed triumphantly.

Alice continued, "Pepper transformed the baby into a pig. Babies are human and can grow to be clever, but pigs will always be pigs, and compared to a human, would seem to be mad. But what turned the pig back into a baby, I wonder?"

"Proper seasoning!" Dorothy exclaimed. "That's what the Cook said. The Gnome King must have stolen some Pepper from the Cook. All we have to do is season him properly and the Scarecrow will be right as rain."

"Scarecrow?" Wendy and Alice said simultaneously. "Your friend is a Scarecrow?"

Dorothy ignored them and was rooting through the bag the cook had sent with their lunch. "Look!" she cried, "here are salt, pepper, oregano, garlic, and thyme. And here is a small recipe book! All I need to do is return to Oz and find the proper recipe! Thank you, Humpta Dumpta and Father Humpty!" Dorothy would have vaulted the fence to kiss the rooster, but Alice held her back.

Behind them, waiting patiently, the Knight coughed artificially. "Oh, and thank you Sir Knight," Dorothy exclaimed. She looked at her watch, and Wendy and Alice looked at it as well. It had several more hands and rings of numbers and symbols than any watch either one had ever seen. Dorothy looked at the watch, made a few quick calculations on her fingers and said, "It is almost time! Quickly, gather our things! I'm going to make the sign and Ozma will transport us to Oz!"

Wendy and Alice picked up their bags, and Alice walked up to the White Knight and bowed low. "You have been a true friend and protector, and I am eternally in your debt. I am sorry I was not properly grateful the first time we met."

Alice kissed the White Knight on his cheek. He blushed, but not so red that he might change sides. Knights never do, you know.

"Farewell, ladies," he said. "I would fain accompany you to finish your quest." He bowed low to Alice. "But I am confident that with the help of my Queen, you will succeed." Now it was Alice's turn to blush.

"Hurry," Dorothy called. "It is almost the moment when Ozma will look in the picture. I will make the sign and she will transport us to Oz."

Wendy and Alice gathered the rest of their belongings, while Dorothy clutched the Cook's bag. The women drew closely together. Alice held onto Wendy, and Wendy held onto Dorothy, who raised one hand and made a series of gestures.

It felt like a tornado was sweeping them up. They held tightly to each other and to their possessions. They passed through a wild, windy blackness and landed with a thump. It took them a moment to regain their bearings.

When at last they were able to stand and look about, instead of standing in the throne room of Oz, with the great queen Ozma welcoming them, they saw that they were imprisoned in a large green cage. Dorothy recognized Ozma's bedchamber, but instead of Ozma waiting to welcome them, the evil little Gnome King stood outside of the cage, pointing at them, and howling with laughter as though he would burst.

CHAPTER TWENTY

PRISONERS OF THE GNOME KING

The Gnome King was small, just four feet high, and he looked as though he was carved out of granite. His skin was rough, mostly greyish white, speckled with flecks of black and pink minerals. When his face moved, as it did now with laughter, it moved like lava rather than a face of muscle and skin. He was dusty, and despite his small size, he moved as if he carried a great weight, and sounded of scraping rocks.

Dorothy looked at the little creature in horror, but as she knew she must when facing this old and powerful enemy, she quickly put on an austere, commanding face.

"Ruggedo, Gnome King" she said in a stern voice, "We have given you so many chances to be good. Why do you always revert to wickedness? Why don't you let us out of this cage, and we can talk about how to help you be good again?"

"Because I don't want to be good," he replied with an evil laugh. "And now, I don't have to. I've got you; I've got Ozma, and your friends are in no position to help you."

He was twirling a gold key on one finger as he spoke. "I suppose you'd like this,'" he taunted. "It would unlock your cage. But oh, look! I've set it just out of your reach." He placed the key on a table, which was, of course, far beyond reach.

"I've been waiting for your signal, just waiting, so I could capture you and take you by surprise. Thought you were coming home to Ozma, and comfort, ready to save your friends. Well, that won't happen! Going to turn you all into something nasty. Or maybe something useful." He reached into the cage and pinched Dorothy's cheek. "Maybe you can be my footstool."

He reached into his pocket, searched about, but his hand came out empty. He searched again, becoming more and more agitated.

"Drat!" he exclaimed. "Got to get more magic spice. Can't do the transformations without the magic spice. Oh well, this will give me more time to decide what to transform the rest of you into." He looked at Dorothy's companions with curiosity.

"You're old," he said to Wendy. "I may not waste any magic on you. You can just die." Then he looked at Alice. "You are a little bit flinty, like me," he said. "You might be fun to keep around for a while."

Alice held her tongue at this but glared at the wicked little man. He blew her a kiss, and said, "Just you wait. You'll become fond of me, and perhaps I may show a bit of mercy to your friends." Then he laughed again, and giggling, said, "Perhaps not. But you...we will have some fun." Alice was so choked with rage she could not reply.

Dorothy looked around the room. There was no sign of Ozma, but there was another cage, with a beautiful golden canary sitting on a perch. The bird seemed to be watching her intently.

Her companions looked at her with fear and questions in their eyes. Dorothy looked back at them, and gathered all her courage. She turned again to the evil thing and shouted, "Ozma will not let you harm us!"

"Oh, I don't think Ozma is in any position to help you," laughed the Gnome King, and he very deliberately threw a sunflower seed to the canary.

The evil little man left the room, trailing rock dust behind him. They could hear his laughter fade as he walked down the hall.

"Dorothy," the canary said, "Is that really you? Thank goodness you are back! The Gnome King has stolen all my magic and transformed me into a bird! It's me, Ozma!"

At the sound of the word "bird," there was a rustling movement from within Alice's handbag. Until this moment, Alice had been too confused and angry to do more than observe.

Now Alice opened her bag, and out popped the head of Ruby the kitten, whom she had stuffed in the bag just before steamrolling down the hall of the medical center to confront Dorothy. Was that only a few hours ago?

"Bird?" the kitten inquired. "Is there a bird here? Show me, I'll catch it!"

When she had first been stuffed into Alice's bag (something, I am afraid, she was already used to in her young life), Ruby had settled comfortably into the bag, and fallen asleep. She had woken up during the ruckus in the courtroom, but was afraid, and had stayed inside. Once the ruckus was over, she had fallen asleep again. But now, she was awake, and here was a bird, and she was hungry.

Alice looked at Ruby incredulously. "You can talk?" she asked.

"I guess I can," Ruby replied cheerfully. The kitten was unsurprised by this development.

"All animals can talk in Oz," Dorothy explained.

"Curiouser and curiouser," muttered Alice.

"What about the bird?" Ruby asked, jumping out of the bag to the floor of the cage, and slipping out easily between the bars. Alice immediately said, "Oh Ruby, that bird is not for you. I can get you such lovely treats, if you bring me that key up on the table."

Ruby looked at the bird in the cage and at the table with the key. The key did seem much easier to reach than the bird, and besides, it was always nice to please Alice. But, as a cat, she could not immediately acquiesce. Even a small kitten knew that.

"What kind of treats?" she asked, licking a paw, and looking again at the pretty bird.

The bird twittered, "All kinds of good treats, anything you like." Ruby continued to lick her paws, ignoring the bird.

Dorothy stepped forward to the front of the cage. "There are two other cats here, and we know what cats like. They are nice cats, and I think you will like them. But if you don't get the key, I can tell you that the Gnome King will not have any treats for cats, and he may even…" She paused for dramatic effect, "Turn you into a mouse!"

"Okay, Okay," Ruby replied, and jumped up on a nearby sofa to reach the table. She swatted the key to the floor, and then swatted it across the floor to Alice.

Alice grabbed the key, and quickly unlocked their cage. Once free, Alice scooped up Ruby and kissed her. Ruby purred and rubbed her face against Alice's. "Am I not the best and most amazing kitten?" she asked between purrs.

"Of course you are!" Alice exclaimed, rubbing her face against the kitten. Then she put Ruby on the table, while they gathered their belongings.

Dorothy unlocked the cage with Ozma the Bird and set her on her shoulder. "We must hurry!" she exclaimed. "The Gnome King will be back soon."

Alice went to scoop Ruby back into her bag, but the kitten hopped lightly away to a nearby window ledge and looked out the window. "There is another cat here!" she cried. "A really big cat! Maybe he can help you."

Alice looked out the window. "I don't see a cat," she said. "There!" Ruby replied, hunching down, and staring at a large rose bush, her tail twitching furiously.

Dorothy looked out the window, following Ruby's gaze. She looked at the rose bush, but at first, she did not see anything. Then, a familiar movement caught her attention. From within the rose bush, a tail, long and tawny, with a tuft of brown fur poked out. The tail twitched again.

"Lion!" she called out the window. The rose bush shook, and for a brief moment, the head of the Lion emerged and looked about. Then, just as quickly, it returned to the safety of the bush and disappeared.

"We should get out of here before that horrid little man returns," said Alice, scooping up the kitten.

"Yes," Dorothy replied. "Let's go!"

"Get the picture!" trilled Ozma the Bird. Dorothy ran to the wall and removed a small landscape painting of a rural countryside.

"We don't have time to pack!" said Alice.

"We have time for this," Dorothy replied, as they hurried to the door.

CHAPTER TWENTY-ONE

CAT AND BIRD

Ozma the Bird peeked out the door to survey the scene. The hallway was empty save for a single gnome guard at the end of the hall, blocking the stairway. Fortunately, the guard was looking towards the stairs when the bird looked out.

"How shall we get past him?" whispered Wendy. "I've got an idea," Dorothy whispered back. She turned to Ruby and spoke in a conspiratorial voice.

"Kitten," she purred, "How would you like to chase the bird… just chasing, not catching?"

Ruby's tail twitched in excitement. "Why can't I catch it?" she mewled, although privately, she thought chasing would be fun even if she did not catch it.

"Because," Dorothy replied, taking care to speak in a very simple and direct manner, "You will chase the bird right past the guard, who will run down the stairs after both of you. The bird will fly very fast, and you will run very fast, and the guard won't be able to catch either of you. While the guard is chasing you, the rest of us will escape and hide. The bird will fly to the kitchen, and we will meet you there, and there will be some lovely tidbits for you. Do you understand? There is a backdoor in the kitchen that opens to the garden. If we can make it out there, the Lion will protect us."

Dorothy turned to the bird. "Ozma, dear, are you brave enough? Do you think you can do it?"

"Yes," trilled the Bird. "Let's go, Kitten!"

Then Ozma flew out into the hall, deliberately brushing against a small table lamp, knocking it over with a crash. Ruby sprang out of Alice's arms after her, leaping over the broken lamp.

The guard whirled round and ran towards them. Ozma flew high, just below the ceiling, and sailed over his head. He turned to chase the bird down the stairs, and the kitten darted between his legs, knocking him off balance. He stood up quickly and ran down the stairs after them, yelling and cursing in the gnomish way.

Wendy, Dorothy, and Alice listened to his steps thunder down the stairs and then quickly slipped out of the room. They followed, and once they came to the next floor, looked for a hiding spot. A large tapestry hung on the wall, and the group quickly slipped behind it.

In another moment, they heard the gnome guard's footsteps tromp past again. Once they heard him start up the stairs, they emerged and began to make their way to the kitchen.

Ozma the Bird knew every hall and room of the great palace and should be able to lead the kitten to the kitchen quickly through back corridors.

Once the guard had given up the chase, she had slowed her flight and advised the kitten not to pounce about quite so much, but of course, Ruby would not listen to the advice of a bird. Ozma knew she had to guide the kitten to the rendezvous point, or the kitten would do as kittens do and get into some trouble.

So Ozma had landed and walked ahead of the kitten. Once the bird was on the ground, Ruby hunched down, coming out of chasing mode and going into stalking mode.

Ozma walked ahead, paused, and allowed Ruby to creep silently up until she was within pouncing range. Then Ozma would fly a distance, land again, and once again allow the kitten to creep up to her. So it was that the bird and the kitten were able to make their way to the kitchen undetected.

Dorothy also knew the palace quite well, and it looked to her that very little had changed since she was last here.

The group stuck close to the walls, ducking behind another tapestry, or into an alcove, if they heard a noise. There did not seem to be a general alarm sounding, and it seemed that the Guard had not thought to open the door and check on the prisoners.

The Guard had, in fact, checked on the prisoners and realized that they had escaped. However, his shift was due to end, and he had decided that he would not report them as missing and instead allow his replacement to take the blame for the escape, as it would be discovered on the next watch.

He had just finished cleaning up the broken lamp when the next guard appeared for his turn. "All quiet in there," he reported. The second guard nodded and settled into position at the top of the stairs.

The women arrived at the kitchen door without incident, just as the bird and kitten also approached the door. Wendy saw how close Ruby had come to Ozma, noting the stalking posture of the kitten and said to Ruby severely, "You were told not to catch the bird!"

"I didn't catch the bird," Ruby replied. "But nobody said I couldn't try, just that I couldn't catch it." The kitten looked about innocently and yawned.

Alice rushed forward and scooped up Ruby. She stuffed her back into the bag firmly. The kitten's head immediately popped out again, but Alice snapped the bag part way shut so while Ruby could look about, she could not get out of the bag.

"Hey," Ruby started to protest, but Alice laid a firm finger on the kitten's nose, and she settled down.

CHAPTER TWENTY-TWO

JELLIA JAMB

Dorothy listened at the kitchen door. She did not hear any voices, but she did hear someone moving about and smelled something baking. "I think there is only a cook in there," she said. "And I don't think it is a gnome cook because the food smells too good. Gnomes are terrible cooks."

She opened the door a crack and peeked in. Then she threw the door open wide and exclaimed, "Jellia Jamb!" Sitting by the stove was a pretty young green-skinned girl, perhaps fifteen years old, wearing a checkered green dress with a white apron and white ribbons in her hair. The girl was at the stove, stirring a pot, evidently the source of the delicious smell.

At the sound of the door, the girl turned around, and looked puzzled for a moment. Then a look of recognition and joy dawned on her face, and she said, "Dorothy? Dorothy, is that really you? You have gotten so tall!"

"I grew up," Dorothy said. "I had to go away, you know. It took a long time, but I think I have found the cure for the Scarecrow. But what has happened here? When I left, even though the Scarecrow had been hurt, Ozma was sure she had the Gnome King on the run. Things are terrible now. Ozma is enchanted, and the Gnome King is ruling the Emerald City! How did all this happen? What have the citizens of Oz been doing all these years? Why has there not been a revolution?"

Jellia looked confused. She replied slowly, "It's only been a week since you left, Dorothy."

Jellia continued, "Ozma and Glinda let you and the Wizard go, since they were sure they had the means to defeat the Ruggedo. He was on the run as you said, or so it seemed. But he had more dirty tricks and stranger magic than we thought, and he took the Emerald City only two days after you left. He is using his awful power to transform us citizens of Oz into whatever suits his whim. I haven't seen Ozma in days, and no one has heard from Glinda at all." The girl was near tears.

"I am Ozma," chirped the bird, alighting on the counter. "The wicked one has turned me into a canary, to sing for his amusement." Jellia now burst into actual tears.

"It's all right," said the bird, soothingly. "Now that Dorothy is here and has brought a cure, I shall be made right soon. We just need to figure out the right recipe. But first we must get out of the Palace and to safety. You must come with us, as you are such a good cook, I am sure that you will be able to figure out the recipe which contains the cure."

At this, Jellia Jamb sobbed loudly. "I can't go anywhere!" Jellia sniffled, tried to compose herself, and once she had calmed down as much as she could, she lifted her skirt. To everyone's shock and dismay, they saw that, underneath the skirt, instead of legs and feet, the bottom half of her body had been transformed to a kitchen stool.

"I'm stuck here in the kitchen," she wailed. "I am such a good cook, Ruggedo wanted to make sure I was always by the stove. I can move just a little bit…"

At this, she rocked and tilted, half walking the stool legs to the table, "But as you can see, not nearly enough to escape with you. This is what he does, he keeps you if you are useful and transforms you so you will be even more useful and trapped." The girl burst into a fresh torrent of tears.

"Then," Dorothy said, "we will stay here and figure out these recipes right now."

But at this, there sounded a loud gong, and Wendy cried, "They must have discovered our escape! We cannot stay here, or we shall all be captured."

Wendy thought for a moment and said, "I will stay with poor Jellia, to help and protect her. The rest of you should all escape. When you have deciphered the cure, you can come back and rescue us both."

"No," said Jellia, wiping away her tears and putting on a brave face. "You all go, all of you, everyone. I am going nowhere, and there is nothing else he can or will do to me. I will be fine here, lonely as I will be."

She rocked back and forth on her stool legs, then, steadying herself, she stood tall, and grabbed a rolling pin and raised it over her head in a sort of salute. Bits of flour drifted down, dusting her hair in white.

Little Ruby, still struggling in the bag, said, "Leave me here! No one will suspect a pretty little kitten, and I can help. I can fetch things for this girl, and she can give me kitchen treats."

With a great effort, Ruby strained against the snaps on Alice's bag, and popped them open. She leapt into the girl's lap and began purring and nuzzling her face.

Jellia, nuzzled back and said softly, "Oh, may she stay? I am so lonely here. I am sure that now that Dorothy is back, you will be able to defeat the Gnome King and return for us."

A brief shadow of doubt crossed Dorothy's face. Dorothy looked at Alice. "She's your cat," she said. "You can say what she will do."

"Yes, stay Ruby," Alice replied with great tenderness as she stroked the kitten. "Just don't forget me." The kitten purred and licked Alice's face.

They could now hear footsteps tromping down the hall. Jellia tucked the kitten under her apron, and the women ran out through the kitchen door to the garden, Ozma flying right over their heads. Jellia busied herself with some pots and pans, trying to appear as if nothing was amiss.

The door burst open and two gnome guards entered. "Has anyone passed through here?" the first demanded. Then he said, "Hey, what's cooking? It smells great!"

"No one has been here," Jellia replied, cool as ice. "And I am baking a cake, light as a feather, special request from Ruggedo, so please be gentle with your boots and stomping, for I would hate for the cake to fall. I should have to tell him the reason and who was responsible for ruining his special dessert."

At the mention of the Gnome King's name, both guards stepped back and replied, "Oh, no, of course not, we would not want to be held responsible for such a calamity."

"So tiptoe out of here, then," the girl replied, "And maybe later, after dinner, you can come and have some leftovers, if there are any." Both guards murmured thanks and left the kitchen with haste.

CHAPTER TWENTY-THREE

ESCAPE FROM THE EMERALD CITY

Outside in the garden, the women pressed up against the wall of the palace and looked out over the ground. There were at least 500 feet between them and the rose bush that concealed the Lion. Even if they could reach it, they would then need to escape the palace grounds, and possibly even the Emerald City.

"I'm not sure what to do now," Dorothy said to herself, and she pressed against the wall, and closed her eyes to try and think. She spoke aloud, in a desperate whisper, "How is it that I have become the hope of all Oz? I can't be. If I couldn't save the Scarecrow, how will I do this?"

"You haven't saved the Scarecrow yet," said Ozma, ruffling her wings. "But we now have the means, and you have brought some good allies to help, and we are always able to prevail when we are brave and true and have good friends."

By the way," the Bird continued, "I have been meaning to ask. Who are these people?"

Meanwhile, Alice and Wendy had both been looking about, to see what they might find to help them in their escape. Wendy had picked up a rope she had found near the door, and Alice had spotted a small wooden wagon off to the side with some gardening tools in it. They put their heads together for a moment, speaking rapidly. Then Wendy turned to Dorothy and said, "This Lion friend of yours, is he strong enough to pull this wagon and us?"

Dorothy looked uncertainly at the ramshackle wagon, but replied, "Oh, yes. He is most wonderfully strong. And brave," she added, "usually quite, quite brave."

"Well then," Alice said, "Why don't we set up a harness with the rope here, and he can pull us all out on this wagon. We can go barreling through the gates before they can stop us."

"We still have to get to him and let him know we need his help without being spotted," Wendy said. "And anyone looking out of a window would spot us going to the rose bush. And by the way, why is he hiding in a rose bush, if he is so brave?"

"Usually brave," Dorothy muttered, recalling the last time she had seen her friend. "Like me, usually brave." She sat with this dark thought for only a moment.

Then, on impulse and without really thinking it through, Dorothy suddenly made a dash across the lawn to the rose bush. She dove right in through the thorns, slid a foot or two, like a baseball runner sliding into home base, and almost bumped noses with the Lion.

The startled Lion was about to roar, but then he pulled his head back far enough to get a good look at the intruder. He sniffed at her for a moment, and then said in a deep whisper, "Dorothy! You've come back!" The Lion rumbled something like a purr and embraced her in his huge paws.

"And you came back too," Dorothy said, hugging the Lion and stroking his mane.

While Dorothy had been talking to the Lion, Wendy and Alice had hooked up a makeshift harness, loaded their belongings onto the wagon, and looked about for anything else that might be useful. "I don't think Margaret is here, do you?" Wendy asked.

"I doubt it, " Alice replied. "But it seems that there are people here, this Glinda for instance, who have power and can perhaps take us to this Neverland, where she must be, if only we can sort out this present mess." She was not prepared to be part of a revolution in this strange land, despite the clear violations of human rights that she had already witnessed.

"Politics," Alice muttered under her breath, "Hate the lot of them. Usually, it is hard to figure out who are the good guys and who are the bad guys, but it seems more straightforward here." Alice had been scuffing about as she ranted to herself, looking for anything else that might be useful. She had been kicking at the ground, sticking the toe of her shoe into the shrubbery, when she came upon a small tin labeled "Pepper." She gasped in surprise, but then quickly picked it up and stuffed it into her bag with a satisfied smile.

Wendy and Alice started at a loud crashing sound. Just as suddenly as she had bolted for the rose bush, Dorothy and the Lion reappeared, bursting out through the thorns, tearing small branches off in their flight. Bits of leaves and rose petals clung to the hairs of the Lion's mane and tail. They headed straight to the wall where Wendy, Alice, and Ozma waited.

Dorothy was riding on the back of the Lion, hunched down and holding tight to his mane. As they emerged from the rose bush, a cry could be heard from above. Dorothy looked up and saw the Gnome King leaning out the window, screaming and cursing at them.

As the Lion quickly reached the wall, Alice and Wendy threw the harness over him and hopped aboard the cart.

Once harnessed, the Lion ran towards the city gates, dodging arrows and stones from the palace and avoiding the guards who seemed to pop up inconveniently in his path. Dorothy clung desperately to the Lion's back, barely holding on. Alice and Wendy clung just as desperately to the wagon. Ozma flew above them, trying to keep up with the Lion's breakneck pace.

The Lion headed for a low spot in the garden wall and leapt over it, wagon and all. They landed in the streets of the Emerald City, and the citizens who happened to be milling about near the palace gave a loud cheer at the sight.

The Lion did not stop but ran towards the exit of the city. As he approached, the Soldier with the Green Whiskers unbarred the gates and bowed as they passed. The Lion ran through the portal, and the Soldier closed the gates swiftly behind them, blocking the pursuing soldiers. As they disappeared into the forest, they could hear the angry, gritty voice of the Gnome King, yelling at the Soldier, "You shall pay for this!"

The Lion tore at an alarming speed down the yellow brick road and passed the poisonous poppy fields so quickly they had no time to breathe in the deadly scent.

Once they were in the woods, the Lion veered quickly and dangerously off the path. After several frightening minutes, leaping over logs and streams and crashing through underbrush, he stopped, panting heavily, in a clearing.

"We shall be safe here tonight," he gasped, and lay down, utterly exhausted. Dorothy quickly dismounted and threw her arms around him. "You are the bravest and most magnificent Lion I have ever known," she cried.

"But am I not the only Lion you have ever known?", he replied sleepily. The Lion put his paws over his eyes and seemed to fall asleep.

"Wait," said Dorothy, shaking him. "You must tell me what has happened since I left."

"And," said Alice to Dorothy, "you must tell us your full story, Dorothy. What kind of place have we gotten ourselves into?"

"Yes," Wendy cried. "We were supposed to come here, cure your friend, and then go to Neverland and find Margaret. How shall we ever get ourselves out of this situation and on to Neverland?"

Wendy did not cry, but after their capture and wild escape, she was clearly distraught. She looked, for the first time since she had first seen her asleep in the hospital bed, like a frail old woman to Alice.

The Lion opened one eye, listening, and Ozma the Bird perched on a branch nearby and cocked her head.

There was no avoiding it. Dorothy sighed. "Yes, I will tell my story to Wendy and Alice, for they deserve to know it all, and to you, Ozma and Lion, for you must know what has happened to me since I left. First, however, Ozma and Lion, you must tell me what has happened here."

CHAPTER TWENTY- FOUR

DOROTHY CONFESSES

W hen I left, although she could not cure our beloved Scarecrow, Glinda was quite positive she had a spell to capture the evil Ruggedo and thwart his wicked nature once and for all. It just needed a day or two to perfect. I wouldn't have left otherwise," Dorothy began.

"Yes," Ozma replied, "When we sent you and the Wizard to find a cure for our poor injured Scarecrow, we believed Ruggedo was on the run and would soon be captured and reformed again. But alas, he was far more cunning than we had ever imagined."

The Lion nodded in agreement. "Cunning," he repeated, "And frightening." The great cat shook his main and shivered.

Ozma continued, "Somehow, before she could complete her spell, he tricked Glinda into drinking water from the Fountain of Forgetfulness herself, and now she does not remember who she is! Ruggedo has told her she is his mother, and that she has been ill, and he keeps her with him to mother him night and day. He keeps the Scarecrow with him too, as a Court Jester. Nick Chopper is rusted solid again, as you know, and Ruggedo has him serving as the royal coat rack."

"Water of Forgetfulness?" Alice said, frowning. "Seems like a dangerous thing to keep about, I would think."

"But it's really been very useful," Dorothy replied. "Whenever the Gnome King is up to mischief, we find a way to make him drink the water, and he forgets all his terrible plans, and he is quite good for some time."

"And how often has he had to drink this stuff?" Alice said, arching her eyebrows.

"Oh two or three times, I think, or maybe four?" Ozma chirped.

"Well, that's your problem right there" Alice snorted. "You made him forget about his evil plans for the moment, but inside, he was still an awful villain, and sooner or later, he came back to that. You might have made him forget, but you didn't really change his nature. Of course, he reverted back to type."

Alice continued, warming to her subject. "Before my work with children, I was a counselor at a prison for the criminally insane. And I was quite successful at turning a bad egg around. I bet that with some intense therapy with me, this Gnome King wouldn't need your Water of Forgetfulness. Sounds like you just medicated him instead of addressing the root causes of his dreadful behavior."

She cast a sidelong look at Dorothy and could not resist saying. "Aren't you the one always talking about not overmedicating, Patient Advocate Gale?"

Dorothy nodded glumly. She gazed down at her hands, lacing her fingers together. Everyone was looking at her, Dorothy knew.

"Alright," she said to Wendy and Alice. "Here in Oz, there is much beauty and love and magic, and almost everyone you meet will be good and kind, although they may have some mighty peculiar customs, which can take some getting used to. But there are also sometimes very bad creatures."

She looked at Ozma and the Lion, who both nodded their assent. Dorothy laced and unlaced her fingers for several minutes. She looked away for a moment, then turned back to her audience. This was difficult for her.

"The Gnome King is a far more dangerous and tenacious villain than the more famous Wicked Witch of the West. Most people know about her reign of terror, because she was more showy, but the Gnome King is so much worse."

"Yes," Ozma agreed, fluffing her feathers. "As he had many times before, the Gnome King once again challenged me, the rightful ruler of Oz. He had planned a clever attack this time, aiming his destructive vengeance not at Dorothy and myself, his true targets, but at our friends, for he knew that harm to our loved ones would wound more deeply than anything he could inflict on our persons. So, in his wickedness, he created a terrible spell, designed to demoralize his true foes, by destroying those they loved most."

Dorothy continued, "The Gnome King had planned this exceptionally cruel revenge on his longtime enemies with care and thought. His first target would be my dear friend, the beloved Scarecrow of Oz." She looked away again and choked back a small sob.

Dorothy was clearly distraught in the telling, so the Lion picked up the thread and said, "Ozma and her subjects still believed that the Gnome King was tamed by the Waters of Forgetfulness, so it was simple enough for him to get close enough to the straw man to cast his curse.

"He had simply ambled up to the Scarecrow, smiling and giggling a bit, and asked if he wanted to know a secret. The Scarecrow had inclined his head to the creature. Although the Scarecrow had no ears, just painted circles, the evil gnome had whispered the spell into the place where ears should be. The effect was instantaneous." The Lion shuddered, and went on.

"The Scarecrow, once the most brilliant and clever being in all of Oz, because of the Gnome King's wicked magic, lost his wits, and now sat babbling meaningless, senseless phrases, in a state of great agitation.

"'Beware the Frumious Bandersnatch!' he had cried out as the spell hit. Now he spends his days spouting such nonsense, with doggerel about walruses, carpenters, and oysters, among others."

"It was horrible!" Ozma cried. "The Gnome King had cackled in glee, and declared that he would curse us all. Most of the courtiers fled the scene, calling for Glinda."

"When Glinda appeared, the Gnome King had fled as well, for though he had been successful in this battle, the war was not won and he was not ready to face Glinda the Good just yet. His spell did, however, have the demoralizing effect he had hoped for."

Dorothy spoke at last. "Nick Chopper, the woodsman, awash in grief over the fate of his friend, had wept without stopping. No matter how quickly or diligently we oiled him, as soon as he was able, he burst into fresh tears, rusting over and over and over. At last, he was left to rust, as that seemed his wish."

Dorothy placed her arms around the Lion, and he ducked his head. She went on, "The Lion, a professed coward, had always, in the moment of truth, rushed into battle despite his great fears. But at this calamity, he had run off to the forest, hiding himself amongst the more ordinary animals, afraid and unable to help his friends."

Dorothy buried her face in the Lion's mane. Ozma flew to the Lion and perched upon his back, trying to soothe them both.

Finally, Ozma went on, "In this crisis, Dorothy had turned to Glinda for guidance. Glinda stepped over to the Scarecrow and looked into his now crazed eyes. She placed his gloved hands in hers and held them. She removed his hat and passed her wand over his head. She tried several more incantations, and finally bowed her head and walked to Dorothy.

"Dorothy looked up with a fragile hope in her eyes. She had been holding back the tears till she heard what Glinda would say."

Ozma looked at Dorothy, then back to Alice and Wendy as she continued.

"Glinda sadly and solemnly informed her, 'I believe I do have the means to overcome the Gnome King again, although it will take a bit of time. This curse is new and powerful. I have never seen its like. But I am afraid there is no magic in Oz with enough power to break this terrible enchantment on our friend, even if I do defeat Ruggedo once more.'

"Glinda placed her hand beneath the child's chin and lifted her face and looked into her eyes. 'We must take as good care of our friend as we are able. That is all we can do. There is no power in all of Oz that can break this enchantment.'"

There was a distant noise, of something like thunder. The Lion rose for a moment, and with his great paw motioned for them to lay down on the ground. He then lay down himself, covering himself with brush.

They all stayed low, as the sound, now clearly not thunder, but carriage wheels and horse's hooves, roared past their hiding place. Once the sound had faded into the distance, they relaxed and sat up again.

Dorothy lifted her head. "Heartbroken as I was, there was something in what Glinda had said that gave me an idea."

CHAPTER TWENTY-FIVE

DOROTHY'S MISSION

No power in all of Oz...if not Oz, where can there be such a power? Dorothy did not know, but she knew she had to find it. So she decided to return to her world. It was the only other world she knew of, at the time. Perhaps there was a power there. Perhaps she could find a way to even more worlds. The cure must be out there."

Ozma nodded, "Dorothy was quickly resolved and told Glinda of her plan. Although risky and uncertain of success, after some thought, Glinda agreed that it was the Scarecrow's best hope.

"But Dorothy was a little girl, and a little girl alone in the world where she came from would soon be put into an orphanage and would have no way to search for the cure. An adult, a parent of sorts, must be selected to return with her."

"I could not go back with my aunt and uncle." Dorothy replied. "Aunt Em and Uncle Henry had emigrated to Oz years ago, and were so very comfortable now in Oz that I could not bear to ask them to return with me. Besides, they were already old, and once back, would begin to age again, so who knew how long they had? Here they stayed just as they had been when they arrived. It would not be right."

The Lion lifted his head, and Ozma flew back to rest on a log by Alice and Wendy, who had been listening rapt to the story.

Ozma said, "There were, of course, many adults in Oz who would gladly accompany her, but they had no experience of Dorothy's world and would be confused at best."

"There were only two adults in Oz who had come from the United States, outside of Dorothy's aunt and uncle. These two were the Shaggy Man and the Wizard. Both were more than willing to act as Dorothy's guardian, but it seemed that the Wizard would be the best choice. Truth be told, the Shaggy Man had been a hobo in America, and he did not like to have any responsibilities.

"The Wizard, on the other hand, had been a humbug in Kansas. He had made his way in the world as a gentle charlatan and trickster. He was quick on his feet, quick in thought, and always up for an adventure. Under the circumstances, being a humbug would come in very handy in this adventure. New identities must be created, a plausible cover story for who they were and where they came from must be established. They must not arouse suspicion but must be able to move about and further their investigations. Who better than a humbug to do this?"

Alice had been bursting with questions all through this narrative, but each time she was about the speak, Wendy had shushed her. Now she could no longer contain herself.

"A Wizard?," she asked. "You grew up with a wizard? A real wizard?"

"Yes," Dorothy replied, in a matter-of-fact way "So back to my world we went. Ozma sent us to my home state, Kansas, along with a sizeable portion of Oz's riches, so that we might establish ourselves in comfort and begin the quest for a cure, while Glinda worked to defeat the Gnome King here in Oz. No one thought that it would take more than a week, a month at most. We would be back for the victory celebration, certainly."

"But this was not to be. I grew up in the care of the Wizard. I went to school and did all the other things young girls do as they mature and grow, but try as we might, never did we find anything that might help the Scarecrow. Weeks turned to months, months to years. Twenty years have passed."

At this, the Lion growled, "Twenty years? You left us at the mercy of the Gnome King and did not wonder what was happening for twenty years?"

Ozma twittered, "It was just days here. How could you let so much time pass?"

Wendy asked, "And when weeks turned to months, did you not miss your aunt and uncle?"

Dorothy swallowed hard and did not answer them directly. "I despaired at ever finding a cure. But we tried, truly we did. We never found a cure in our world or found a way to another. However, in our investigations, it became clear to me that I was not the only child who had traveled outside her world, and that Oz was not the only world. I met other children, many of whom were not doing nearly as well as I had, after travelling."

"Frightened children, depressed children, children who were not believed and were medicated—these children had immediate needs that I was uniquely qualified to meet. While the Scarecrow was ever in my thoughts, the hope of finding a cure slowly moved to the back of my mind, and the children became my primary purpose. It was good to see that I was actually able to help someone."

Wendy spoke, "So even if you could not help the Scarecrow, you were resolved to help these troubled children. And perhaps you might find a way to these other places where these children had been and discover the cure. If it were not to be found here, perhaps in another elsewhere."

"At least that is how I rationalized it." Dorothy replied. "Life with the Wizard was good. He was a kind and protective guardian, helping me to walk the line between the quest we must never forget and yet still live in the present, giving me a full and happy childhood, with school, friends, and a loving home. The one thing he did not do was prepare me for the possibility that we might fail."

Wendy asked, "So you never considered just returning, even after so much time had passed? Didn't you worry about your friends, your aunt and uncle?"

"Of course I did," Dorothy replied. "But the Wizard and I pushed on. We met many children, a boy who went to a hundred acre woods with his toys, a girl who stepped through a wardrobe closet to a land of eternal winter, a chimney sweep who transformed into a water fairy…I could help them cope but never could I find a way to cross over."

"The Wizard died peacefully when I was in college. After that, I fully committed to a new quest, not totally abandoning the hope of a cure for the Scarecrow but putting it on a back shelf in my conscience. I was *almost* at peace with the satisfaction of the work. I was helping people, people marooned in this world, when their hearts were elsewhere, people who no one but I believed."

Alice nodded, "But really, the important word in what you just said is almost. Am I right? You could never quite escape your worry for your friends in Oz and your guilt at what you perceive as a failure."

"Yes," Dorothy replied, "The Scarecrow has always haunted me in what ought to have been quiet moments.

"And now I am back, and the cure is within my reach, if only we could get to the Scarecrow. But the Gnome King has all but conquered Oz!" she concluded.

She looked around at the faces of her companions, hoping for understanding. Wendy went over to her and patted her on the shoulder. Alice smiled kindly. Ozma and the Lion were looking at Dorothy with unreadable expressions on their faces.

"Well…" said Wendy. After an uncomfortable silence, she repeated, "Well, there is not much to be done at the moment. We are all exhausted, and we must take the time to study the contents of the Cook's basket. I suppose we ought to make camp."

CHAPTER TWENTY-SIX

GIRL SCOUTS IN OZ

Wendy pulled a few dirty and tattered drop cloths from the wagon and laid them out. She drew a circle in the dirt with her toe, and began to gather some twigs and logs. She piled them high in the center of the circle, and said, "I don't suppose anyone knows how to start a fire."

Alice shrugged, dug about her in bag and produced a cigarette lighter.

"Oh, that's quite helpful!" Wendy said happily. "Perhaps we ought to take an inventory of all of our possessions to see what we can make use of in the upcoming rescue."

Alice shrugged again and dumped the contents of her bag out onto the ground. With a wry smile, she held up the flask of brandy with the words "Drink Me" etched on it. A pack of cigarettes, which Alice at first seized upon, but then, looking thoughtful, put down again. Keys, wallet, chewing gum, gloves, and a cellphone all lay on the ground. Alice picked up the cell phone curiously and swiped.

"No signal," she said with a half smile. She shook the bag again, and out tumbled a notebook, several chewed pencils, a packet of tissue, some loose change, a ball of yarn, and some catnip in a baggie. The bag had been carelessly shut, and there were tiny claw marks piercing the plastic. The Lion raised his head and inhaled deeply.

Now it was Dorothy's turn to empty her pockets. Her inventory also yielded a useless cell phone, keys, and wallet. In addition, she had a pair of sunglasses, a bright red lipstick, a compact with face powder, sunscreen, a hairbrush, a bag of saltwater taffy, two pens, a bottle of aspirin, a Swiss army knife, and several green hair ties.

Wendy stepped forward. She was still wearing her robe and slippers, and she turned out the pockets. Nothing but a few tissues and a blue hair ribbon fell out and drifted slowly to the ground.

Wendy looked down at the meager contents of her robe, and then smiled. She reached around her neck and took off a thin chain, with an acorn, clad in silver hanging from it. She looked at it tenderly and held it out for all to see. It sparkled in the moonlight and, almost prism-like, seemed to cast reflected colors about the campsite. She cupped the acorn in her hand, kissed it, and returned it to its place around her neck, tucking it back beneath her nightgown.

Ozma (being a bird) and the Lion (being a lion) had nothing to offer. Dorothy then stepped over to the cart and produced the picture they had taken from the Gnome King, with a triumphant smile. "This had better be good," Alice muttered to herself.

"This," Dorothy said, holding the picture above her head, "is the Magic Picture. With this, you can ask to see anyone, anywhere. It is how Ozma was able to keep an eye on me and how I was able to signal to her when I was ready to return to Oz…although, I guess, now that I think about it, after Ozma was captured and transformed, the Gnome King was keeping an eye on me too."

"That will be very useful!" Wendy exclaimed. "Can I see Margaret?"

"Why, yes, you can," replied the Bird, "But only for a few moments. That's how it works. Come here." The Bird gestured with her wings. "Stand in front of the picture and think about the person you wish to see."

Wendy stepped forward eagerly and stood in front of the picture. She closed her eyes, and whispered, "Margaret." She stood silent for a moment, and her hand unconsciously touched the silver acorn beneath her nightgown.

She opened her eyes. As she opened them, she saw the surface of the picture shimmer and melt. Everyone crowded around to see what would be revealed. "It's Margaret!" Wendy exclaimed.

There was a small girl, in a nightgown, sleeping beneath a rough blanket, which appeared to be made from leaves sewn together. It looked as though she was in a cave of some sort, and there was flickering light…candles, perhaps, as the light flickered and was not steady. Beside her there was a cup, which looked to have been carved of wood, and an empty plate, also of wood. The child stirred, still asleep, and made a sound like a sob.

As the image began to fade, Wendy cried out, "No!" and took a step towards the image, her hands outstretched as if to take the child in her arms. Abruptly, the image disappeared, winking out like a light. Wendy slumped and buried her face in her hands.

Alice stepped up to stand in front of Wendy and lifted Wendy's face. She looked into her teary eyes and said in her most convincing (and well-practiced) therapist's voice, "This is good. We see she is alive, and unharmed. We see that someone is taking care of her, although she may be that person's prisoner. She is in no immediate danger. This means we have time, and once we get ourselves out of this Oz place, we have a great chance of rescuing her."

"But where is Peter?" Wendy asked. At this, the picture shimmered and melted, and revealed a boy, no more than ten years old, sitting on a cliff in the moonlight, looking pensively out to sea. He was clad in a suit that was made from leaves, like the blanket that covered Margaret. He did not move or speak during the entire time they watched him, and finally the image faded.

"So, Peter is alive, too," Wendy said. "Thank goodness! Whatever has befallen Margaret, he will make right. I am sure he is thinking up a plan right this very minute. He is awfully clever."

Alice rolled her eyes, cleared her throat a little too loudly, and said, "Okay, so we have this pretty amazing spyglass. Everything else we have is practically useless. But before we go any further, let's take a serious inventory of the Cook's basket. We may find something valuable there, and even if we don't, I am hungry."

Dorothy brought the basket out and knelt down before it. She opened the lid and began to set the contents out on the ground before her.

The first thing she removed was the thermos. She opened the lid, and at once, the intoxicating aroma of warm soup filled the air. The Lion roared, the bird flitted about, and Dorothy breathed in the scent and stepped back. "I have never smelled such an incredible soup!" she exclaimed.

Wendy stepped forward, and looked into the thermos. "It looks wholesome," she declared. "And now that I think about it, I am also frightfully hungry."

Alice cautioned, "You have to be careful about what you eat from Wonderland or the Looking Glass world," she said. She picked up the thermos and examined it carefully from all sides. She smelled the soup, and finally, experimentally, she dipped her pinky into the soup and took a taste. She waited a few minutes and then declared, "Soup's on!"

Just below the soup thermos were three mugs and two shallow plates. "I wonder how the Cook knew how many dishes we would need," said Dorothy, dishing out a mug for each of the women and a plate for the Lion and the Bird.

Alice laughed, with a touch of bitterness, and said, "Oh, those places know just what you need, when you need it. The trick is to figure out how to make the best use of it. Took me a while to work that out."

Wendy said, "Well, if Alice thinks the soup is safe, let's eat and then continue the inventory of our resources."

They ate in silence, not because of any emotional awkwardness, but just because the soup was so delicious. The thermos also seemed to be much larger than it appeared, for everyone had at least a second helping. The Lion had a third helping, and a fourth.

At last, too full to eat more, the women turned their attention back to the remaining contents of the Cook's basket.

Dorothy drew forth a number of ingredients...salt, pepper, cardamom, ginger, thyme, oregano, several lemons, a small flask of oil, a hard-boiled egg, a head of elephant garlic, a loaf of cinnamon bread, three potatoes, a bag of sugar, a square of butter, a block of some soft white cheese, several squares of baking chocolate, a bag of walnuts and a fairly wicked-looking cleaver. She also brought forth a red-checked picnic blanket and a set of matching napkins.

Finally, she produced the recipe book.

Dorothy opened it and paged through it. "Proper seasoning," she mused. She frowned and turned the pages rapidly, back and forth. "Why, this cookbook makes no sense!" she exclaimed. "How can I find the cure for the Scarecrow with this nonsense?"

CHAPTER TWENTY-SEVEN

THE RECIPE BOOK

"Welcome to my world," Alice said, with a wry smile. "Allow me."

Alice looked through the book, turning the pages much more slowly, and occasionally making a note in the margin with one of her pencils. Finally, she said, "Okay, so there are some pretty good recipes in here. Most of them are for soup, but a few of them are for spells, I guess, like turning something into something else..." and she began reciting:

> *"Once there was an ear of corn,*
> *Gripening in the Spring.*
> *Now the ear is forgottenlorn*
> *Don't know anything."*

She continued:

> *"Make it happen, make it work,*
> *Add a pinch of thyme,*
> *I hate writing recipes,*
> *Why does it have to rhyme?"*

Alice looked at Dorothy with a serious look, and said, "I think that this is what happened to your Scarecrow friend. Listen to this...it is a spell. I'm guessing your friend is stuffed mostly with cornstalks, yes? So thyme was the ingredient that activated the spell.

To reverse it, I think we need to add a different seasoning to counteract the effects."

Alice turned to Ozma, flipping through the pages of the cookbook. "And Bird, can you tell me what happened just before you became a bird? I think I know, but I must be sure."

"My name is Ozma," the Bird replied primly. "I was in my chamber, and the Gnome King burst in. He threw this black powder over me, and I began to sneeze uncontrollably. And then, before I knew what had happened, I had become a bird! And while I do love birds very much, I did not want to become one! He threw a net over me and put me in the cage, which is where you found me."

"Ah," Alice said thoughtfully, "So very much like the pig-baby." She continued flipping through the pages of the cookbook, and paused at one page, reading silently to herself.

Then she closed the book in triumph and declared, "It says here that too much pepper will cause the person so seasoned to sneeze themselves into whatever animal they most sympathize with. And proper seasoning will restore them to humanity."

Alice once again opened the book. She paged through back and forth, but finally shook her head. "These recipes don't really have directions about what to do if you have over-seasoned someone," she said sadly.

"Well," said Wendy in a confident voice, taking the book from Alice, "I have cooked under the most primitive of conditions, as well as in the most elegant of kitchens, and if I can't fix a dish gone wrong, no one can." She smiled and tied her hair back with the blue ribbon from her pocket.

Wendy used one of the napkins to clean out her mug as best she could. She seized a lemon and some sugar and the cleaver. She cut the lemon in half and squeezed some lemon juice into the mug. She added some sugar and stirred them together. Finally, Wendy took a small bit of the cheese and crumbled it up into a napkin.

Then she stood up, holding the mug with the lemon juice and sugar in one hand, and the napkin with the crumbled cheese in another. She walked over to the Bird and poured the lemon-sugar mixture over her. The Bird shuddered, and a wisp of smoke appeared, swirling around the Bird. Wendy sprinkled the cheese over the Bird, as the smoke thickened and completely enveloped both Ozma and Wendy.

Once the smoke thickened, neither Wendy nor Ozma could be seen. Then just as suddenly as it had materialized, the smoke cleared, and standing before them were Wendy and Ozma, the true Princess and ruler of Oz.

Where once there had been a bird, now stood a beautiful young woman with golden hair cascading down her back, with a silver tiara upon her head, dressed in a gown of silver gossamer with a sweet, merry face.

Dorothy cried out in delight and ran forward to embrace her friend. Ozma looked down, ascertaining that she had indeed been restored to her proper shape, and embraced Dorothy. Then she looked to Wendy, then to Alice, and said, "Thank you, kind friends! You have restored me to my proper form, and together we will defeat the evil Gnome King."

Ozma looked at Wendy with gratitude and asked, "However did you know what to do to remedy my situation?

Wendy casually replied, "You work in enough soup kitchens, you will learn how to fix any soup. A little lemon and sugar will cut the pepper, and a little dairy will help as well."

"But what about the Scarecrow?" Dorothy asked. "How can we make him right?"

Alice had taken back the book during Wendy's preparations. She had been looking through the cookbook during the entire transformation of Ozma.

"Listen," she said, "You have no idea how often and how many times stuff from there will transform you into goodness knows what. I was six inches tall, for pity's sake! Then I had a neck like a snake that fit up a chimney. But there is always a way back! And I have been thinking…your Scarecrow is reciting Wonderland poetry, right? And something from there might have affected his brains, right again? So maybe his Oz brain straw was changed to some Wonderland straw and that's why he seems crazy and is reciting poetry from there."

"I do hate poetry," she murmured under her breath. "But I think your Scarecrow is fine, he is just confused with foreign stuff in his brain. He was the first…" she hesitated. "The first being the Gnome King affected with the magic, which he stole from who knows where, but it's from my lands, of that I am sure. I'm betting the Gnome King is still figuring out how to use what he has. Otherwise, he'd have taken the whole kingdom by now."

CHAPTER TWENTY-EIGHT
A PLAN IS MADE

The Lion stepped forward. "Here is what I know," he said. "I did not spend all my time hiding in the rose bushes. I have been gathering intelligence. There are many in Oz who would rise should a leader emerge."

The Lion continued, "Here is more of what I know: Nick Chopper will be found in the front hall of the throne room, rusted solid and holding the coats of those who dare to visit the Gnome King. The Gnome King is planning to journey south towards Glinda's Castle to take possession of all her magic. He keeps the Scarecrow with him for amusement. I am guessing that your appearance and subsequent escape will not delay this journey."

He paused, and bowed his magnificent head, then continued, "Yes, I ran," he confessed. "I ran when two of my three best friends were defeated and destroyed so swiftly. The Scarecrow's wonderful brain was utterly scrambled, and Nick Chopper rusted completely when his heart would not let him go on without the Scarecrow. I did not wait to see what the Gnome King had planned for me."

At this, he raised his head and looked at Dorothy with deep sorrow. "Dorothy, I lost my faith in you, and I ran. I spent a day or two in the forest, but I came back. I had no plan, but I came back because I knew where I had to be."

The Lion shook his mane till it cascaded down his back. He stood tall and proud, looking at last like a King of Beasts.

He spoke, "I have not been able to figure out a plan as clever as the Scarecrow might, nor as kind and sparing of violence as the Tin Man might, but I am here. I am terribly frightened, but I will face anything to defeat this evil and restore Ozma to the throne of Oz."

This was the first time Alice and Wendy had really been able to study the Lion. He was huge, with powerful muscles and frighteningly large teeth and claws. His mane was long and tangled, and his voice was deep. Yet, there was a kindness and wisdom in his brown eyes, and a tone in his deep voice that assured them that he was the most gentle of animals.

The Lion held his noble pose for a moment, then looked around uncertainly. Ozma raced forward to embrace the Lion, with Dorothy not far behind, while Alice and Wendy stood uncomfortably in their places, glancing back and forth at each other, looking for some sort of direction in this emotional and highly personal situation.

Fortunately, the Lion reluctantly shook himself from their embraces and continued. "Nick Chopper has been standing in the throne room rusted, but undoubtedly he has heard all that has been said there. He will have valuable information. And if the Gnome King is travelling, it should be easy enough to rescue Nick. Then we can follow and rescue the Scarecrow and Glinda."

"But how shall we restore Glinda's memory? That magic is not from the Wonderland recipes, but from the Fountain of Forgetfulness here in Oz," Dorothy asked.

"Oh," the Lion replied confidently, "Once we have restored the Scarecrow to his wits, he is sure to figure something out." Dorothy looked relieved, but Alice and Wendy looked doubtful.

Wendy cleared her throat a trifle loudly and said, "Well, it seems we have much planning and travel to do in the next few days. Perhaps we should try and sleep now, so we can face these problems with fresh minds in the morning. It is sure to grow cold in the night, so we should use Alice's lighter to make a small fire and make what beds we can from these sacks." At her words, all the company immediately stretched and yawned.

"Yes," Dorothy said, "I am most certainly tired and must be ready for tomorrow."

Ozma also yawned and said, "It was incredibly tiring being a bird, even in a cage." And she curled herself into a little ball and drew one of the burlap sacks over her. The Lion was already asleep, or so it seemed, although his tail twitched from time to time.

This left Alice and Wendy to make the fire. Wendy gathered some more wood and some round stones. She placed the stones to make a circle, surrounding her pile of wood. Alice watched, and said, "I've never camped or made a fire. What should I do to help?" Wendy replied with a smile, "Watch me this time, and make a fire tomorrow night."

Alice opened her cell phone and began playing solitaire, "At least until the battery dies," she said to Wendy.

Once the fire was built and burning evenly to Wendy's satisfaction, she lay down, but did not close her eyes. She looked up at the night sky of Oz, searching for a certain constellation. The stars were all unfamiliar to her.

Wendy murmured, "Second star to the right, and straight on till morning." She shook her head. Even if that star were somewhere in this sky, she could not find it. And if she could, well, she could not fly any longer. She picked up the Cook's recipe book and began to read in earnest.

It was difficult reading. First of all, it was handwritten, and the Cook's handwriting left much to be desired. Second, it was a well-used cookbook, and food stains spotted many pages.

"Although," Wendy thought, "this must mean that the recipe is well-used, so it must be a good one and worth studying."

Finally, after thumbing through the book for some time, she came upon some words she did not recognize. There was so much information, yet so confusing. It was like deciphering a code.

"This must be it!" she thought. Wendy decided to concentrate on the recipe next to the poem Alice had quoted, the spell that had enchanted the Scarecrow.

She looked over to Alice, who was still playing Solitaire on her cell phone. "Alice," she asked, "What does 'Gripening' mean?"

"Oh," Alice replied, "a lot of words in Wonderland are sort of mushed together to pack them with meaning. Sometimes there is a pun. 'Gripening" is to grow and ripen, I imagine. And 'forgottenlorn' is to forget something and be sad about it, you know, a combination of forgotten and forlorn. It takes a bit of practice to figure them out, like the London Times Cryptic Crossword puzzle, which I am rather good at deciphering."

"I'm afraid I was never much good at that," Wendy said, "Or puzzles in general. I like things to be straightforward."

"Well," Alice replied, "I suppose that is one of the things I got from my experiences. I'm a crackerjack at puzzles and have actually won some cryptic crossword competitions. Only at the regional level, of course."

Alice glanced over at Dorothy, who was asleep and cuddled with Ozma and the Lion, like a heap of kittens.

"Must be nice," she thought, "to have friends you are so comfortable with." She turned towards Wendy and said, "I can't sleep either. Let's put our heads together and see if we can make sense of this."

CHAPTER TWENTY-NINE

DOROTHY AND THE LION

The morning sun was filtering through the trees, casting long shadows across the campsite. Dorothy was awakened by the Lion's tail, switching back and forth in sleep, and hitting her on the nose. She tried to snuggle deeper down into his fur, but the tail was insistent.

She quietly and gently extracted herself from the comfort of the Lion and Ozma's embraces and looked about. The campfire Wendy had started the night before was down to embers, so Dorothy threw a few more armfuls of twigs and leaves on it.

She was hungry, and doubtless, so would everyone else be once when they awaked. They had finished all the soup the night before, and while there were some other items in the basket that might make up a meal, Dorothy felt they should be saved for an emergency. Besides, there were always plentiful nuts and berries in the forests of Oz, so she emptied the basket and set off to gather some breakfast.

Just a short distance away, she found a patch of green and yellow mushrooms, which she recognized as being both safe and delicious.

Nearby, she found a patch of blackberries, a bit thorny, but worth the effort.

Despite the serious danger of their situation, she felt very happy to be back in Oz. Somehow, when in Oz, she had always known that she had friends around her, and that things would work out for the good. At least, it aways had.

A shadow passed over her, briefly darkening the forest. She looked up, and thought she saw a flying monkey. They had been her friends, after she had freed them from the Wicked Witch. But whose side were they on now?

*Yes, Oz had always felt safe, like home, until the Scarecrow had…*she could not even finish the thought.

After that, Oz had been tainted for Dorothy, and going back to Kansas with the Wizard, undertaking the mission of finding a cure for the Scarecrow had been an escape. She had to admit herself that she had welcomed the relief from the guilt of thinking there might have been more she could have done, and that she, not the Scarecrow, should have suffered the Gnome King's vengeance. The memories overwhelmed her, and she sank down on her knees and sobbed.

"There, there, Dorothy," a familiar voice rumbled. "We've all had these moments, no one more than I."

She looked up through her tears to see the Lion standing before her. "Everyone thought you were so brave, to go back to your dull and dreary world to grow older with the Wizard and search for a cure for the Scarecrow. And I know that that was true, you made a huge sacrifice to do so. But I also know that a part of you was going back to be somewhere safe and familiar, even if a bit dull, where you knew the rules and there was no magic to rob you of your brain or turn you into a footstool."

Dorothy gasped. The Lion continued. "No one is more of an expert on cowardice than I. You know me. I am afraid all the time. I am afraid now, fearful that in telling you this hard truth you may not be my friend any longer. But I am telling you anyway, despite my fears, and that is how I am able to hold courage and cowardice in the same place."

"Dorothy," he continued, "you are as brave as I, and as cowardly as well. But when our friends are in danger, when our backs are against the wall, when there is a wrong that must be made right, we act despite our fear. We shall save our friends, we shall save Oz, even though it will be quite frightening."

The Lion shook his head, tossed his magnificent mane over his forehead, and leaned forward. "Look at all these white hairs."

Dorothy looked. Although you could not see them with his mane brushed back, she now saw many white streaks. The Lion lifted a paw and touched one.

"This one appeared when you were captured by the Wicked Witch." He touched another. "And this one when General Jinjur attacked the Emerald City." He swept his paw across a score of white streaks, then abruptly lifted his head and tossed them back under his mane.

"Here is what I finally concluded," he said. "The Wizard (God rest his soul) did not really give me courage. I always had courage. But I also had a very real and not unreasonable fear of danger. I worried and trembled when danger was present. But I always acted to save our friends and to do good. As have you.

"You ran at first, but like me, you have returned. Like our friend the Scarecrow, you may not be sure of what to do, but you'll figure it out, for he is not the only one with brains. And like our friend Nick Chopper, you have a heart that breaks at any sorrow or pain that a friend suffers, but also like him, your heart will not allow you to give up." The Lion paused and placed his heavy paw on Dorothy's shoulder.

"You must stop blaming yourself for the Scarecrow's misfortune. It is true, the Gnome King is your enemy, and his actions were meant to hurt you, but he is the villain, and he made his own choice. Your choice, now, is to save our friends."

The Lion swept her up with his great paws and put her on his back. "Put on a few pounds, I see," he growled. "Although I think you were seven the last time I carried you thus," and he started back to their camp.

Wendy had apparently followed the same train of thought as Dorothy about breakfast. When Dorothy and the Lion returned, Wendy was just emerging from the woods with her own gleanings. She had a great number of mildly bruised apples and several small green eggs. She also had the soup tureen, and the sloshing sound told Dorothy that she had found water.

The others were stirring, still wiping the sleep from their eyes. "I don't suppose you found coffee?" Alice inquired.

"Afraid not," Wendy and Dorothy replied simultaneously, and laughed. The women laid out their provisions, and Dorothy said, "I think it best to preserve as much as we can from the Cook's basket. One never knows what might be useful, and I have never gone hungry in the woods of Oz."

Wendy laid one of the Cook's plates on a flat piece of bark over the fire and added a small bit of butter from the basket. She mixed the eggs and began to slice up the mushrooms Dorothy had found. At the sight of the mushrooms, Alice grimaced and declared, "None of those for me, thanks." Wendy pushed them aside and said, "Omelets alright for everyone?"

Meanwhile, Dorothy washed the fruit they had found and began to slice the apples. "Take care with those apples," Wendy said. "They were not easy to come by." Dorothy exchanged a quick look with Wendy, and a smile passed between them.

Once everyone had eaten to their satisfaction (although the Lion did seem a bit peckish, even after breakfast), it was time to decide on their next move.

"Back to the Emerald City, I think," said Dorothy, "to rescue Nick Chopper and learn what intelligence he has about the Gnome King's ultimate plans. Then on to rescue Glinda!"

Everyone agreed, but the question of how best to return safely to the Emerald City was in doubt.

"It would seem to me," The Lion said, "That the citizens of Oz cannot be happy with this turn of events. They have cooperated thus far because they fear the Gnome King. But if he has left the City and we approach with Ozma, the true ruler, in our company, I have to believe that we will be admitted to the City without question, and that the people will rally to our cause."

Alice said, with disbelief, "So let me get this straight. You are proposing that we just walk up to the City gates, with Ozma on display, and the guards will open the gates and escort us to the palace?" She shook her head and muttered under her breath, "The idea is crazier than a Mad Hatter."

"Yes," replied the Lion calmly, ignoring Alice's obvious skepticism. He turned his head to the others, to see their responses.

Dorothy, Ozma, and Wendy all clapped their hands and with one voice cried, "Yes!"

Alice sighed, and began to gather up their belongings. She came to the rejected plate of mushrooms and looked at it. She took a sniff and looked at them quizzically. The mushrooms did smell quite tempting. She took the tiniest bite and rolled it around in her mouth. Then she took a few minutes to look at her fingers, toes, and body to make sure everything was quite what it should be. Then she packed up the mushrooms and cheerfully declared, "Might be good for supper."

CHAPTER TWENTY-NINE

RETURN TO THE EMERALD CITY

Incredibly, they arrived at the gates of the Emerald City without incident. Walking through the forest, there had been little conversation, but a sense of optimism prevailed. The forest seemed peaceful, the sun dappling the ground as it shone through the canopy of leaves. It seemed that there was always fresh water nearby and plenty of wild food to gather. When at last they reached the edge and saw the yellow brick road stretching out towards the Emerald City, the group as a whole let out a sigh of relief.

The sun was just setting, and Dorothy said, "We should wait and approach just before dawn. Darkness will cover our approach. Once we enter the City, dawn will have broken and the people will all be up and about."

They made camp just inside the forest's edge. No campfire burned tonight, and there was not much talking. The danger of being discovered was great, and the need to conserve energy for the difficult day ahead was imperative.

Dorothy and Wendy took the first watch. The two women sat together, huddled for warmth, gazing out at the green lights of the Emerald City. There was no moon, so the City looked as if it were floating above the meadow of poppies.

Dorothy gazed at the jeweled metropolis, lost in memories and regrets.

Wendy looked over at the young woman, who was cupping her face in her hands, leaning forward and looking at the lights with a single tear rolling down her cheek.

Wendy had cared for enough children to know that speaking is not always the right thing to do. She drew Dorothy as close as she could and stroked her hair until the tears stopped and their watch was done.

Alice and Ozma took the second watch. Burning with curiosity, Alice plied Ozma with questions about Oz, and most especially about Dorothy Gale.

Ozma whispered answers to the first few questions. She told Alice very little and soon seemed disinclined to talk more, holding a finger to her lips to indicate the need for silence. From their brief conversation, Alice gathered that Dorothy was some sort of heroine who had saved the kingdom multiple times. "Huh," she thought, looking over at the sleeping woman.

The Lion took the third watch, and he awoke them with a rough tongue shortly before dawn. Without speaking, they gathered their belongings into the wagon and silently set forth to the gates of the City.

The poppy flowers were still closed for the night and would not open till the sun was much higher in the sky. As they drew closer, they could see the head of the Guardian, poking through the window in the gate.

"Do you think he will admit us?" Dorothy asked in a whisper.

"One way to find out," replied Ozma, drawing herself up to her full, regal height. The Fairy Queen of Oz strode down the yellow brick road with alarming speed, and the rest of the party had to run quickly to catch up to her.

She approached the guard and said in her most imperious voice, "I am Ozma, rightful ruler of Oz. Know me! I and my companions are here to defeat the Gnome King and rescue my people!" She stepped back, placed her hands on her hips, tossed her shining hair over her shoulders and smiled.

At these words, the Guardian began weeping copiously, to the alarm of the group. This was not a reaction they had anticipated.

"Tears of Joy, your Royalness," he explained between sobs. "All of Oz, myself especially, knew you would return to save us. Of course I will admit you." At his words, the handles turned and the gates opened. The party proceeded into the city.

As they closed, Ozma turned to thank the loyal Guardian. She gasped, as she saw that there was no body behind the door, just the small inset door through which the Guardian thrust his head and a pair of hands. She knew at once that the same terrible fate had befallen the Guardian as Jellia Jamb. The Gnome King had cruelly anchored all the servants to their posts and removed anything not necessary to their function.

She wanted to cry at this sight, but instead her look grew grimmer and more determined. She called back to the Guardian, "We shall save you all, and the Gnome King will sorely regret the pain he has caused the people of Oz."

She strode forward through the streets. "If," she said, "the Lion's intelligence is correct, we shall reach the palace unopposed."

As they made their way along the streets of Oz, it appeared that Ozma knew her people well. There were cheers, and flowers were tossed and strewn along the road. As she looked out over the crowds, Dorothy was overcome to see the change. Instead of the gay green garments, which were the usual garb of the citizens of Oz, most wore drab greys and browns.

Even more saddening was the sight of the occasional servant who had been transformed, welded to his work—the carriage driver without legs, attached to his wagon, or the gardener rooted to his plot. Dorothy looked at Ozma and saw a hint of grief, but the more prominent expression on Ozma's face was the fierce and righteous anger of the Fairy Queen of Oz, full of wrath for the terrible harm done to her subjects by the Gnome King.

Dorothy looked behind, to see Wendy was lagging, looking older and more tired than she had ever seen her, with Alice, gently supporting her with an arm around her waist.

The people continued to cheer, and it looked as though they might make the Palace without incident. But just as they turned the corner to the boulevard that would take them to the palace gates, they were confronted by a squadron of evil-looking gnomish guards, less than a block away.

Though small in stature, their foes were nevertheless very intimidating. They wore scraps of metal armor, which hung randomly from their frames, clanging with each movement. Their skin was gray and riddled with veins, like marble. When they moved, a fine layer of dust arose from their joints, and the sound of rock scraping against rock accompanied each movement. They seemed to be living stone, like their King, and each footstep fell with a dull thud, as if a great weight had been dropped.

The people, who had been following behind and cheering, suddenly fell silent. The Guards raised their crude stone weapons threateningly.

Looking at the fear in her citizens' face, Ozma rose up with a look of determination. She gazed about, trying to meet the eyes of her people, but most turned away.

The Fairy Queen marshalled her strength, and with a confidence she did not fully feel, called out.

"People of Oz! We are here to take back our Kingdom from the treacherous Gnome King. Will you not rise up and resist these villains?"

The citizens of Oz, it was clear, were terribly frightened now. They looked about wildly, first at Ozma and her party, then at the gnome soldiers, and finally they looked with new horror at those amongst them who had been transformed to suit their function. They raised no cry, nor made any motion.

The apparent leader of the Gnomes chuckled and took a slow step towards Ozma.

Seeing his queen in danger, the Lion stepped forward and roared at the crowd, "Cowards! Of course, you are afraid." He growled and glowered at the frightened people. Then, in an almost amused voice he spoke. "Me personally, I am so terrified, I can hardly bear it."

He shook his fabulous mane and looked with great kindness at the frightened people. He continued, "But despite my fear (and let me tell you again, my fear is great), I will act with Courage to defend Oz to the last. If I can act bravely, despite my overwhelming fear, can you join me?"

A murmur ran through the crowd, and a few courageous souls stepped forward. But most hung back, whispering among themselves while the Gnome guards continued to advance.

With a mighty leap, the Lion placed himself between Ozma's party and the gnomes. He was trembling, but stood firm. The guards paused.

Alice had been watching this unfold with an unreadable expression on her face. Unable to contain herself any longer, she stood up and scolded the crowd, "Are you kidding me? Are you prepared to live the rest of your lives poisoned with regret that you did not do the right thing today?"

She raised her voice, speaking with great passion. "As a professional, I can assure you that my work is filled with people who cannot come to terms with their regrets, people who failed to do the right thing, who did not follow their heart when the moment called."

Alice leaped up on a nearby bench and she pointed at the crowd. "Do you want to spend the rest of your life saying, 'Oh yes, I was there when Princess Ozma stormed the gates of the Palace, but I hesitated and hung back. I wanted to see how it would turn out.'"

"Or…" and here she paused dramatically, "Do you want to say, 'I was there when Ozma stormed the Palace. And I joined in the push, despite the danger, and we took back Oz and our freedom!'"

The crowd was watching and listening, but still most hung back.

"Besides, we outnumber them!" Alice shouted with exasperation. "Do the math!"

For a moment or two, there was a low buzz of voices, and the people looked about, some trying to count on their fingers. The buzz rose to a roar, and then the people began to cheer again. As one, the crowd rushed at the enemy.

Alice was correct in her calculations, for the crowd did indeed far outnumber the guards. The citizens surged forward, knocking the first row to the ground.

To everyone's astonishment, as the guards hit the cobblestone streets, they shattered like sandstone tossed upon granite. As the dust sifted through the air, the people at first shook their heads in disbelief and wonderment, and then began laughing. The remaining guards raised their weapons, but just as the people lost their fear, the guards began to experience real fear themselves.

The battle was swift and bloodless. Seeing their comrades smashed, the remaining gnome guards scattered like rocks tumbling down a mountain.

Alice looked quizzically at Dorothy, who shrugged her shoulders and spread her hands out, with a "Who knew?" look on her face.

Wendy was laughing, but Ozma knew that though the battle was won, there was still a more dangerous foe ahead. Her face was stern. She gestured silently, pointing towards the Palace. Her companions fell into place and followed. The party made their way to there in relative triumph, followed by the festive crowd.

At the Palace doors, the crowd seemed to hesitate. Understanding, Ozma turned to her people and said, "Good people of Oz, you have been brave and true. Now my companions and I will go and vanquish the Gnome King. I do not ask that you come with us, as I value your safety and we are more than prepared to end this tyranny."

The people cheered again, less enthusiastically, most secretly relieved that their moment of bravery was over. Ozma and her group opened the doors and advanced inside.

CHAPTER THIRTY-ONE

NICK CHOPPER

Once inside, behind the closed door, Ozma turned to her friends and said, "It is true, I wish my people to be safe so I did not ask them to accompany us, though their numbers might help. But Lion, as you also know, finding courage is the first step. Becoming courageous is harder. I wish to let my people be comfortable in that first step."

The palace was almost deserted, save for the occasional anchored citizen whom Ozma hushed with a signal as they passed. Each time they passed a beloved servant transformed, Ozma's face became darker. Dorothy had never seen her Princess look so stern.

Silently, they made their way through the halls. They had been prepared to break through a barrier when they reached the throne room, but to their surprise the door was open and the room appeared deserted, save for an untidy heap of cloaks piled on a coat rack.

"Search the room," Ozma commanded in a whisper. "We must find our enemy and any battle plans or spells he has concealed."

Everyone began to search the room for clues, weapons, or anything that might prove useful. But Dorothy walked directly over to the rack and began removing the coats. She pulled off garment after garment—green velvet capes, leather jackets, peasant aprons, rain cloaks, farmer's overalls, chef's jackets, flannel nightgowns, and several interesting hats. The pile grew bigger and bigger.

At last she had cleared it. Underneath the colorful pile of cloth stood Nick Chopper, the Tin Woodsman, rusted solid with his tears.

"Oh, you poor thing," she cried, throwing her arms around him. Dorothy was rewarded with the tiniest of squeaks and a brief movement of the tin eyelids.

"We must find the oil can and oil him up so he can move!" she cried. They searched the throne room to no avail. The oil can was not to be found.

"What can we do?" Ozma cried. Dorothy's look of despair slowly changed to a smile, and she looked towards Alice.

"If we do not have oil," Dorothy said, "We must find another way to loosen the mechanical joints in our friend. Something smooth, something silky, something that will allow his joints to move without sticking. Something good for mechanical devices, mechanical things like a watch..."

Alice looked confused for a moment and then her face lit up. "Of course!" she exclaimed. "It is, after all, the best butter!" She rustled through the cook's basket and found the butter. It was already quite soft, as it had been a warm day.

"Thank goodness we used very little for breakfast," Wendy said.

Everyone gathered round, and dipping their fingers in the soft yellow lubricant, massaging it into the frozen joints. The Tin Man shook and shuddered as he was slowly freed from paralysis. Finally, he was able to say, "Dorothy!" He tried to hug her, but his arms were still too stiff.

Dorothy embraced her old friend, and as he regained movement, he was soon able to embrace her as well. He held her in his metal arms for just a moment, then turned and bowed to Ozma.

"Your Majesty," he said, "I am sorry that my emotions got the better of me and I allowed myself to fall under the Gnome King's control." A tear began to trickle down his cheek and ran towards his jaw, which began to seize up.

"None of that," Alice snapped. "Wish you were out in the street, so I wouldn't have to give my regret speech again. What's done is done, move on!"

Wendy could see that Alice's approach, though it had worked on the people of Oz, was not quite right for this situation. She stepped forward and said, "I don't believe we have been properly introduced. I am Wendy…" She thought about going on with all the other names, but then settled on, "Just Wendy. You are Nick Chopper. I've heard so much about you."

Wendy tried to conceal her astonishment at the being before her. He was a metal man, crafted of tin sheets, rivets, gears, and bits of odd machine parts she could not identify. Quite frankly, he was just a bit scary looking. But his eyes, even though made of tin, were friendly and kind. Bravely, she thrust out her hand.

The Tin Man was charmed and bowed low. He had always fancied himself a ladies' man (although he had no idea what that meant). Clearly, though, here was a lady. Wendy laughed a bit, as the metal man kissed her hand.

Then Nick stretched his arms, listened for a creak, and hefted his ax. "This butter isn't bad," he said, "But I do prefer machine oil. I smell like popcorn."

Ozma, having watched the encounter with interest and amusement, now stepped up. "Faithful Friend," she said, "you have stood here as a coat rack for some time and have no doubt heard the evil scheme of the Gnome King. Where is he headed and what are his plans?"

The Tin Man looked at Ozma and said solemnly, "He has taken Glinda and the Scarecrow to Glinda's palace to claim her most powerful magic. He tricked Glinda into drinking the Water of Forgetfulness, and he has convinced her that she is his Mother."

At this, Nick paused and waggled his jaw, which creaked uncomfortably. He took a fingerful of the butter and rubbed it into the bolt anchoring the lower half of his face.

He continued, "And my dear friend the Scarecrow has lost his mind and is now the court jester. They are less than a day ahead on the road, so you might easily catch up to them."

"And we shall!" cried Dorothy.

Ozma touched her on the shoulder with a serious look. "Dorothy," she said, "friend, sister. I must make my kingdom right, and my people need me here." She picked up the Cook's book. "I have the means here to restore my people—Jellia Jamb, the Guardian of the Gate, and all of Oz, to their rightful form. You and your party alone must rescue the Scarecrow and Glinda."

She looked towards Wendy. "Only Glinda has the magic to help this woman find her grandchild. Save Glinda, and you save Margaret."

CHAPTER THIRTY-TWO

THE KITTENS COME THROUGH

Ozma strode to the throne and sat down. She did her best to assume an air of royal authority, but then she stood up and knelt down at the foot of the throne. Ozma had put on a brave face during the entry to Oz and while facing the Gnome guards, but this adventure had tired her. She knew she was going to have to send Dorothy and her friends back into danger, and quickly.

Finally, she rose up, seated herself on the throne, took the crown, which had been lying on the floor, and placed it on her head. "It was all much easier," she thought, "when I was just Tip, with only a simple country witch to deal with." For long ago Ozma had been enchanted and had forgotten who she was. She had simply been a boy called Tip who worked for a witch. It wasn't pleasant, but her life had been straightforward, with no difficult decisions to make. Here was a difficult decision. Ozma knew what she had to do, and was ready to do so, as a ruler must.

Just as Ozma was prepared to make her pronouncements, three cats paced into the throne room, followed by a nervous guard. First was Ruby, Alice's kitten, then Eureka, a pink kitten who had been brought to Oz by Dorothy many years ago, and finally the Glass Cat.

This creature, although catlike in all ways, was as transparent as glass, for that is what he had once been. The only parts that were not clear glass were the emerald eyes, the ruby heart, and the pink brains, visible in its head. Like many of Oz's more unusual citizens, the Glass Cat had been brought to life by the Powder of Life many years ago. He was exceptionally proud of his pink brains, which rolled like marbles, as he thought.

"We found each other!" said Ruby excitedly. "Once we found each other, we worked together to get you some important information. Cats don't usually work together, but we made an exception this time. This seemed particularly important, and besides, Jellia Jamb is crying all the time, and I like her and I want to help her."

Eureka stepped forward and said, "Hi Dorothy! I helped too, because, well, I like living in Oz, and it hasn't been very nice lately, and I like you, and I just hate the Gnome King."

The Glass Cat slowly stepped forward his pink brains whirling round in his Glass head. Alice and Wendy could not take their eyes off him.

Speaking to them as if explaining something to a particularly dull child, he said, "It's a map of the Gnome King's itinerary. He's going to Glinda's Palace, but he is going to detour through several Munchkin Villages along the way to display his powers."

The Glass Cat yawned, and continued, "Don't thank me, or the other cats, we just did what had to be done to remain comfortable."

Then the Glass Cat curled into a ball and appeared to fall asleep. Eureka and Ruby ran forward, purring madly, and leapt into the arms of Dorothy and Alice.

"Well, where is this map?" Dorothy asked. The Glass Cat opened one eye and said sleepily, "It was all my idea."

"It was only your idea after I told you about how Ozma and I helped everyone escape!" exclaimed Ruby.

"And after I heard the Gnome King talking about his route and sketching it on a piece of paper!" said Eureka.

"And after I ran in front of the guards packing for the trip and made them chase me!" said Ruby.

"And after I took the paper and hid it in a Mousehole," said Eureka.

"And after I got away," said Ruby.

"And after I put another piece of paper in their bags so they would not know it was missing," said Eureka.

"It was all my idea," said the Glass Cat, opening the other eye, "Although the kittens did have some part in the execution."

"This is excellent!" cried Ozma. "We no longer need to catch up to him. We can move ahead of him to his destination and ambush him there! Kittens, lead this man to the map! Despite this advantage, we must outfit our party at once, to leave before sunset."

The kittens dashed down the hall, followed at first by the Glass Cat, who refused to run, and then followed clumsily by the palace guard, who cried, "Wait, wait!"

Ozma picked up the Cook's basket. "This must remain here in Oz, to aid us in restoring my people to their natural forms. Wendy, if you can restore Jellia Jamb, she is such a good cook that I think she can make the other transformation recipes, freeing you for the journey. But you, Dorothy, and Alice, must prepare to leave as quickly as possible while Wendy works on Jellia."

"As must I," said the Lion. "I will not leave Dorothy."

The kittens came dashing back into the great hall, followed by the guard, wheezing and out of breath. He handed the map to Ozma. Ruby weaved in and out between Alice's ankles, and looking up at her said, "Alice, do you have any treats?"

Automatically, Alice thrust her hands into her lab coat pockets, and felt not cat treats, but the pieces of the mushroom she had gotten from the caterpillar. She had forgotten about them when they had been inventorying their resources in the forest. She looked at Ozma, holding the Cook's basket and thought to herself *These are mine, from my adventure, and I don't think I want to put them on the communal table.* To Ruby, she replied, "No, darling, I am all out."

CHAPTER THIRTY-THREE

PREPARATIONS

Wendy spoke up. "What about the Magic Picture? Can I see Margaret again? And must it stay here in Oz?"

Ozma replied, "It must, so I can keep watch on you and the Gnome King and be able to send aid or rescue if needed. But before you go, of course let us look in on Margaret."

Ozma held up the Picture. There was a shimmer, then a soft focus that slowly cleared to reveal the child sitting near a fire, with a rough blanket tossed over her shoulders. Her back was to them, and although they could not hear anything through the picture, it was obvious someone had spoken to her, for she turned suddenly and looked up, her face streaked with dirt and dried tears. She bit her lip in a defiant gesture all too familiar to her grandmother, and then the image faded.

"Now Peter!" said Wendy. Again, the Picture shimmered, and Peter came into focus. He was standing in his customary stance, arms akimbo, with his head cocked to one side. He was scowling. Although she knew the picture was a one-way window, she felt as if Peter was scowling at her. His eyes seemed to be looking right into hers, his pretty boyish face unlined except for the furrow in his forehead made by the scowl.

Wendy put her hand to her own forehead, feeling the years etched in her skin. When Peter had come for Margaret, she had been careful to stay in the doorway of the nursery, so she had been backlit, and Peter could not see how old she had become. It had been traumatic enough for both of them when he had come for Jane, and had seen her as a grown-up woman, but at least she had been a pretty, young woman. She did not like to think how Peter would react when he finally saw her again, so old. Peter turned to face the other direction, and the image faded.

"There," said Ozma, "They remain safe for the moment. And moments are all we have, for we must get your party on the road as quickly as possible if you are to overtake the Gnome King."

Nick Chopper spoke up at this point. "One more point of information. The spell that was used on my dear friend…" He began to tear up at the sad thought, but Dorothy and Alice simultaneously stopped his crying, Dorothy wiping the tears and Alice hissing, "Your weeping will not help your friend. Tell us what you know."

Nick composed himself and went on, "The spell that was used on my dear friend was a little different than most. The Gnome King did not transform him as he did the others. He made a substitution. His spell substituted straw from the other land for the Scarecrow's magnificent brains. It was not enough, you see, to turn his brains back to straw, for then he would still be himself, only his old brainless self. This foreign straw has left him not only stupid, but disoriented and mad."

"Ah," said Alice, "That explains the poetry he was reciting."

Things began to move quickly. Wendy headed to the kitchen and was soon able to find the recipe to restore Jellia to her natural form and passed the book and basket to her. There was little time for much else, and after thankfully hugging Wendy, Jellia turned to studying the recipes.

Ozma ordered a covered wagon and a pair of swift ponies to pull it. "I could pull it all myself," the Lion rumbled.

But Ozma replied, "Yes, but I would not have you tethered to the wagon, for you must be the protector and guardian of these women."

The wagon was stocked with provisions, and Wendy was given some proper clothing and shoes. The servants of Ozma wanted to take her robe and nightgown to wash, but Wendy insisted, "No, I shall keep these with me."

Within two hours, they were packed and ready to head out. Although Ozma had kept the cook's basket and book, Dorothy had asked for the egg and for the page with the spell used on the Scarecrow, as well as a good supply of straw from a Munchkin farm and some bran and some sharp pins and needles.

"I spent a number of years with the Wizard," she said, "and we talked about many things. I do believe this was the mixture he used to provide the Scarecrow with his magnificent Brain. The pins and needles were to make him sharp and bright, so all we need do is put them back in. He did become very sharp and bright, did he not?" The Lion and the Tin Man nodded in agreement.

Once everything was packed into the wagon, Ozma gave Dorothy the map the kittens had acquired.

"Stolen!" said Ruby proudly. "We stole it!"

"You acquired it for the greater good of Oz," replied Ozma, with a reproving tone. "There are very, very few circumstances in which taking the possessions of another can be sanctioned, but this is one of those rare occasions. I trust that if you decide to remain in Oz with us, you will be an honest kitten." Ruby nodded her agreement.

Ozma turned back to the wagon. After the night in the forest, her royal attire was a bit worse for wear. A small pearl fell from her dress, and Ruby deftly caught it and batted it to Eureka, who batted it under the throne (for later).

Finally, Ozma gave them a large flask of the Water of Forgetfulness, "For the Gnome King, when you catch him. Perhaps if you can get him to drink it, he will forget his wickedness again."

Alice replied. "I keep telling you, medicating him is a short-term solution. If you want real change, give me a few weeks with him and I'll make a new gnome of him."

Ozma replied, "Right now, we need an immediate solution, short-term or not."

CHAPTER THIRTY-FOUR

ON THE ROAD AGAIN

Dorothy, Alice, Wendy, and the Lion set out to overtake the Gnome King, restore the Scarecrow and Glinda to their right minds, defeat their enemy, save Oz, and find a way to Neverland to rescue Wendy's granddaughter. They had the help of two healthy ponies, a wagon with supplies for camping and travel, the egg, some of the Water of Forgetfulness, the straw and other items required to restore the Scarecrow's brains, and not much else, besides their own courage and resources.

Still, their spirits were high, for they had stormed the city, healed the Tin Man, and devised a clever plan, although there were still a few details to work out.

The only one who did not share in their high spirits was Wendy, who was anxious and troubled by the last glimpse into the Magic Picture.

She was also physically exhausted, for she was not used to so much walking, much less running. The pony cart was an improvement, but not much. Wendy almost wished she had allowed herself to become a bit plump, for then at least there would be something to cushion the bumps. But somehow, as she had aged, she had done her best to keep light and strong, perhaps in an unconscious effort to be prepared to fly again. *But I don't suppose I ever will* she thought sadly.

Wendy closed her eyes, leaned on Alice's shoulder, and tried to rest. Alice was initially startled at the intimacy, but softened as she looked at the old woman, who somehow also seemed quite girlish, and drew her under her arm and wrapped a blanket around her.

Dorothy and the Lion were chatting about old times and catching up. For the Lion, it had not been so long, so he had little to add. Many years had passed for Dorothy, and the Lion was especially curious about the Wizard and Toto.

"I was glad that Toto came back with me," she said. "And the Wizard…you remember when we found out he was a humbug? He told me then that he was an exceptionally good man, just not a good Wizard, although he did eventually learn quite a few good magic tricks—real magic, which worked here in Oz. But it turned out that it was much more important that he was a good man."

The Lion nodded, and replied, "Indeed he was, both a good man and a passable humbug."

Dorothy continued, "When we went back to Kansas, being a humbug helped too. Here in Oz, you are who you are, and you don't need anything to prove it. But back in Kansas, you need proof of who you are, and paperwork, to get a job, go to school, or even find a house to live in. A wizard could not make these happen, but a humbug could. He provided us with a house, and I was able to go to school, and we were able to search for some way to help the Scarecrow."

The Lion paused, and looked at Dorothy, and said quietly, "You searched, but had no success?"

She looked down, momentarily flustered by the question. The Lion gave her a moment and swatted casually at a butterfly that happened to pass, making no real effort to actually catch it.

At last, Dorothy replied hotly, "We did look, but we also had many days when there were no clues! So, then we would go to town to buy groceries together, or sit on the porch and watch the sunset, and he would tell me stories of his days before Oz, when a humbug might make a very good living in a carnival. Or he would tell me about his time as the Great and Powerful Oz. You know he was able to give you courage because you believed he could, didn't you?"

The Lion growled gently, almost a purr. "I believe I did figure that out," he rumbled.

CHAPTER THIRTY-FIVE

THE FAIRY

Suddenly the party came upon something blocking the way, a strange creature, huge and radiating a silvery light. It was seated across their path with its back towards them and seemed unaware of their approach. Gossamer wings, rumpled and filthy, torn in a few places, covered most of its back.

They could see shoulders hunched over, but not much else. It was holding its head in its hands and crying softly, great tears as big as if they had been flung from buckets were splashing down, and the path was now soft with mud. If this went on much longer, the path would soon be flooded.

One of the ponies whinnied, but the creature did not turn around. Leaves were being sucked from the trees each time it gasped between sobs, and they whirled through the air.

Dorothy stepped from the wagon and laid her hand on the Lion's back for courage. Alice also stepped from the wagon, after laying the still-sleeping Wendy down and pulling the blanket over her. The Lion and the two women stepped forward.

"Hello," said Dorothy, in her bravest voice. "Can we help you?"

The being turned around. If there had been no visual cues, if the creature had been seen against a featureless background, you might guess that she was tiny, delicate and fairy-like, with a sharp feminine face. Something about her just seemed to suggest daintiness. But she was as big as tree, a monster-like size, and was clearly in distress.

She started to speak, but instead of words, there was a loud clanging of bells, as if they were trapped in the bell tower of Notre Dame, with Quasimodo ringing for all he was worth. The poor thing placed her hands over her mouth in embarrassment and began sobbing anew.

Wendy, of course, had been awakened by the clamor, sat up and exclaimed, "Why it's a fairy! A Neverland fairy!" She leapt from the cart spryly, forgetting her earlier aches and pains.

She addressed the fairy. "However did you get here? And how did you become so large?"

The fairy sighed and gestured. The gesture made no sense to any of them.

Alice, who had plenty of experience in growing and shrinking unexpectedly and the disorientation that can accompany the phenomenon, asked, "Did you eat or drink something? Something you found just lying around? Maybe a bottle with some enticing words, like 'Drink me' written on it? Or a cookie with 'Eat me' written in raisins?" The fairy nodded miserably.

"Well," said Alice, "I'd venture to say that the Gnome King brought a few snacks back from Wonderland when he went there to pilfer magic."

She addressed the giant again. "I don't suppose you found anything else?" The fairy shook her head, just as miserably as before.

"I suppose there is nothing to be done for her then," said Alice. "If we weren't on a quest, I would use my clinical skills to help her adjust to her new size."

Wendy's eyes blazed at this statement, and she clenched her fists. Dorothy stepped back in alarm, for she had never seen gentle Wendy quite so agitated. Alice was oblivious, stepping towards the gigantic fairy and speaking in a soothing voice, "So you are huge. Is that so bad?"

Wendy stepped forward and screamed "No!" silencing Alice immediately. She said, "A fairy depends upon belief for her existence. Belief or disbelief can cure or kill a fairy."

She walked up close to the creature before her and said, "I believe you are a fairy." Then she closed her eyes and said, "I do believe in fairies, and the fairies I believe in are small delicate creatures with voices like tiny chimes. They live in Neverland, and this is a fairy." She repeated this, and as she did, she gestured to the others to join in.

Wendy began again, "I do believe in fairies, and the fairies I believe in are small delicate creatures, with voices like tiny chimes. They live in Neverland."

Dorothy and the Lion began to repeat with her. "I do believe in fairies, and the fairies I believe in are small delicate creatures with voices like tiny chimes. They live in Neverland and this is a fairy."

Wendy opened her eyes, but the fairy had not changed. Then she caught sight of Alice, who was not speaking but instead had folded her arms and was shaking her head. Wendy gestured for Alice to join in the chant. Alice shook her head again and sighed, but did not join in.

Wendy then turned on Alice in fury. "Do you mean to tell me that after all we have been through, both now and in our childhoods, you do not believe in fairies?"

Alice shook her head and looked thoughtful. "This is hard for me," she replied. "I am not the sort to believe in impossible things."

"Do I believe in fairies? I never did before, you know. But of course, I believe in fairies now! I am seeing one! Who wouldn't believe in them, after all we've been through?"

At Alice's words, the giant fairy began to shrink and shrink until it was nothing more than a ball of light, which darted about the woods in obvious delight, tinkling with the musical bell-like speech which is the language of the fairies.

"Oh, I do wish Peter had taught me the fairy tongue," Wendy exclaimed, as the grateful creature lit briefly upon her open palm. The fairy then flew away, but she left behind a small pouch. Wendy opened it and poured a few grains of some glittering dust into her hand. "Fairy dust!" she exclaimed. "If only we were children."

Alice smiled ruefully. "I guess I really do believe in fairies," she said. Somewhere, far, far away, a fairy who had been near death suddenly revived.

CHAPTER THIRTY-SIX

THE RESCUE OF THE SCARECROW

The rescue of the fairy had reenergized Wendy, and she urged the ponies to pick up their pace, and said, "It's clear that whatever borders have been established between all these places are not impenetrable. If the Gnome King could travel from Oz to Wonderland and back, and a fairy was able to come to Oz from Neverland, then surely, we can find a way from here to Neverland and rescue Margaret."

"Yes," replied Dorothy. "But our best chance is still to find and restore Glinda and the Scarecrow, for between his brains and her magic, we will find a way."

Alice had been studying the map that the kittens had stolen. They had left the great yellow brick road shortly after leaving the Emerald City and had been following a smaller road paved with blue cobblestones. A pretty little brook, which had been running alongside the road for most of their journey, now began to meander away from them and head into the woods.

"We should be very close to Ruggedo's first stop, she said. "It looks to be a fishing village. This brook will eventually feed into a lake near the village. If we wish to approach the village unseen, we could follow the brook instead of the road."

"Good idea," Dorothy replied. "We can stash the wagon in the woods and ride up on the ponies and the Lion. We can observe from a distance. If we have managed to arrive before Ruggedo, we can enlist the aid of the villagers. If he has already arrived, we can wait until night and then see if we might find the Scarecrow. Once we have him back to his clever self, we can decide on the best method for dealing with the Gnome King."

"I think we have some cleverness among us already," replied Alice. "But a little more couldn't hurt."

They brought the wagon as deep into the woods as they could, and concealed it in the brush, packing a basket with only the most essential items. Then Dorothy mounted the Lion, and Alice and Wendy the ponies, and they made their way along the brook, which grew wider as they traveled, first becoming a stream and then a smallish river. They could see a few turtles sunning themselves on the opposite bank and some silvery fish swimming between the rocks.

Soon the lake was visible through the trees and the little village on the opposite shore. The woods had begun to thin out, and there was little cover between them and the village. The sun was low in the sky, and soon it would be dark.

The Lion said, "We will not be able to approach unseen as a party until it is dark. Let me go ahead now and scout out the situation. I have become quite good at hiding and stealthy movement."

Without waiting for an answer, he crouched low and began creeping along the edge of the lake, taking cover where he could, in a stand of reeds, a deepening shadow, and a ruined boat that had been beached on the shore. In a few moments, they lost sight of him.

"My, he is quite good at that!" said Alice admiringly. Dorothy nodded, and then noticed some berries growing on the bushes nearby. The women busied themselves in picking berries for their supper.

The Lion soon returned with news. "The Gnome King was just arriving when I came to the village. Naturally, the Munchkins were terrified, as was I. But I stayed and was able to discover their plan for the evening. They immediately took possession of the grandest house—that large blue one by the edge of the lake," he said, pointing.

"The Gnome King and Glinda are to stay there, and his guards will be housed in all the other homes to keep an eye on the inhabitants. The Scarecrow is to be posted outside the house where Ruggedo and Glinda will be staying. He never sleeps and continues to recite senseless poetry, but they have induced him to whisper at night. When I saw him, he was going on and on about the antics of an old father who was performing miraculous feats of strength and agility. But in his madness, he will strike up a loud conversation with anyone who approaches, and the sound of conversation in the night will alert Ruggedo to any stranger's approach."

At the mention of the subject of the poem, a curious look crossed Alice's face.

"Well done!" said Dorothy. "Once it is night, and everyone but the Scarecrow is asleep, we will go there and see if there is a way to keep him quiet while I replace his brains. I will have to remove his head, of course, but just for a few moments."

Alice smiled. "I may have an idea," she said, but refused to elaborate. "Just trust me," she replied to their questions. "That poem is from my world."

As planned, they waited until they were sure everyone except the Scarecrow would be asleep. Creeping towards the house where they knew the Gnome King and Glinda slept, Dorothy looked anxiously at Wendy. "Do you think Alice knows what she is doing?"

Wendy replied. "At some point, we all really need to trust each other." They crept towards the house, and as they approached, they could see the Scarecrow, standing by the entrance. Dorothy, of course, knew what to expect, but Alice and Wendy did not. Despite what the women had already heard, the sight of a living Scarecrow dancing, capering, and reciting poetry was extremely disturbing and peculiar, to say the least.

Both Alice and Wendy stared at him in disbelief. Although they had met the Tin Man, he had been somewhat like a robot, and therefore more familiar. This being, however, confounded them. They watched as he performed, his limbs bending in all the wrong places and directions for a man. He was speaking, but his mouth did not open, and although the painted face did not change, the surface of it rippled and bulged, giving a sort of expression. The two women were transfixed.

Dorothy was transfixed as well, but not for the reasons that Alice and Wendy were. She was quite used to the Scarecrow and didn't even think of him as a peculiar creature. She was focused on the sad fate of her friend, her wise and noble friend, who was now leaping about and babbling the utmost nonsense, as he had been the last time she saw him. Here was the Scarecrow, the smartest, wisest being in all of Oz, reduced to a clown. It was awful.

At this moment, he was juggling some crockery, and singing in a low voice, "Twinkle, twinkle, little bat. How I wonder what you're at! Up above the world you fly, like a tea tray in the sky…" At this, he flung a tea tray up into the air and tossed all the other dishes into the flower bed, fortunately not breaking anything but a few flowers.

Alice had been listening closely to the Scarecrow, and as he launched the tea tray, she stepped forward and waited beneath. As the Scarecrow was tossing the rest of the dishware, she deftly caught the tray.

The Scarecrow's painted smile seemed to stretch ever so slightly, as if he were trying to smile even more, but before he could speak to her, Alice folded her arms in front of her, standing like a schoolgirl, and recited, in the same low singsong voice as the Scarecrow,

> "'You are Old, Father William,' the young man said.
> 'And your hair has become very white,
> and yet you incessantly stand on your head.
> Do you think, at your age, it is right?'"

Delighted, the Scarecrow replied,

> "'In my youth,' Father William replied to his son,
> 'I feared it might injure the brain;
> But now that I'm perfectly sure I have none,
> Why, I do it again and again!'"

With this, he flipped himself over, wobbling quite a bit, until he was standing on his hands, his straw body swaying this way and that. Alice shot an urgent look at Dorothy and pointed at the Scarecrow.

Dorothy rushed up and firmly pulled at a thread hanging from his neck, and the head tumbled off. Just as quickly, Dorothy dumped out the contents.

The flat face smiled up at her, and she impulsively bent forward to kiss the burlap cheek. Then she began re-stuffing it with the new brain ingredients.

Without the head, the body had begun to sway in a most frightening manner, so Alice and Wendy ran forward to hold it in place. The arms flapped about, but fortunately, without the head attached, it was no longer inclined towards conversation or sounding the alarm.

Finally, Dorothy was done refilling the Scarecrow's head. The head turned to her, and the eyes once again shone with recognition.

"Dorothy! Is that really you? Oh! Thank you!" he said.

"Hush," she whispered. "We are in great danger."

They quickly reattached the Scarecrow's head and stepped back into the shadows, hidden but with a clear view of the house where Glinda and the Gnome King slept.

CHAPTER THIRTY-SEVEN

THE SCARECROW FIGURES IT OUT

I remember everything that happened," the Scarecrow told Dorothy. "But I was so confused all the time. All I could think about were these poems and songs. Say Dorothy, why haven't you introduced me to your friends? And hello, Lion, nice to see you." The Scarecrow held a white gloved hand out to each, his left to Alice and his right to Wendy.

Dorothy said, "This is Dr. Alice Liddell, and this is Wendy Winthrop. They came with me to help save you, and now we must save Glinda, for only Glinda can help Wendy save her granddaughter."

"That's a lot of saving," replied the Scarecrow. "Dr. Liddell, don't you need any saving?"

Alice smiled wryly, "Thank you, but actually, I do believe I have already been saved, although I wasn't aware I needed it at the time."

Wendy cast a meaningful look at Dorothy, but Dorothy was too preoccupied with the present situation to notice. But Alice caught it and grinned, shrugging her shoulders and opening her hands in a sign of surrender.

Dorothy said to the Scarecrow, "You do remember! You know Glinda drank the Water of Forgetfulness, and the Gnome King has convinced her that she is his mother. What can we do?"

"Yes," said Alice tartly, "We had a plan to rescue you, but after that, we figured, what with you being so smart and all, you could figure out what to do next."

Wendy now cast a frowning look at Alice, the silent and universal look of mothers everywhere for "Don't be rude."

The Scarecrow scrunched up his face and his brow furrowed with deep wrinkles of concentration. The new brains had not yet settled, so a few needles poked out through the burlap. He scratched his head, and furrowed his brow even further, so his painted eyebrows disappeared.

After much thought, he leapt up. "She drank the Water of Forgetfulness!" he said. "All she has to do is to drink it again, and she will forget that she forgot!"

"Brilliant!" Wendy and Dorothy exclaimed in unison.

His painted face was lit momentarily with joy, but then his expression fell. Sadly, he went on, "But the Fountain is back in the Emerald City. How will we get some in time to cure her before the Gnome King reaches her palace?"

Alice followed with, "Actually, yes, it is brilliant," and she reached into their travelling pack to produce the Water of Forgetfulness, which she had initially been so reluctant to bring.

Fate is sometimes kind, for at that moment, a voice called out, "Jester, where are you? I woke up and did not hear your soothing voice." They looked towards the house, and saw Glinda, at a window. She did not look as Dorothy remembered her, regal and elegant, clothed in royal garb, with a tiara set with jewels that had been worked with magical symbols.

Glinda was now wearing a white nightcap with earflaps and a long nightgown with a too busy pattern of poppies in the cloth. Her long flowing hair was all tucked under her cap.

She had opened the shutters and was leaning out the window, looking for the Scarecrow. He quickly somersaulted into view and tried to recite poetry as he had been doing for days. But now, in his right mind, nothing came to him. He looked worriedly towards the bushes where the rescue party has hastily concealed themselves at the noise.

Alice rolled her eyes and knelt down. She crept through the bushes until she was close enough so the Scarecrow could hear her, but Glinda would not, and recited in a whisper,

> *"'Will you walk a little faster?'*
> *said a whiting to a snail."*

The Scarecrow immediately repeated her words. She went on,

> *"There's a porpoise close behind us,*
> *and he's treading on my tail."*

And as Alice recited, the Scarecrow repeated every verse of the Lobster Quadrille. He ended with an elaborate bow, tumbling over headfirst, as he had bowed a trifle too deeply.

"I cannot believe I still remember all that," Alice thought to herself. "Lucky, though."

Glinda clapped her hands and laughed. "You are so amusing! I must wake up my son so he can hear your latest jest!"

"Oh no, Ma'am," said the Scarecrow, picking himself up and dusting off. "Don't you know how much he hates to be disturbed while getting his beauty sleep."

Glinda looked a bit confused at hearing the Scarecrow talking sensibly. However, here the Scarecrow proved that he was indeed quite sharp, for he said to her, "Now, let me get you a nice cool drink of water, and I will sing you my best jest ever!"

He ambled backwards, hands behind his back, the white-fingered gloves urgently gesturing. Alice understood, and as the Scarecrow backed up to the bush where she was concealed, she handed him the Water.

Dorothy, Wendy, and the Lion watched from their hiding places. Dorothy reached out and squeezed Wendy's hand. The Lion rumbled low in his throat and hunched down, prepared to pounce if the need arose.

The Scarecrow produced the Water of Forgetfulness from behind his back with a flourish, as if performing some great magic trick. Glinda clapped again, and said, "Well, now that you mention it, I am a bit parched," and she reached for the flask.

Everyone held their breath as Glinda took a long draught from the Water of Forgetfulness. For a moment, it seemed to have no effect. Then, she shook her head slowly. She reached up to the top of her head, pulled off the nightcap, and stared at it incredulously. Then she looked at the Scarecrow and held her arms out to him. He ran forward, and they embraced. through the window. "Oh, my friend," she whispered, "you are saved, and I am saved! But how can this be?"

The Scarecrow put a gloved finger to his painted smile and gestured for quiet. He lifted Glinda and helped her to climb out the window.

Alice stood up and led the Scarecrow and Glinda back to where Dorothy, Wendy, and the Lion were hiding. Glinda held her arms out again, and they all came together for a moment.

The Scarecrow stepped back, and now that the immediate danger had passed, studied Dorothy more closely. "I thought it was just a week," he said. "And I think it has been a week for me. But you... I can see that you have done more than a week's worth of growing. How long has it been for you?"

Dorothy lowered her eyes and spoke quietly, "It has been twenty years for me."

Although the Scarecrow's face still held its painted smile, it was clear he was distraught. "Twenty years? You thought you had left me in that terrible condition for twenty years?"

Dorothy nodded miserably. "We tried, the Wizard and I," she said. "Truly we did. But we came up empty, time and again, until now. And in the meantime, I have helped many others, I have!"

Dorothy turned to Alice for confirmation, who nodded and gave her a quick thumbs up. Wendy pinched Alice's arm, and Alice spoke up, "Of course she has! Ms. Gale has helped so many people."

Wendy pushed Alice towards the Scarecrow and whispered, "Doctor, do what you do best."

Startled, Alice took a moment and composed herself. Then she addressed the Scarecrow, "I can see you are hurt, and perhaps feeling abandoned by Dorothy in this instance. That is quite natural, and to be expected. But you do not know what she has been going through, and all the possible reasons for delay, not the least of which is that until this moment, no cure was found."

She continued, pulling Dorothy to her. "You both have a long history of friendship and loyalty. Scarecrow, you know this person, the innate goodness that is the core of her being. There will be time for you to talk in depth with her, but for now, in this perilous situation we are in, can you not have faith in your friend and her motives?"

The Scarecrow looked thoughtful and cocked his head to one side and placed a hand on his cheek. Dorothy walked to the Scarecrow and whispered, "But I never forgot about you, truly." She stifled a sob.

He wrapped his soft arms around her and held her close for a few moments. Finally they parted, and while it did not seem possible, there were tears leaking from the painted eyes and, the painted smile looked even more kindly than usual .

CHAPTER THIRTY-EIGHT

GLINDA'S PLAN

D orothy," said Glinda, looking at her with care and tenderness. "More time has passed for you than for us here in Oz. We are not judging you for the time it has taken. But you did succeed in finding the Scarecrow's cure, and it seems you have brought some powerful allies to help us."

"Yes," Dorothy replied, "But we need your help as well."

After some quick introductions, Dorothy recounted their adventures to Glinda and the Scarecrow. When they reached the present point, Wendy said, "And now, it is of the utmost importance that we find a way to Neverland and rescue Margaret."

Glinda listened with attention, and said, "It would be good to have the help of Dorothy and her friends in the battles ahead. But it is clear that the safety of Ms. Winthrop's granddaughter takes precedence."

She looked at Dorothy. "Child, I think I can help your friend and any who choose to travel with her to find this Neverland. But Oz had been your home, more of a home in some ways than that Kansas has ever been. But then you left us for such a long time. Child, where do you think your home is?"

Dorothy bit her lip. "That's hard to say," she replied. "Oz is where my friends are, and now, Uncle Henry and Aunt Em. And I am a Princess of Oz. I love it here, even though it is sometimes dangerous. But when the Wizard and I went back, I grew up in

Kansas. And I found people who needed my help. I did good work. I made friends there too. How can I choose?"

Dorothy was on the edge of tears again, and Glinda reached out to touch her cheek.

Glinda smiled, "Why did you think you had to choose? You belong in both worlds, and you may travel between them as you choose."

Dorothy looked at Glinda, "But how?"

"The Gnome King has been scouring Oz and any other world he can find for magic to aid him in his quest. My palace was to be his final stop, but there is much magic already here in this house, gathered by the Gnome King to further his evil ends. And since I am his 'mother,' he has been careless about concealing his treasures. Wait here."

Glinda replaced her nightcap and disappeared into the house. A few minutes later, she returned, holding a silver shoe in each hand.

Nice shoes, Alice thought. *But I imagined magic shoes would be flashier, maybe in red? If this was a movie, they would be red.*

"But those were lost in the Deadly Desert! They fell off my feet the first time I left Oz to return to Kansas." Dorothy said.

Glinda replied with a wise smile, "Just because something is lost, does not mean it cannot be found. Very few things are lost forever."

Glinda touched Dorothy's cheek again and said, "You may use these shoes to take your friends to Neverland. They will not fall off this time, so that when your mission is fulfilled, you and your friends can return here to Oz, and then, if you wish, back to your other land. Do not worry about the fate of Oz. The Scarecrow and I are in a perfect position to infiltrate the Gnome King's defenses. I was but one ingredient away from the spell I was intending to bind him, and if we continue to my palace, I shall be able to complete my spell and defeat him. All that is needed is that the Scarecrow and I continue to play our parts until then. Have faith, we shall prevail."

The Scarecrow looked a little doubtful, but Alice said, "Don't worry, I'll write you a script that will see you through. If you run out, just repeat. No one is listening anyway."

CHAPTER THIRTY-NINE
FAREWELL TO OZ

Just as their departure from the Emerald City had been rushed, so was their departure. Alice returned to the wagon to pack as much as each woman could carry.

While Glinda instructed Dorothy in the proper use of the shoes, Wendy, feeling a bit useless, sat down between the Lion and the Scarecrow. She was shivering, both from the cold of the night, but also from fear and anticipation.

Finally, they were going to Neverland, and Wendy had to come to terms with what she would do when she saw Peter again. She had no doubt that her companions would succeed in helping her rescue Margaret from whatever held her captive. In this, she was confident. But seeing Peter again…in this, she was not settled. She shuddered again, and the Scarecrow threw a soft, wobbly arm around her shoulder. The Lion nuzzled her elbow, nudging her with his great muzzle, and she placed her other arm around him.

"You are afraid of something?" the Lion inquired.

"Or is there something I can help you figure out?" asked the Scarecrow.

Wendy sighed, "I think that the only one in Oz who can answer my question is not here. I need your friend, Nick Chopper, for this is a matter of the heart."

The Lion replied, "I understand. But know that in matters of the heart, one must also be brave. If you need help in being brave, I am here."

The Scarecrow added, "And even when you know the path your heart is taking you, you must still be wise in your choices."

"You are all so incredibly kind," Wendy said. "I see why Dorothy loves this place."

Dorothy had come up beside them quietly. "I do love this place," she agreed. "Did you love Neverland?"

"Did I love Neverland?" Wendy echoed. "I loved being a mother to the Lost Boys. I loved that there were fairies and mermaids. I loved that I had a pet wolf. I didn't love that there were pirates and dangerous animals. And Peter…" Here she trailed off, and a distant look crossed her face.

"And you could fly," Dorothy said. "Didn't you love that?"

"Oh, of course," Wendy replied, "I could fly. I'm not sure how I feel about that. Sometimes it was thrilling, but sometimes it was frightening, or just tiring. When we first flew to Neverland, it took forever, and if we started to sleep, we would fall. That will wake you up, let me tell you! And sometimes Peter flew so fast…"

Again, the distant look crossed her face. She looked up at the stars, and suddenly said, "Oh, there it is after all! Second to the right and straight on till morning!"

They were interrupted by the sound of someone stumbling through the brush. Alice was returning from the wagon, carrying a bit more than she ought to have been. She had bags slung over her shoulders and around her waist and a large basket in her arms. Everyone hurried forward to help her, and they proceeded quietly to a small clearing out of sight of the house.

"Wasn't sure what we might need, "Alice said rather breathlessly, "so I took all I could carry."

They sorted through the supplies, but since they didn't know what they were preparing for, it was hard to decide. In the end, they took food and water, some ropes, and a tinder box, and Wendy also took her nightgown. The egg was to be left with Glinda, to help her deal with the Gnome King, who had an abnormal fear of eggs. Glinda had drunk all of the Water of Forgetfulness, so the flask was of no use.

Glinda appeared at the window again and beckoned. "You must leave," she whispered. "The Gnome King will awaken soon, and the Scarecrow and I must continue our deception. Have you packed, are you ready?"

Dorothy nodded, and she hugged the Lion and kissed the Scarecrow. She stepped up to the window, and Glinda leaned forward and placed a kiss upon her forehead. "This kiss means something here in Oz, "she said. "I hope it will mean something where you go."

Wendy hugged the Lion and the Scarecrow as well and stepped to the window. "Thank you," she said to Glinda, as the kiss was placed on her forehead.

Alice stood awkwardly, then finally hugged the Lion and Scarecrow a bit stiffly. She passed a sheaf of notes to the Scarecrow and said, "Here are the Wonderland poems and songs, all that I can remember. And like I said, just repeat them if you need to. I don't think the Gnome King is paying much attention."

The Scarecrow hugged her back with as much strength as a straw man can muster. "Oh, thank you, thank you," he said. He looked over the papers and said, "Oh, 'The Walrus and the Carpenter'...this one looks quite nice! I do hope it has a happy ending."

At last, Dorothy took off her own comfortable shoes, and put on the silver slippers. "I will be able to take them off when we're done?" she asked.

"Of course," Glinda replied. "They are only on loan to you, and I expect you to return them to me in good time."

Dorothy and her friends gathered all their supplies and stood close to each other. Dorothy threw her arms around each of their shoulders and pulled them in tight. Wendy and Alice each wrapped one arm around Dorothy's waist, and the other around each other, forming a small circle. Dorothy looked at Wendy. "You must help me. When I click my heels, you must say where we want to go."

"Neverland," Wendy breathed, "to save Margaret and Peter." Dorothy clicked her heels once.

"Neverland," Wendy repeated, and Alice and Dorothy echoed, "to save Margaret and Peter."

Dorothy clicked her heels again. In unison, the women said, "Neverland, to save Margaret and Peter." Dorothy clicked her heels one final time, and they were suddenly enveloped in a great swirling wind.

It was deafening, and it battered them, as if it wanted to tear them apart. They clung more tightly to each other, and they felt the ground beneath them slip away, as they were lifted up and whirled around the vortex that had formed around them. They had to close their eyes, as the winds were stinging. It seemed to go on forever, but afterwards, checking her watch, Alice saw that it had been less than a minute.

Finally, the winds subsided, and they landed suddenly on a sandy surface. All was calm. They opened their eyes and looked about. Dorothy quickly checked her feet. The shoes were still there.

CHAPTER FORTY

THE NEVERLAND

The three women found themselves on the shores of the Neverland. Wendy gasped. The sky was gray, there was a chill from the ocean and the scent of salt water on the breeze.

Wendy studied the horizon, picking out landmarks, the hills that surrounded the mermaid's lagoon, the bay where the pirate ship would dock, and the forest where she had been a mother to the Lost Boys.

She saw unfamiliar landmarks as well. Now there was a high cliff above Pirate Bay, and what was that tower? Why, it was a lighthouse! There had never been a lighthouse before. And to the east, she ought to have seen smoke from the native village, but she did not. This was a very different Neverland.

Wendy looked at the two women, who had helped her come this far. They each looked back at her questioningly. This was her land, and they looked to her for direction.

Finally, now that she was actually back in Neverland, Wendy gave in fully to her fears. She closed her eyes, and thought, *Something terrible must have happened to Peter, or he would have brought Margaret home. Was Peter dead? Had someone worse than Captain Hook come to Neverland, someone crueler, meaner, more clever? Had someone or something gotten Peter?* She found herself gasping, almost sobbing, as Dorothy reached out and held her close.

Alice looked over the landscape and with her cool analyst's voice asked, "Is this your Neverland? Is there anything out of place, or anything that seems to merit caution, or seems odd, or that calls to you?" Wendy pointed immediately at the lighthouse.

Dorothy said, "The lighthouse is a long way off and very high up. I think we should walk along the beach. Perhaps we will find a path to make it up the cliff."

They walked along the sand, and Wendy could hear the sounds of the forest drifting on the wind. She heard animal calls, she heard a drum, but not the drum of the natives. She did not hear any voices, and most importantly, she did not hear the sound she wanted most to hear—Margaret's laugh and Peter's triumphant crow.

She looked again at the sky. She saw the Never bird and her fledglings, she saw darts of light that might have been fairies, but she did not see Peter or any flying child.

Dorothy was picking up seashells as they walked. Alice, who had a bad feeling about it, was keeping her eyes on the lighthouse, barely noticing the scenery.

The path along the beach took them past the mermaids' lagoon. It has been so many years since Wendy had seen a mermaid, and though they were not friendly to her, she longed to see them again. It would be good to see that something of her Neverland remained.

Wendy turned and walked to the edge. She looked into the water and saw to her surprise that it was muddy and rank. No mermaid had been here in quite some time. The mermaids were gone, there was no fire from the natives, no noise from the woods but the animals...what had happened here? Wendy sank down and exhaustion overtook her. It felt like it had been days since they had slept.

Dorothy said, "Let's rest a bit. We will need our strength and wits about us."

"Yes, "said Alice. "It is clear from what we have seen in the Magic Picture that while Margaret may be captive, she is at least safe. If whoever has taken her meant to harm her, they would have done so already."

Wendy's heart would have urged her on without rest, but her body would not allow it. And it seemed that night was falling. The sun was already low on the horizon, sending red and gold reflections across the water. Reluctantly, she agreed, and they set up camp.

Alice lit a small fire with the tinderbox, and Dorothy portioned out some of their food. It was agreed that Dorothy would take the first watch, Alice the second, and Wendy the third. As weary as she was, Wendy did not believe that she would be able to sleep at all, but once she lay down, she fell into a deep but troubled sleep.

Dorothy sat by the fire, letting it burn low before restoking it to avoid calling attention to their campsite. She looked up at the stars, and they seemed to be winking at her.

She was not worried about affairs in Oz. She was confident that Glinda and the Scarecrow and the Lion would defeat the Gnome King, as they had in the past. She wondered however, if this would be the final battle with Ruggedo.

She looked at Alice, snoring quietly in a rough blanket before the campfire, and tried to picture her as the difficult Dr. Liddell with whom she often clashed.

Although she and Dr. Liddell had been at odds most of her time at the hospital, she tended to agree with Alice's assertions about the Water of Forgetfulness and Ruggedo's reformation. After all, had not Glinda remained helpful and good despite the water's effects? Perhaps that really had been the problem all along, for the Gnome King had returned many times to vex them.

Dorothy sighed, not unhappily, but with something like relief. She thought back not just upon the past few days, but further. Days? Hours? Weeks? How long since they passed through the mirror in Wendy's room?

She knew that it had been twenty years to the day by her reckoning since she and the Wizard left Oz to find a cure for the Scarecrow. But in Oz, it had been just a few days.

Somehow, she had been given the years to find what she needed to find, and in that time she had been allowed to grow up, go to school, make friends, help people, and have the Wizard as her truly good and loving father, while her friends only suffered for a few days. She felt blessed.

The stars were quite definitely winking at her. If she could have understood their language, as Peter did, she would have heard their warning. But she did not, and could only sit, poking the fire to stay awake, until it was Alice's watch.

She did not know is that there was another watcher looking out for them. Wendy's pet wolf, which has endured through recent changes in the Neverland, had detected his mistress's scent on the island and was standing just out of sight in the shadow of the ferns, guarding them.

CHAPTER FORTY-ONE

INTERLUDE: THE NATURE OF THE NEVERLAND

They were finally in the Neverland, the real Neverland. Unlike the childhood fantasy of Neverland, where there were adventures and dangers, when children woke up after dreaming of the Neverland, they were always alright.

In this Neverland, there is no guarantee that things will turnout alright. In fact, many times, they do not. The real Neverland is dangerous.

In our plain ordinary world, things do not change, unless someone or something makes them change. A bridge is built, a storm knocks down the levee, or seeds are blown by the wind and plants grow.

It is much the same in Oz, although it may be that a witch enchants a forest and the trees become greedy and will not share their fruit. It is the same in Wonderland, for a girl might drink a potion and grow so large as to break your roof. These changes may happen quickly, or slowly, but you can always figure out why it has happened.

Not so the Neverland. The Neverland is always changing.

Was it a lucky accident that when Wendy, John and Michael went to Neverland they found pirates, Indians and mermaids? No, John was mad for pirates, and had a well-thumbed copy of Treasure Island tucked beneath his mattress. Michael had been given a splendid playset for Christmas the past year, with cowboys and Indians, and he much favored the Indians. And Wendy, who had taken swimming lessons the past summer, had become an accomplished swimmer by pretending to be a mermaid.

The Neverland, you see, usually only comes to children when they are asleep, and it holds whatever adventure they are dreaming of. So, one child's Neverland might have Ninja assassins, while another might have Centaurs. But these are dream Neverlands. There are so many out there, as there are so many dreaming children.

Fortunately, there are often common fantasies, or the Neverland would become too crowded. The rage for pirates, for example— John was not the only boy with a copy of Treasure Island stuffed under his mattress at that time.

These Neverlands often blend and overlap, and this blended Neverland is where Peter lives. He had lived for quite some time in Kensington Park, but the fairies had filled his ears with talk of the Neverland, and not one to pass up an adventure, Peter had begged them to take him there. He quite likes that the island changes in this way, otherwise he would become bored.

Generally, as the island changes, it tends toward the most popular of children's dreams, and before Peter came, it would drift lazily between pirates, mermaids, knights in shining armor, evil sorcerers and whatnot. Still, it was always dangerous and exciting.

However, once Peter arrived, he made it his own. Since Peter often visits children in their dreams, he gets to pick and choose what is on the actual Neverland. He does it rather impulsively, and then he must live with his choices for a while. The island will still have its say, and sometimes there will appear some thing or other, which Peter did not expect or choose. This thrills him no end, but more and more the island had been deferring to Peter's choices. You see how it is.

The physical Neverland, where the women now slept, does have some constants. Its geography is more or less fixed, in that the island is small enough to go anywhere in a day and still be home by nightfall.

We see that the lagoon is still there, although mermaids seem to have fallen out of fashion with children for the moment. Although the water is murky now, it is actually in flux, changing to suit the present rage amongst children for dragons. Soon the water will clear, and the lagoon will sink deep, and a cave with dragon eggs will be found there.

The Neverland will always have fairies, for they are not just an imagining of children, but are quite real, and this is where they live. They all love Peter, and that is why they brought him here long ago. Peter is also one of the constants.

Because Peter must have a crew, and because boys are always getting lost, there are always Lost Boys. The actual boys may change, for any number of reasons.

Some join other factions. Peter lost quite a few boys to the Gypsies when they were part of the Neverland. Gypsies, of course, like the Indians have fallen out of fashion in children's fantasies, not merely because they are old-fashioned, but are now recognized as an offensive stereotype, and are no longer found in the Neverland.

Sadly, some are killed by the dangers of the island.

Finally, despite all of Peter's admonishments, some of them seemed to insist upon growing older. Once any boy had grown taller than he, Peter banished that boy back to whence he came. Some cried, some pleaded, but most just went with a touch of relief, which puzzled Peter.

Just now, the Neverland was between. Peter had been rooting about in children's dreams, looking for just the right mix of danger, adventure and fun, but other than the dragons, he had been strangely unsatisfied with anything he found. He was even starting to doubt that the dragons would prove worthy, and he wondered if it was too late to stop it. He had never before had second thoughts.

So, Peter had left the Neverland to its own devices, and it was out of practice. The Neverland had begun to depend on Peter, you see, to supply the adventures.

The fairies at first tried to help him, directing him to this particularly imaginative child or that, but after the incident with Tinker Bell, they left him on his own. The Neverland had never been "between" for quite this long a time. It was troublesome to all the inhabitants, but especially the fairies.

And it is at this strange time of flux that the women now camped.

CHAPTER FORTY-TWO
MORNING IN NEVERLAND

D orothy's watch ended without incident, and she woke Alice. Second watch is the most beastly, for you have only just fallen asleep, when you are awakened for your shift, and just when you finally are alert and awake, your watch is done, and you must try and go to sleep again.

Alice had been sitting up, half awake, fighting the urge to sleep, poking the fire, and listening to the night sounds. It was nearly time for her to wake Wendy for the third watch. A soft and sweet part of her thought about letting her sleep, and taking both watches, but she knew that Wendy would be offended if she were not allowed to do her part.

As she weighed the pro and cons of waking Wendy or letting her sleep, she was startled by a ball of light, which darted here and there throughout their campsite, emitting the most beautiful bell-like tones. The ball circled her head, and the tinkling noises woke up Wendy. She sat up and watched the ball of light with surprise and delight. "Tinker Bell!" she cried. "You are alright!"

The ball finally lit on Alice's shoulder, and by turning her head slowly, out of the corner of her eye, Alice could actually see the fairy. She was incredible…a small, delicate, and beautiful creature, like a tiny person, with gossamer wings. The fairy was repeating the same tinkling sequence.

"She is saying 'thank you,' I think," said Wendy. "I don't understand much of the fairy language, but I do understand this."

Alice was confused. "What is she thanking me for? I never met this fairy, and until we met that great huge one in Oz, I wasn't sure I believed in them."

Tinker Bell was trying to thank Alice for saving her life. Back in Oz, when Alice had said that she believed in fairies, Tinker Bell had heard her, and instantly recovered from a terrible hurt that had been inflicted on her. Wild with gratitude, she had been flying all over the Neverland to find her savior.

Now, having recovered and given her thanks to Alice, Tink flew off to have some fun with the other fairies, forgetting completely about the cruel attack which had almost killed her until Alice's belief saved her. This is how it is with fairies, who are such tiny creatures they can only hold on to one feeling at a time.

Wendy and Alice watched the fairy depart. "I suppose it is my watch now," said Wendy, looking at the sky. There was already a suggestion of pre-dawn light, and the Neverland was slowly warming to it.

Alice nodded and settled in for sleep. Wendy sat before the fire, hugging her knees. Sleep would not come to Alice, however, toss and turn as she might. Finally, she sat up and turned to Wendy. "Is there anyone here, you suppose, who might be able to help us?"

Wendy looked thoughtful. "I suppose," she said, "that there will be a new crew of Lost Boys. Undoubtedly, they will know where Peter is, or at least where he was last headed. Although I feel that the lighthouse is our goal, it might be best to find the Boys."

"Besides," she added wistfully, "I don't suppose they have had a mother in quite some time, and I am sure their clothes need some mending." Wendy trailed off, looking at the furiously winking stars.

Alice once again settled herself in her rough bedding, muttering under her breath, "I knew there was a reason I never wished to go camping."

Once the dawn had truly broken, Wendy woke Dorothy and Alice, and after a simple breakfast of gathered fruit, they resolved to find the Lost Boys. This seemed their best hope of finding out what had happened and of rescuing Peter and Margaret.

Wendy remembered the island perfectly, and although some features had changed, the basic topography was still the same. She could lead them through the forest to where the Lost Boys and Peter had lived, but in all the intervening years, it was quite possible they had changed locations.

Wendy led them down the beach, looking for a certain path through the trees, which would be concealed by a large palm with drooping leaves.

CHAPTER FORTY-THREE

INTERLUDE TWO:
WHAT THE STARS TRIED TO SAY

Dorothy had been sleeping fitfully, awakening again and again to look again at the stars, still puzzling at their behavior and wishing she could understand. It seemed important.

The stars had seen it all, from the time Peter first brought Wendy and her brothers to Neverland, till this moment, where Dorothy lay vainly trying to sleep, while the stars, just as vainly, tried to tell Dorothy and her companions what had happened.

The stars, like the fairies, are generally loyal to Peter, but this had been too much for them. Peter, you see, is sadly mixed up in this whole affair of Margaret's disappearance, and he does not come out of it in the best light.

"You won't forget to come for me, Peter, will you?" Wendy had said that first night she had returned home.

Of course not. He did not forget; he just did not choose to come. She had taken everything from him…his boys, herself (his mother, and maybe something else), and most importantly, his heart. A part of him wanted to grow old with her, and he hated that part.

For making him feel that way, he decided she would be taught a lesson, a hard and cruel lesson. He told Tinker Bell. "Peter Pan will never be crossed by a mere girl. fairies, mermaids, and Indian princesses carry torches for me. You too, Tink! No simple London girl will break my heart".

Tinker Bell laughed at him, and said, "You think you will go back, and Wendy will see the error of her ways and stay with you forever. Let's see how that will work for you."

Peter did come back for Wendy the first year, sure that she would stay with him in Neverland forever this time. But she was an inch taller, and he saw at once that she would not stay more than the expected two weeks for spring cleaning.

On his return, he told Tink what had happened. "I pretended to forget about the Lost Boys, about the pirates, and even you. I said you must be dead, as fairies do not live long. I think that hurt her," he said with satisfaction.

"You are such a liar!" the fairy laughed. "You know we fairies can live almost forever as long as someone believes. And you believe!" She nuzzled Peter's cheek, and he carelessly swatted her away.

Her mood changed at the swat from amused to angry. She hung in the air near his ear, and then, in what was a most complicated thought for a fairy, she whispered, "Oh Peter, you never forget. Sometimes it amuses you to pretend to forget. You like to see the shock, the hurt, the bewilderment on one or another person's face. Sometimes it is convenient for you to pretend to forget. That way, you do not have to do anything you did not really want to do."

Peter scowled and replied. "That is not true!"

She continued, seemingly oblivious to his anger, "Sometimes, you really wished you could forget. But you remember everything."

Tinker Bell then laughed, but not an amused laugh, and flew away. He shouted angrily after her, "You will see! I will show her! I am never going back for her!"

Peter did not come the following year, but he missed Wendy. He told Tink that if he neglected her for a year, surely, she would see that her place was with him in Neverland. "She will be so grateful to see me, she will never return to dreary old London. I just hope she has slowed down on the growing."

Tinker Bell said primly, "I don't see what is so special about her anyway. But let's see if it works out for you this time."

So, Peter came one final time, and Wendy went again for spring cleaning, but he could see that she was already growing up. Things were not the same between them.

When he returned this time, Tink could not resist. She taunted him, saying, "The little London girl is getting older, and she wants more than you and the Neverland can give her. Give her up and stay here with me. I won't grow old. But I won't take care of you or your boys either," she said and tugged at his hair.

Peter bitterly resolved to not return again until Wendy was all grown up and could not fly and let her see what a mistake she had made. He would mock her, tell her about all the adventures she had missed, and fill her with regret.

He did not tell Tink of his plan this time, as he was tired of her inexcusable lack of complete support.

He kept track of the years by marking the start of each Spring on a tree trunk. Once he decided enough years had passed, he flew to the nursery window.

There he found Wendy the grown-up and her daughter. Impulsively, he gave up his plan of revenge and decided that Jane would do as well as Wendy to fill that void in Peter's brave heart. So off to Neverland with Jane!

He was initially very proud of this innovative solution to his problem, and bragged to Tinker Bell, "She'll be just as good, and maybe even better! She will want to stay. Who needs that old Wendy?"

Tink replied, "If you say so. I never liked that Wendy girl, anyway. This one will probably not work out either, and will be wanting home before you know it."

This angered Peter, for he needed unquestioning loyalty.

Jane, alas, was not the child her mother had been, and Peter soon realized that he could not replace Wendy, not even with her own daughter. It must be Wendy or no one. Angry and heartbroken, a very new and strange thing for Peter, he again decided to make Wendy hurt as he did.

He spent a few more spring cleanings, with Jane, for appearances' sake, and then did not return for many years.

While he did not return to the nursery window for entry, he did, from time to time, check up on Wendy.

"Just curious," he would casually reply when Tink asked him why he did it. Each time he swore it would be the last, but it never was. So, he had seen when Jane died, and silver-haired Wendy brought Margaret to the nursery.

Peter still struggled with his thoughts, both foreign and troubling to him. He did not know how, but he had to find a way to make them go away. For a long time, he had no solution.

Then, one summer night, when the window had been left open to the warm night air and moonlight, Peter perched on the eaves above the window, and sat listening to Wendy singing a song to Margaret, a lullaby he knew all too well, a thought came to him. A thought that might, at last, soothe him.

What he was now considering was evil and cruel. Peter, while careless and thoughtless, did not fancy himself evil or cruel. He let the thought lie for a while, hoping it would go away, distracting himself with this adventure and that, but it did not go away, this hurt, or this idea. He really did not know what to do.

This was his plan. He meant to take Margaret and never return her, so Wendy would know the pain and loss he has lived with all these years. And surely, if he took her while she was young enough, Margaret would grow to love the Neverland and never wish to return home. It seemed perfect.

Peter decided to talk with Tinker Bell. True, they had not been as close of late, but, like he had assumed with Wendy, he convinced himself that Tink had been pining away for his company and would assist him.

He thought that Tink would agree wholeheartedly with his plan, as he knew that Wendy was far from being a favorite of the fairy's. He had not spoken to Tink in some time, but he was confident of the fairy's friendship and conveniently pretended to forget that they had ever had a falling out. So just before he set off to claim Margaret, he told her of his brilliant scheme.

"And," he concluded, "I will have a mother who will stay forever and Wendy will get what she deserves! Imagine, thinking she could grow up and leave me like that. What do you think?"

While he told her his intentions, he expected that she would be pleased, and that, as always, she would help him. Instead, she had buzzed around more like a bee than a fairy, scolding him and calling him much cruder names than her usual, "You Silly Ass."

That was okay, sometimes he and Tink did have a falling out, but they always made it right. She would fall in, as she always did.

This time, though, she said in her tinkly fairy voice, "This is not right. I won't let you do this! I will stop you; I will warn Wendy. Peter, you are WRONG!"

Peter was infuriated, but he did not show it to Tink. He tried one more time to convince her that his plan was good, but she became even more insistent, saying, "This is not you, Peter. You are supposed to be the hero, not the villain. What has that Wendy done to you?"

Peter's face darkened, and he said, "You know, Tink, maybe you are right. But even if you are, what can a fairy do about it? You know, I do believe in fairies, but you know what else I believe? I believe that the fairies are dying off, because fewer and fewer children believe. It is not that they stop believing, they just never start. As a matter of fact, I believe that a fairy will die tonight, just before dawn. You know why I believe that a fairy will die? Because just before dawn, I don't think I will believe that you are real anymore. And if you aren't real, it must be because you are dead. Because if you were the real Tinker Bell, you would help me with my excellent plan."

Tinker Bell let out a pitiful scream, and without another word to Peter, flew off as fast as she could to warn.

Peter sat back against a tall tree and looked up to the sky, peeking at him between the leaves. He winced a bit at the brightness and scowled. His plan was perfect, he thought. What was Tinker Bell's problem?

Peter was surprised when the fairy did not return. He thought for sure his bluff would have worked. Oh, well, she will probably be back, and they could make it up as usual. He would tell her that he did believe, and it would be all right. Then, pulling his hat over his eyes, he fell asleep.

CHAPTER FORTY-FOUR

OLD FRIENDS

As they walked, Wendy talked about Peter and her time in Neverland. "The last thing Peter ever said to me as a girl was, 'Just always be waiting for me, and then some night you will hear me crowing.' But of course, he did forget about me, and then he did come, and took Jane with him. I was all grown, you see. And when Jane started growing, he stopped coming, until he came for Margaret."

Wendy began crying softly, but bravely wiped the tears aside. The other two just listened, for it was clear Wendy was not looking for a response or advice.

They turned a corner on the beach, and to their left, was the palm tree Wendy had been searching for with the path into the forest, and to their right, scuttled on the shore, was a large ship. It was clear that it had not been at sea for many years. The bow had several holes, and the main mast was broken and lay across the deck. But someone had taken the trouble to hoist the flag, although the flagpole was listing alarmingly. The flag was almost tattered beyond recognition.

Not quite beyond recognition, however, for surely it was the skull and crossbones of the Jolly Roger. Wendy would know it anywhere. And, as they looked more closely at the ship, they perceived a small but steady stream of smoke coming from a cabin towards the back.

Alice and Dorothy looked at Wendy. "We should investigate," she declared. The women approached the pirate ship. The barnacles on the hull were dry and desiccated, the timbers as well. There was an odor of the sea about her, just a faint echo of what the ship had been.

A semi-rotted rope ladder still hung from the bow of the ship. Wendy, who realized that here, she was the leader, tugged on the ladder. It seemed to be sound. Wendy tugged on it again, and then began to ascend.

Alice and Dorothy followed, and the three women reached the deck of the ship. The smoke came from somewhere to the aft, so they slowly made their way to the back end of the rotting pirate vessel. Wendy paused as they passed the mast, saying, "This is where I was tied and forced to watch my children walk the plank. Of course, Peter saved the day."

They continued along the deck, and as they approached the rear of the ship, they heard a whirring sound, occasionally interrupted by a pirate-style oath "Ods Bodkins!" or a simple cry of "Ow!"

They reached the back, and Wendy opened a hatch leading to the decks below. The sounds grew louder, and it was clear where they were coming from. Wendy approached a large wooden door with a small grimy window and used her handkerchief to clean a small spot to peek in.

Sitting at a foot treadle sewing machine was an old pirate, or at least one would assume he was a pirate, for when he went to cut the cloth he was working on, he used a cutlass instead of scissors. Wendy knew this pirate, and so she knocked gently.

"Who's there?" replied a voice which Wendy recognized all too well. "It's Wendy," she replied. "Mr. Smee, is that you?" In answer, the door opened suddenly, causing all the women to step back.

A plump old man, with a stocking cap and a sweet baby face, rushed from the cabin and enveloped Wendy in his arms. Wendy was startled, for while Smee was really quite loveable as far as pirates went, he was nevertheless a pirate, and the last time she had seen him was when he jumped overboard and swam towards shore after Peter's defeat of Captain James Hook and his crew. Smee, she thought, was probably the only survivor, and he could not have been pleased to lose his captain, his mates, and his ship.

However, the old pirate seemed genuinely touched to see her. He stepped back, keeping his hands on her shoulders, and peered deeply into her face. "Sure, 'tis good to see you again Miss Wendy. Grown up quite a bit, all the better, I think. Those boys have so been needing a mother. I do my best to help as I can, but none can do quite what a mother can, and you were the finest mother they could have."

He went to his sewing machine and lifted up the small pair of pants he had been working on. They were a patchwork of animal skins, sailcloth, and flannel.

"See," he said proudly in a lilting voice which seemed to shift from an Irish to Scottish accent, "I've made pockets for the wee bairns. I do my best to keep up with the mending and such for them. In exchange, Peter lets me alone, holds no grudge, nor do I."

"Oh, poor Mr. Smee!" Wendy exclaimed.

"Not at all," he replied. "For now, am I Captain of the Jolly Roger, and I have my lovely companion here to keep me company."

The women had not heard her footsteps, but Tiger Lily had come up silently behind them. She had a freshly caught bass fish tied to her waist and was carrying a wicked looking knife, which she had raised at the sight of the strangers. To Wendy, it looked at first as if the native Princess had not aged a day. On a closer look, though, while her face and garb were unchanged, her eyes were not the same. They had a sadder, older look to them, as though she had seen much more than she had ever wanted to see.

Seeing the upraised knife, Smee said, "No dear, these are friends. Look, don't you remember Wendy?"

The Princess lowered her blade, gazed hard at Wendy, and then, with a look of disgust, turned and silently sat next to Smee.

"Oh dear, I was forgetting that you two never quite got along," apologized Smee. "Now don't you be thinking there is more between us than friendship. Poor Miss Lily, after Peter defeated us pirates and had become friendly with her people, there was not much excitement for the tribe."

Wendy said, "But I would have thought they would be happy to be rid of the pirates…no offense intended, Mr. Smee."

"You would think so," he replied. "But it weren't so. With no one to fight, and with Peter moping about as he did after you and the boys sailed off, they got bored and went to look for some real adventure. Sailed away in their canoes, they did."

Smee patted Tiger Lily's hand. "Miss Lily, as their leader, ought to have gone with 'em, but for some reason, she stayed behind. Don't know now that she doesn't regret it, but it was what she did."

Alice looked over at the Princess, whose face remained as impassive as stone.

Smee continued, "Then, what with me being the last pirate and her being the last native on the island, we sort of gravitated together, becoming a sort of a wee family. She's like a daughter to me, and quite a comfort, although I don't think that I am such a comfort to her. She's a sad lass. But here I am forgetting my manners, an old sea dog like meself. Who are your lovely companions, Miss Wendy? I don't think the Boys will need but one mother."

"This is Dr. Alice Liddell, and this is Miss Dorothy Gale," said Wendy. "And I haven't returned to be anyone's mother. Mr. Smee, you must help me. Peter has taken my granddaughter Margaret to do his Spring Cleaning. That was weeks ago, and neither has returned. I am so afraid that something dreadful has happened to them!"

Smee's kindly face wrinkled into a frown. "No, that can't be right," he said. "I do remember that for a time or two you came back for cleaning and mothering. Peter said after that there would be no more mothers, but then he brought little Janie, who was mother for a time, although not so good a mother as you. Peter as much as said so, for last time he took her home, he was clear that she had not quite lived up to expectations, so while it had been a bold experiment, he was done with mothers. So, I can't see him coming and taking your granddaughter, now."

Smee screwed up his face as he was thinking deeply, something he did not do very often. "Peter does come and go all the time, you know, fetching boys and such, and he did go off for a bit a few weeks ago. I don't know as he's returned, though, for I haven't seen him. He may have, though. The Boys would know."

"The Boys!" Wendy exclaimed. "Where are the Boys and how many are there now?"

"Well," Smee replied, "there are but four of them now. I had been thinking Peter had gone to locate another one or two, for he generally likes to have about six. Right now, what with the island in between adventures, so to speak, the boys would be hibernating, awaiting Peter's return and some new excitement. They've taken to sleeping in the old underground home. You remember, Miss Wendy?"

The old pirate insisted they join him for lunch. From a kettle sitting on the potbellied stove, he dished out a savory clam and corn chowder, along with some biscuits and mugs of apple cider. Although Tiger Lily joined them at the table, she spoke not one word, nor ate one bite, despite all of Smee's cajoling, and stared with clear animosity at Wendy.

The pirate was an excellent cook, and as they ate, provided some information about the current crop of Boys.

Rascal was a mischievous boy just a hair shorter than Peter himself. Fatty was not really all that plump, but he did enjoy cooking and was always being teased that he would grow fat. Smee seemed to have a particular affection for this one.

Bear was quite plump and when wearing his clothing of fur and sailcloth did resemble a child-sized teddy bear. Finally, there was Mite, the youngest and smallest, who was still given to the occasional sniffling and crying. Smee felt that Mite, at least, needed a mother.

"Won't you reconsider, Miss Wendy?" he asked after describing poor Mite. "Or perhaps one of you other ladies? Miss Lily, you see, hasn't a motherly bone in her body."

At this Tiger Lily turned her steely gaze from Wendy to the pirate. "No offense," he said gently, "But we both know it is true."

CHAPTER FORTY-FIVE
PETER, AGAIN

Lunch concluded, and with no more information to be had, the women thanked Smee, and led by Wendy, set off to find the Lost Boys. As they picked their way back across the deck of the scuttled Jolly Roger, Wendy stopped by the one remaining mast.

She placed her hands on it and sighed. Here was where she had once been tied, where the dastardly James Hook had meant to make her watch her children walk the plank. Here was where Peter came and rescued her and the Boys, and here is where, because of Peter's heroic actions, she had almost changed her mind. Instead, she had steeled her resolve and taken her brothers and the Boys home.

What if she had stayed? Would she still be young Wendy Darling, mother to the Lost Boys? For all children grow up, except for one. Even here, in Neverland, from time to time, although Peter had forbidden it, a lost boy will grow, and of course, once he is taller than Peter, he is banished. Wendy had seen it happen on her second visit. She was reasonably sure that, even if she had stayed, she would have started to grow up. Indeed, part of the appeal of Neverland for her had been that she really was almost a grown-up, for only a grown woman can truly be a mother.

What would she have been to Peter, who had once told her, in answer to her question, "Peter, what are your exact feelings for me?" that his feelings were "those of a devoted son." No, that had sealed it for her.

Wendy pulled the acorn necklace out and sighed. She kissed it and thought back on the innocence with which she and Peter had exchanged an acorn and a thimble for "kisses".

Dorothy and Alice stood back, giving Wendy her privacy. It was clear that something more than concern for her granddaughter was at play here.

Alice, ever the analyst, thought, *Is there something more that she is dealing with from her childhood adventure? Is it grief? Regret?*

She cupped her chin as she watched Mrs. Winthrop at the mast. "Curiouser and curiouser," she muttered to herself.

Dorothy finally walked over and gently took Wendy's hands from the mast. "Come," she said. "It is already past midday, and we should find the Lost Boys, and see what they might know of Peter and Margaret." Wendy nodded, and Dorothy put an arm around her waist and guided her to the ladder.

They disembarked from the ship and stood on the beach. Wendy shielded her eyes with her hands and looked up to the lighthouse. While it was certainly much more sensible to find the Lost Boys and see what they could tell them, she was nevertheless drawn to the lighthouse. However, she could see no way to approach it. The only way, as far as she could see from the beach, was to fly.

As Wendy gazed up, someone unseen up on the cliff was also looking down at her and her companions.

Peter stood on the cliff, gazing at the three strangers on the beach. No one ever came to Neverland, unless Peter brought them, or the island manifested them as part of the current adventure. These three did not look like anything the island would produce, and Peter had not brought them here. He was disturbed by a loud sob.

Peter looked over his shoulder at the crying child and scowled. He did not like how he was feeling right now. An unpleasant mixture of disgust, self-pity, and confusion were rolling around in his head. Peter did not like mixes.

Things were not going according to plan. Margaret was to come, be the mother to the Lost Boys, and never go home. How could he have ever thought she could be anyone's mother? She was actually a very small child, far younger than Wendy or Jane had been when he brought them.

Now she was crying, and Peter was unsure. Peter did not like being unsure of anything. He did not know what to do, and he did not like that either. Usually, Peter knew just what to do, and if he didn't, well he did something anyway, and it usually worked out.

Finally, he patted the child on the head and whispered something soothing and meaningless to her, and she seemed to calm down.

Peter turned from Margaret and looked down at the beach at the three women again. He did not recognize them, and he did not know how they had gotten here, but one of them, the oldest one, bothered him greatly.

She should not be so old, he thought. He wondered if she were under some sort of spell. *It's just not right somehow.* Behind him, Margaret had stopped crying, but she was still sniffling. Peter could not bear it.

The child sniffed once more, loudly and finally, and walked to the cliff edge and stood next to Peter. She tried to take his hand, but he folded his arms against his chest and tried to look very stern. Margaret looked down at the strangers on the beach. She gasped and ran to the very edge of the cliff. "Grandma!" she cried.

Peter ignored her. The child was always calling for her Grandma.

Peter pulled her back and leaned over to have a close look. He pulled out Hook's spyglass and gazed down at the women on the beach. Who was that old woman? She was dangerous, he was sure now. He was somehow reluctant to study her too closely, so he first turned his attention to her companions.

The first one he focused on was old, but not nearly as old as the other. She was wearing a long white coat, with deep pockets and some sort of symbol across the right side. Peter recognized the coat as the kind that doctor's wear. The doctor looked rather drab, and Peter disliked her instantly.

The second was younger, but this did not matter to Peter. If they were adults, he had no use for them. She was pretty, and dressed in a more colorful fashion, which pleased Peter.

He was especially attracted to the silver shoes she was wearing, which caught the afternoon sun and cast rainbow reflections across the sand. Was she a gypsy? Once, long ago, before Wendy, there had been Gypsies on Neverland. It might be fun to have a Gypsy caravan again. Had she been a little younger, she might have been a suitable mother, but she was not, and so Peter lowered his spyglass for a moment.

He hesitated, but it was time to see who the old woman was. Perhaps she was a witch. Neverland had not had witches before, and they might be even more exciting than pirates. For a moment, Peter's hopes rose.

She did not look like a witch, for her face was too kind. And she was not wearing witchy clothing. Besides, why would a witch travel with a doctor and a Gypsy?

He screwed the lens to focus even closer and studied the old woman. He started at her feet. She was wearing some green boots, suitable for hiking. A witch would not wear boots like that. He slowly raised the glass to take in every detail. Her clothing reminiscent of the Gypsy girl's, colorful and suitable for hiking. When he reached her neck, he stopped and stepped back. What was that around her neck? He screwed the lens of the spyglass as tight as he could.

He saw it now. It was the kiss he had given Wendy on the night they met (now, of course, he knew that it was an acorn, but then it had been a kiss). He thrust his hand into his pocket, pulled out his kiss (the thimble) Wendy had given him that same night, and threw it to the ground.

Peter was enraged, and there is nothing more terrifying than an enraged Peter. He threw the spyglass to the ground after the thimble and started stamping his feet and pacing around. He yelled, "No, no, NO!"

CHAPTER FORTY-SIX

LOST BOYS

Wendy led her friends into the Neverland forest. It was clear that the island was in the midst of some dramatic transitions. Parts of the forest were subtropical, with a canopy of trees interlaced with air ferns and parrots flying through the understory. Orchids bloomed, and in the distance, the chittering of monkeys could be heard. And yet, as they passed through this forest, despite the noises and riotous plant growth, they felt somehow sad and alone.

They turned a corner, and then the forest was completely different. The trees were now towering Redwoods, and the hawks circled above. Instead of monkeys, small animals, squirrels, and chipmunks cavorted. A herd of deer blocked their path for several minutes, as the stag stood guard while the herd crossed the path. Walking here, the women felt rejuvenated, alive, and Dorothy began singing.

As they had passed through the tropical jungle, it seemed that it was slowly dying. The parrots seemed old, and the trees were browning. In the Redwoods, however, although they must have been hundreds of years old, the trees were green and fresh, and the forest was filled with their scent. There was the sound of water burbling in the distance, absent from the tropical forest.

"It's like we are in two different forests, "said Dorothy.

"Yes," Alice replied. "One is ascending, and one is passing away." Wendy shuddered, although the day was warm.

It did not take them long to reach the clearing where the underground home could be found, for remember, the Neverland is small so that you may always be no more than half a day away from your next adventure.

Wendy stood for a moment, looking at the clearing. Here were the trees by which the boys could descend to their home. Above her, rotting in the branches, was the remains of the little house that had been built for her when she first arrived, and which the fairies had carried up to the treetops after Peter defeated the pirates. That was where she had spent her first Spring Cleaning with Peter. It was obviously abandoned, and it looked both uninhabitable and dangerous.

Now that she was looking with adult eyes, it seemed ridiculous to her that it had taken so long for the pirates to discover Peter and the boys. The clearing was ringed with trees, all hollow and leading down to the underground home. All one had to do was to peek down and see where it led. The chimney, clumsily disguised with a mushroom cap, was smoking merrily. Further, if one put his ear to any tree, the voices of children were clearly to be heard.

Wendy knew that she would have to coax them out, as they would not willingly let the women in without Peter there. She smiled mischievously and went over to the chimney and rapped loudly. Then she went to the nearest tree and called down, "Yo, Boys!" The chatter below fell silent instantly.

Wendy smiled and held a finger to her lips, indicating that Alice and Dorothy should be silent. She gestured towards the other trees, and Alice and Dorothy each crept to a tree and cocked their heads towards the openings to listen. They could hear some scuffling as the boys shifted nervously. Finally, they heard a whisper, "Is it gone yet?" followed by a chorus of "Shush!"

Wendy then tiptoed over to their provisions and sought out the sweetest thing she could find. She came up with a small bag of chocolate covered nuts, which she tied up in a napkin to keep it from spilling. She again tiptoed over to one of the trees and tossed the package down.

Immediately, there was a rustling of feet, as the boys rushed to investigate. But then, one voice, a little younger sounding than the others, whispered, "We mustn't. It might be a trick. Not until Peter brings back our new Mother. She will know what to do."

An older voice replied with scorn, "That Mother was too little. That's why he took her away after just one day. Even Peter thought she needed to…" and here the voice fell to a stage whisper, "grow up a bit!"

The voice continued. "He took her up to the old lighthouse, to decide what to do with her. I don't think he means to take her back, for he did say as much to her when she asked to go home. She's never going home, that one, if Peter has his way."

Wendy covered her mouth with her hand to keep from crying out.

"He should give her back," replied a third voice. "She is a little one, not much bigger than the Mite. I wish Peter could get that first Mother back, that Wendy. Peter talks as if she were the only proper Mother to have."

Wendy was beside herself, now with both hands clasped over her mouth and was shaking, soft sobs escaping. Dorothy ran over to her and pulled her back from the tree and wrapped her jacket about her. She drew her towards a large rock and sat her down. Wendy cried silently, still holding her hand over her mouth, while Dorothy ineffectively rubbed her back. Alice put a finger over her lips to silence them and leaned closer to hear what else might be revealed.

While Wendy sat on the rock with Dorothy, Alice listened by the tree. She thought she could identify the boys by their voices. The older voice she was reasonably sure was Rascal, who was assuming the leadership role with Peter gone.

The younger one was obviously Mite. The third voice, thick and slow, was saying, "What about Peter's story? He says...This isn't going the way he tells it. Peter said we would get a new mother who would be young enough to never want to grow up and who wouldn't mind a bit never seeing that old Wendy mother again."

This, she thought, must be Bear. Her suspicions were confirmed when the final voice, sounding a bit more thoughtful, with a touch of dignity replied, "Well, it's just Peter's story. Who knows if a story is true, or if it's going to turn out the way you think it ought?" This was obviously Fatty.

Fatty's remark set the Boys off, for they fell to arguing and telling bits to make their point. Alice slipped her notebook out of her lab coat pocket and began taking notes.

Although the Boys spoke in fragments, interrupting and talking over each other, with quite a bit of arguing and shushing, she was starting to piece together what had happened.

Slowly the arguments about Peter's story were replaced with arguments about eating the sweets, which Wendy had tossed down into the underground home. This argument was more easily settled, by having Mite take the first bite, and when no harm befell him, the Boys all greedily ate the rest.

Alice closed her notebook, put it carefully back into her pocket, and walked over to the other women.

"Should we speak with the Boys?" whispered Dorothy. Alice shook her head indicating "No."

By this time, Wendy had recovered from her initial shock. She was still shaking, but it was not from grief or fear, but anger. Her eyes were lit with a dark passion, and neither Dorothy nor Alice was inclined to start a conversation with her in this state.

CHAPTER FORTY-SEVEN

ALICE EXPLAINS

Silently, Wendy led them through the forest and back to the lagoon by a new path. In the few hours that had passed, the lagoon water had changed marvelously. It was now a brilliant aquamarine, and so clear they could see almost all the way to the bottom.

The sun was setting, and the early stars were beginning to peek out. They could see the lighthouse, through a gap in the trees.

Dorothy began to make a small fire, and Alice poked through their provisions for some food. Wendy sat down, her grim look giving way to one of despair, and she began to weep softly.

She put her hands over her face and said, "I was a fool. Peter is not the person I thought he was, and I should never have trusted him to take Margaret. We are nothing to him but playthings and surrogate mothers. But how could he take her and keep her from me? I could accept indifference towards me, but how could he hate me so?"

Alice immediately went to sit by her and replied softly, "No, dear, I'm afraid the problem isn't that Peter hates you. The problem is that he loves you."

Wendy lifted her head and looked at Alice in disbelief. "Peter never loved me," she said brokenly. "He never tried to stop me from leaving when I wanted to go home, and he was awfully forgetful about coming back for me. All he wanted was a mother to take care of him and those boys. And when he came back for me, he had forgotten about everything we did together. He was just as happy to have Jane, and then he forgot her, and now he has Margaret, and he is keeping her. Why?"

Alice took her notebook out. "Look," she said. "I may have been completely off on my theories about childhood trauma and fantasies of magical lands…"

Dorothy interrupted, "Actually, not always," she told Alice. "While it is true that this sort of thing has happened to children like us, there are just as many children who do make up a fantasy world after some terrible trauma. Do you remember that little girl, who was so convinced that her childhood playmate had been turned wicked and had his heart frozen by an evil ice queen?"

Alice nodded and replied, "Yes, I used to count that as one of my great successes. She was eventually convinced to give up the fantasy. I had thought that her childhood friend had somehow changed and had simply turned out to be a heartless prick of child, who would grow up to be a heartless prick of a man."

Alice sighed. "I was solely concerned with helping the victim, you know. My method didn't involve recovering memories or reliving the horror or supplying the authorities with evidence of a crime. I was focused on a path for my patient to move forward. So whatever awful thing he had done, if it was more than just childhood cruelty, well, that was for the police or others to discover. She was able to move on from that nasty friend and live a normal life."

"Well, that boy had done an evil thing to her, or so I believe," Dorothy replied. "I worked with her too, and there were all sorts of inconsistencies in her story. It was clear he had broken her heart and betrayed her friendship, but I did not believe her story of a Snow Queen to be true, so I was happy to have you work with her. You did help her tremendously! Further, did you ever follow up on that friend of hers? He's been in and out of prison, and his own mother has a restraining order against him. I still do not know what he did, but thank goodness she has forgotten, and you have moved her beyond the icy world of the Snow Queen."

Alice opened her notebook. "Look," she said. "As I said, I may have been completely off on my theories about childhood trauma and fantasies of magical lands, but I do have some talent in listening to children and sorting out what is really going on inside their heads and their hearts. I listened for quite a while, and there was much talking and rambling, but I think I know what Peter did and why. Margaret is in no danger from Peter. Although she may have some sad and frightening moments, he will not let any harm come to her."

During the conversation, Wendy had drifted back into a state of almost catatonia. Alice walked over to her and cupped Wendy's chin and so she could look directly into her eyes.

"Peter always thought you would come back someday, you see," Alice said. "For a long time, that is what he told the Boys, that once their mother returned, all would be well. But you never really came back, not the way Peter wanted. He wanted more than just two weeks for spring cleaning from you and then home again. He wanted you to stay, forever. That is why he stopped coming for you. He was sure that if he left you alone for a few years, you would be anxious to return for good, forever."

Dorothy moved to sit beside Wendy as well, placing an arm around her shoulder as Alice continued.

"But he waited too long. Then Peter tried with Jane, but it was not the same. You are the one, you see. And Margaret…this whole thing has nothing to do with Margaret, it is all about you and Peter."

As Alice recounted what she had surmised from her eavesdropping, Wendy's eyes grew wide, and she shook her head. "I don't believe it," she said slowly, shaking her head "no" again. "And besides, it doesn't matter. What matters is that we find a way up to the lighthouse first thing in the morning so that we can save

Margaret. I will take the first watch tonight, for I am too overwrought to sleep now."

Alice and Dorothy both nodded and exchanged looks. Wendy would need time to accept the truth, but at least she was again roused to action.

CHAPTER FORTY-EIGHT

PETER AND DOROTHY

They ate a simple supper from the provisions Ozma had sent, and since the water had cleared in the lagoon, they took a quick swim to wash up. The water was just the right temperature, cool enough to refresh but not so cool as to give them chills upon emerging. It was also just salty enough to make them a bit more buoyant, yet not salty enough to sting their eyes or their scratches.

Dorothy floated on her back, watching the stars emerge from the twilight. Again, the youngest stars tried furiously to twinkle a message to her, but again, she could not hear them. One star, in its great effort, came free from its hook in the heavens and raced across the sky, leaving an arc of light in its wake.

Dorothy was thinking about all Wendy had told them about flying, and what made it work, and why grownups seemed to be unable to fly. Perhaps the stars were getting through to her a bit, for she had an idea of what it might take to enable Wendy to fly. She needed a little more time to mull it over, but perhaps by morning she would be sure.

The women finally emerged from the water and readied themselves for the night. Although she was on first watch, Wendy changed into her nightgown after the swim. It was agreed that Dorothy would take the second watch, and Alice the third.

Alice and Dorothy dropped off to sleep, perhaps an after effect of the swim. Wendy sat by the fire, her arms wrapped around her knees, with the story Alice had told rolling round and round in her head. She could not make sense of it.

Suddenly, she was dreadfully tired. It was far too soon to wake Dorothy, but she thought that if she closed her eyes for just a minute, she would be able to make it through her watch. Besides, she needed to stop the racing thoughts if only for a minute. She laid down on her blanket and closed her eyes.

The full moon had just risen, and seeing what was happening, the celestial lady struggled to move higher and higher into the sky to better illuminate the campsite and alert the women. But she was still too low to cast any sort of meaningful light.

Eventually the moon crested the treetops, and moonlight streamed into the lagoon, making it almost as bright as day. Alice had the covers over her head and was undisturbed by the light. Wendy, lying uncovered by the shore of the lagoon, was still deep asleep. Dorothy alone was awakened by the light, and she sat up to look about.

Out on the flat rock in the middle of the lagoon, which would be covered by water when the tide came in, the rock where Peter and Wendy almost perished, stood a boy. He was dressed in an outfit of leaves and was preoccupied with something, for he was looking downward, not at the women's camp. She could not see his face, for he was backlit by the moon, and his shadow stretched out across the still waters, darkening the reflection of the night sky.

Dorothy was startled by how truly young he was. When you hear about Peter, and his brave exploits, though you know that he is a boy, you tend to make him as old a boy as you can in your mind, for how could a child do all these things? But Peter is really a very young boy, nowhere near to being a teenager.

She knew it must be Peter. He had not seen her. She felt it was best not to wake the others yet, as she did not want to startle Peter.

He was looking at a small object cupped in one hand. Was he crying? Dorothy was too far away to tell.

He looked up and gazed towards the camp. His eyes were fixed on Wendy, so he still had not noticed Dorothy. Suddenly, he threw the object right at Wendy.

Dorothy leapt up to protect Wendy from the projectile. When he spotted her, he scowled at her and jumped into the air. Dorothy bent down to retrieve the object. It was a small, battered silver thimble, meant for a child's hand. Before she could touch it, Peter flew past her and scooped it up. As he passed, she could see that, yes, there were tears in his eyes.

"Boy," she said, "Why are you crying?"

He hovered in the air close to Wendy. "Not crying," he replied. "Just angry, and righteously so."

"Why are you angry at Wendy?" Dorothy asked. "All she has ever done was love you, and take care of you, and when she could not, she sent her child to do so."

Peter's face darkened, with rage and he flew dangerously close to Dorothy's face. "She left me, she took my boys, and I came back for her faithfully, but she never, ever asked to stay. She always went back. I told her, 'Just always be waiting for me, and some night you will hear me crowing.' But she stopped waiting."

"Did you ever think of staying yourself, instead?" Dorothy asked. "I know that Wendy wanted that very much."

"And grow up?" Peter replied scornfully. "No, I just stopped coming back for her. And then I tried to make it work with that Jane, but she was just not Wendy. And Wendy is all grown, and now it can never be right!"

Peter wiped away the remains of his tears, and said to Dorothy, "Now it will be the same for both of us! I cannot have her, and she will not have Margaret!" His face was contorted with anger, and

Dorothy could see, small boy though he was, how powerful he was. She feared for her safety.

Surprisingly, after that angry outburst, a soft tender look crossed his face. He flew over to Wendy and alighted. He bent down low, close to her face, and placed the thimble just in front of her lips. He gazed at her for a moment, although Dorothy could not see his expression. She was about to creep forward should Wendy be in any danger from the boy, but instead, he stood up, let forth with a lusty crow, and flew away.

CHAPTER FORTY-NINE
CAPTURE OF THE SHADOW

At the sounding of the crow, Wendy instantly awoke. She leapt to her feet and saw Peter flying towards the lighthouse. The moon was in front of him, and she could not see his face or whether he looked back to see her. She raced after him.

The moon was now very bright, almost as bright as the sun, and it shone with a pale and cold light. The moonlight, though not as warm and richly colored with gold as the sun, was nevertheless strong enough to cause Peter to cast a shadow, which flew after him across the glittering sands of the beach.

Peter was already out over the water, and the shadow was racing towards the water's edge. Wendy did not hesitate but ran after the shadow, and just before it reached the tide line, she fell upon it, digging her hands into the sand beneath it and scooping it up in her arms, holding tightly. "Dorothy, help me!" she called.

Dorothy looked up to the boy. He hung in midair, unable to move as his shadow was trapped under Wendy's body. For a few moments, he tugged against his shadow, trying to break free. Wendy was kneeling on the sand, trying to reel Peter in with the shadow as her line. But before Dorothy could reach Wendy, Peter somersaulted in the air, disconnecting himself from his shadow, and flew on.

Once Peter released his shadow, it lay limp and motionless on the sand. Dorothy helped Wendy to stand, and Wendy gathered the shadow and folded it neatly into a small square.

"Now," she said grimly, "He has something I want, and I have something he wants." She slipped the shadow into the pocket of her nightgown.

Amazingly, Alice had slept through the entire encounter and was just stirring. She sat up sleepily and asked, "Did something happen?"

Dorothy walked Wendy back to her blanket, bent down, and picked up the thimble. "He left this for you," she said. "I'm afraid you dozed off for a moment. The moon's light woke me up, and I saw him over there on the rock, looking at you. At first, he was angry and threw it at you."

Dorothy recounted her conversation with Peter. As she talked, Wendy's eyes at first misted with tears, and then grew distant and fierce. Her face was unreadable.

Alice yawned, and asked, "Will anyone be able to sleep after this? Or should we just accept that we are up for the day and plan our next move? Frankly, I'm stumped. Margaret and Peter are up in the lighthouse, and there seems to be no way to get there other than flying, and we cannot fly."

"Yes," said Wendy. "That is true. I could easily fly when I was a child, as could my brothers. But as we grew up, we lost that ability. When you are a child, things are so clear cut, black and white. A bit like fairies, I suppose. You can think lovely, wonderful thoughts, and up you go. There are no worries, no doubts, no holding back. You just feel that joy, purely and completely."

"I've been thinking about that," Dorothy replied. "It's true that once we lose our innocence, we can't really experience the pure happiness a child can feel. There are always questions and second thoughts. But there are other feelings, even more pure and powerful than a child's joy. I haven't felt it myself, but I've heard true love can be like that. But even more powerful than true love is the love of a parent for a child, or a grandmother for her only granddaughter."

She looked at Wendy. "Your love for Margaret is as powerful and pure as any childhood happiness. If you can concentrate on that feeling, that love, I think you will be able to fly. Doesn't every nerve in your body, every pang in your heart, draw you to her?"

Wendy looked thunderstruck, then became very calm and still. She stepped towards the edge of the shore. The lighthouse was now silhouetted by the full moon and she could see, small and distant but still clear, the outline of a small boy and a smaller girl, standing on the cliff.

Wendy looked up at the cliff where Peter stood with her grandchild. She beckoned Dorothy and Alice to her. Dorothy immediately ran to her. Alice, sensing what was up, took a moment to grab two nearby packs of supplies, and joined them at the water's edge.

Wendy took the bag of fairy dust they had been given by the giant fairy in Oz. She walked around her friends and sprinkled the sparkling dust on them. When it touched their skin, there was a moment of something, almost ticklish, and then it disappeared. It seemed to be absorbed into them, and yet there was a faint glow around them. Wendy at last stood between them and dusted herself.

She closed her eyes, took their hands, and thought only of the moment of Margaret's birth—holding her daughter's hand, looking across the bed at her dear son-in-law, wiping Jane's forehead as she pushed the beautiful baby out into the world. The umbilical cord was cut, and Tootles held the baby, kissed her forehead, and passed her to Wendy.

Then, a kaleidoscope of images and feelings spun inside her—joy, sorrow, love, despair—Jane, her baby, Jane—flying off with Peter, marrying, dying. She felt a weight on her heart too heavy to ever lift. She thought again of Margaret, and suddenly the weight was gone. Margaret, her granddaughter, so precious and full of light and laughter, without a father or a mother but with a grandmother to hold and cherish her. An overwhelming feeling of love and protectiveness enveloped Wendy. The instinct, the desire, the need to love and protect Margaret was all she felt. She willed herself to go to Margaret and pictured the lighthouse in her mind.

She had a sense of peace, of completeness. Somewhere outside of that peace, Wendy could vaguely hear her friends, calling out in distress. She could still feel their hands in hers and she gripped them tighter. She willed the peace, which surrounded her, to expand, to envelop her friends, and they became silent. The weight had been lifted from her heart, and now another weight was being lifted from her body. "Margaret," she breathed, and then, surprisingly, "Peter."

After a few moments, the lightness she had been feeling drained away. Wendy opened her eyes, and found that she, along with Alice and Dorothy, had somehow risen to a grassy field atop the cliff. "I flew," she said wonderingly. "I can fly!"

Wendy looked around. She still held Dorothy and Alice's hands. Dorothy looked a bit shaken, but none the worse for wear. Alice looked a bit green and was holding her stomach. She pulled both of them close to her and put her arms around their shoulders to steady both herself and her companions.

The lighthouse loomed before them. Beyond the lighthouse, near the edge of the cliff, looking out across the ocean, stood the small boy and the smaller girl. They were not looking towards the women but were gazing out across the sea.

CHAPTER FIFTY

PETER AND WENDY

Wendy stepped forward, her head held high. The wind caught her long grey hair, still loose and tousled from sleep, and gently waved it around her head like a halo. She still wore the plain white nightgown, and her feet were bare. Her right hand was closed into a fist, holding the thimble. Her left hand was in her nightgown pocket, resting on the shadow.

Peter turned to look at her over his shoulder. He was again backlit by the moon, while she was illuminated by it. At last, he truly recognized her, his Wendy. She was changed, and unchanged. She was still lovely and young, and yet she was lovely and old as well. Peter almost turned to step towards her, but he stopped. This was far too confusing, and Peter was never confused. He frowned at the old woman.

Dorothy stepped forward to place herself between Wendy and the boy, but Alice pulled her back. "No," she whispered. "They need to work this out for themselves."

Peter and Wendy stood silently this way for a moment. Then Margaret, twisting around as only a child can, although Peter held her hand tightly, saw Wendy and cried out, "Grandma!"

"Oh Margaret!" Wendy called, and held out her arms to the child, still keeping the thimble tight in one fist. But Peter held Margaret fast. He turned them both around to face Wendy.

"Peter," Wendy said softly. "Oh, Peter." For a moment, the fierce mother goddess persona, which had transformed Wendy, broke. Her shoulders slumped and she let out one small sigh.

Then, slowly, her steely resolve returned, and Wendy reached into her pocket and pulled out the shadow. She waved it above her head defiantly, like a victory flag.

As she did so, she could see that the toes still had a few torn threads, from where she had sewn the shadow onto Peter so long ago. The last of the stray threads fell from the shadow, leaving small pinholes, which caught the moonlight and made tiny stars on the grass.

Peter howled in anger. But in a moment, he came to himself, for no one gets the better of Peter. He composed himself, and then asked casually, "A trade, then, is that it?" Wendy nodded. She did not trust herself to speak aloud.

Wendy stopped her taunting waving of the shadow, gathered it respectfully and draped it across her outspread arms. She walked towards Peter and Margaret, holding the shadow out to Peter.

Peter stepped forward, dropping Margaret's hand. She ran to Wendy, and Wendy scooped her up in her arms, flinging the shadow to Peter. It floated on the wind for a moment, and Peter caught it.

Wendy held her granddaughter tight. She would never let her go again. Margaret nuzzled her face against Wendy's shoulder, burrowing under her hair.

"Oh, Grandma," she sighed. "Peter didn't think you would come for me, and then I would have to be all his, like you were supposed to be, but you did come, and I don't have to be his. I'm your little girl, aren't I?"

Wendy nodded and hugged the child tighter still, and Margaret continued, "Peter is very sad, aren't you Peter? Don't be sad, she's here."

Margaret turned her head to look back at Peter, and Wendy looked over Margaret's shoulder at him. He was miserably examining the shadow with a tragic look on his face. The shadow lay limp and dead in his arms. He would not look at Wendy or Margaret.

Tenderly, Wendy said, "Here Peter, let me help." She gestured to Alice, pointing at the pack Alice had thoughtfully brought. She then beckoned Dorothy and handed Margaret off to Dorothy's waiting arms. She looked through the pack for the first aid kit, and at last produced a needle and thread.

All during this time, Peter had remained focused on the dead shadow and still would not look at Wendy. One could not say for sure, for now his face was in shadow, but he might have been crying.

Wendy looked at the boy, and a tear crept from the corner of her eye. Then she knelt and picked him up in her arms (he was, after all, a small boy, and she a full-grown woman) and carried him to a nearby boulder. She perched him on the rock so that she could reach his feet without bending over too much and began to sew on the shadow.

Margaret clung to Dorothy, and Dorothy held her tight, stroking her hair and cooing meaningless comforting sounds.

Alice watched the proceedings with a clinical eye. It was impossible to tell what was going on with Wendy, as her face was hidden as she bent over Peter's feet, intent on her task, although it looked to Alice like she was shaking. Peter's face was also hidden, as he gazed down to observe the operation, but he too seemed to be shaking. Out of habit, she thrust her hands deep into her pocket, hoping to find a kitten, but something else was there.

The shadow had been hanging in a tangle beneath Peter while Wendy sewed. All at once, it sprang to life and became Peter's mirror. Peter stood up and looked below at the lively shadow. Now that he had revealed himself, it was clear the boy was crying and had been doing so for some time.

Wendy, who had been standing in front of the rock, sank to her knees, and she was wracked with sobs.

Margaret wriggled out of Dorothy's arms and ran to her grandmother. Wendy was still kneeling on the ground in front of Peter, and Margaret came up behind her and threw her arms around her grandmother's waist and lay her head between her shoulder blades. The little girl hugged her with all her might.

Peter stood up and roughly wiped his face with the back of his hand. "Wendy," he said with some bravado, "You should have stayed home. While you were sleeping in your silly bed, Margaret and I were flying about, saying funny things to the stars."

He tried to look defiant, but as he looked at Wendy, he could not maintain the expression and his face fell.

Wendy looked up at him and stood up slowly, taking Margaret by the hand. "Peter, you should have come with us. We could have grown up together and had a life together. We could have had children; we could have had happy thoughts all our lives."

"Grow up and be a man?" he replied. "All dreariness and solemn things and no adventures? Wendy, it would have been better for us here. You should have stayed with me." Wendy had never known Peter's voice to sound so lost.

She held one hand out to him and said gently, "Peter, there are many ways to be a man."

The two stood there, facing each other, each unwilling to move towards one another or to move away, not knowing what else could be said.

CHAPTER FIFTY-ONE

SECOND CHANCES

Dorothy and Alice watched the tragedy unfold. Dorothy was in tears at the heartbreak playing out before her. Time and age had separated these two, who clearly belonged to each other, and there seemed no way to undo that distance.

Alice was watching with a more studious intent, trying to think of what she could do or say to ease these two out of their pain. She was, after all, a professional. This was her job.

Suddenly, she heard a familiar purr in one ear. Dorothy had heard it too, for she turned to look at Alice and was startled to see a large, semi-transparent cat, floating in the air quite close to Alice's ear. The cat appeared to be whispering something to Alice, but all Dorothy could catch was the phrase, "Remember, these ones work a little differently."

The Cheshire Cat whispered a few more words, then turned to Dorothy and smiled the most beautiful smile.

As the Cat had been speaking to Alice, her eyes grew wide at first, then filled with understanding, and finally with determination. She reached into the left and right pockets of her lab coat, and from each she drew forth the Mushroom pieces that she had been given by her friend, the Caterpillar, back in Wonderland.

She walked slowly towards the sobbing boy and the broken old woman and offered the boy a piece from the left pocket, and the old woman a piece from the right.

Each stood, unable to say anything more, so Alice went first to the boy and coaxed him to take a small nibble.

Then she went to Wendy and gently fed a morsel to her, as one might feed an invalid or a small child. Once Alice had managed to convince each of them to take a bite and swallow, she turned to Dorothy with a look of triumph.

Dorothy watched in amazement. Each of them seemed to shimmer, shifting out of focus. The boy began to grow taller and broader. A beard began to grow quite rapidly on the boy, no, on the young man's face. He gave a startled cry and clapped his hand to his chin.

Wendy's long grey hair grew dark and turned a rich chestnut brown. The lines on her face rippled and rolled away like waves.

Within a matter of just a few minutes, the transformation was done. Peter stood, looking to be about twenty years old, feeling the hair on his face in astonishment and looking at Wendy. She appeared to be just a little older, perhaps twenty-three or twenty-four.

Margaret, still holding Wendy's hand, looked up at the beautiful young woman and said doubtfully, "Grandma?"

"It's your second chance," Alice said. "You can be who you might have been. Or not," she said, giving Peter a bit of the mushroom Wendy had taken that had made her young again, and giving Wendy a piece of the bit that had aged Peter. "You can always go back to the way you were."

Alice sat back on her heels to see what would happen. Wendy and Peter continued to look at each other in silence and wonder for a few more minutes.

Although neither spoke, it was clear to both Alice and Dorothy that something profound was happening. Finally, Wendy handed the thimble to Peter. He took it gravely, and pulled an acorn button from his pocket and handed it to her.

Wendy scooped Margaret up in her arms. She turned to Dorothy and Alice and said, "Peter and I need to discuss a few things privately. You will excuse us. Margaret, darling, you will come with us."

Peter nodded decisively, as if this was his idea all along. He took Wendy's hand, and the three of them walked off and disappeared down a small path.

CHAPTER FIFTY-TWO

THE NEVERLAND AWAKENS

Alice and Dorothy watched as Peter, Wendy, and Margaret walked along the path that wound towards the back of the lighthouse. Then, a few moments later, they saw three figures fly across the face of the moon and dive down towards the island proper.

Dorothy looked back down at the beach, far below them. Even from the great height, although she could not make out their individual footprints, she could see the disturbance in the white sand below which marked their passage along the beach, ending abruptly at the spot they had flown from.

She looked back to where Peter and Wendy had been standing, and while her eyes could trace their path, there was no trace of their footprints on the cold stone of the cliff. It was as if they had never been there.

The sun was beginning to rise, warming both the light and the temperature. Dorothy looked at Alice, who was still holding the backpack she had managed to grab before their frightful dash to the lighthouse and smiled, "You are quite the Girl Scout," Dorothy said. "Always prepared."

"Actually, I think that is the Boy Scouts," Alice replied. She looked through the pack, to see what provisions they had. "This may take some time," she said. "Perhaps we should explore the lighthouse while we wait."

They walked towards the lighthouse. Up close, it appeared to have been abandoned for some time. Once they entered, however, it was clear that someone had been caring for it and staying here. Dorothy spotted a small cot, with a blanket tossed over it, and a stuffed tiger.

Dorothy seized the blanket. "This is the blanket we saw Margaret sleeping under in the Magic Picture," she exclaimed. "This is where Peter has been keeping her, and it looks like he has been taking good care of her." She turned and pointed to a small table, which was set with rough-hewn wooden dishes. There were fruits and nuts and a scattering of leaves. Dorothy picked up the stuffed tiger and said with exasperation, "Must there be cats everywhere?"

"Yes, there must," Alice replied. They continued to explore the lighthouse. There was nothing else of any great interest on the lower floor, but when they came to the lantern room, at the very top, they found an excellent spyglass, mounted on a pedestal, from which they could view any part of the island in detail.

There was nothing for Dorothy and Alice to do but wait.

And they waited, for almost two days. They spent the time speculating about what Wendy and Peter would do. "For you know," Alice told Dorothy, "With the mushrooms, they could be any age they like."

Wendy and Peter might choose to be the same age. If they did, would Peter choose to become a man, and return with her and Margaret, to a place where he would keep his beard? Or would Wendy choose to become a girl again, and stay here in Neverland with Peter and be the mother of the Lost Boys? Margaret could be the first Lost Girl.

Or Wendy might return to being Wendy Moira Angela Darling Winthrop, grandmother to Margaret, benefactor to lost children everywhere, and Peter could remain in Neverland, an eternal boy, young and heartless as children can be.

They spent several days in wild speculation. Both agreed that they would not leave until Wendy and Margaret returned, but they agreed about little else.

Dorothy was sure that Peter would become the man he was always meant to be. He loved Wendy, that was clear, and Wendy would never raise Margaret on this dangerous and god-forsaken island.

Alice was equally convinced that Peter would never change or mature, and that Wendy would return alone with Margaret, to either resume her very fulfilling life, or perhaps come back a bit younger and have another ride on the merry-go-round.

Either that, or Wendy would stay, become a girl again, and raise Peter and the Lost Boys and the Lost Girl for all time. Alice was pretty sure that Peter was not going to grow up, not even for Wendy, and if she wanted to be with him, this would be the only way.

In addition to the speculation about what Peter and Wendy might decide to do, they passed the time in looking through the spyglass at the island. For the first day, there was not much to see. They did spot the Lost Boys emerging from their underground home, but mostly they seemed to be foraging for food, and nothing of any significance seemed to be happening there.

They were able to spot what looked to be a celebratory gathering of fairies, in a glade of fairy ring mushrooms. It was incredibly beautiful, and it went on for quite some time, well into the evening, but again, nothing of significance seemed to occur.

The women spent the night in the comfort of the lighthouse. The next morning, after breakfasting on bread from the knapsack and on the fruits and nuts found in the pantry, they climbed the stairs to the Lantern room to the spyglass and looked out across the island, searching for signs of Wendy and Peter.

At first, there seemed to be nothing different from what they had observed the night before. There were no signs of Wendy,

Peter, or Margaret, and though they scanned the entire island, nothing seemed to have changed. The Lagoon did appear a little clearer, but other than that, the island was stagnant.

Lunch conversation was disagreeable, as both Dorothy and Alice still had their very opposing views of where Peter and Wendy might end up. Dorothy held fast to her belief that Peter would become a man and go back with Wendy to live as a man, raise Margaret, and perhaps even the current crop of Lost Boys. "He loves her, you see," she explained to Alice.

Alice was equally vehement in her argument. "Peter will never grow up! Why should he? Here, he is a hero, a leader, and has no real responsibilities. Wendy, if she loves him so much, may choose to remain here with him as a girl, for he certainly won't have any grown woman. Or she might finally be able to close the door on this last bit of unfinished business in her extraordinary life and go home and care for her granddaughter and all the other children who depend on her charitable foundation."

The argument was interrupted by a loud noise, something like and yet not like an explosion. Both women rushed to the lighthouse and up the stairs to the spyglass.

Dorothy, younger and stronger, reached the spyglass first. She looked out over the island. The forest was now lush with new foliage. Winged lizard-like creatures (dragons?) were emerging from the lagoon. On the far side of the island, it looked as if a long dormant volcano was becoming active. The island was undergoing a sudden and fabulous transformation. It had seemed half-dead when they arrived, but now it was crowded with life and adventure.

Alice, huffing and puffing a bit, entered the lantern room. "What is happening?" she cried.

"The island!" cried Dorothy. "It's coming alive!"

"Do you see Peter and Wendy?" Alice asked anxiously.

"No," Dorothy replied. Alice pushed her aside and looked through the spyglass. The island was indeed awakening. There were dolphins in the surf, dragons circling overhead, and on the beach, a group of people Alice could not identify. Although she was sure they were not Lost Boys, they were doing some sort of dance. It did not look peaceful.

The forest rippled as if a strong wind had passed over it, and a great flock of birds rose into the sky.

Most of the birds circled, dove, and disappeared into the forest, but one bird took a different course. It wheeled round and headed directly for the lighthouse.

CHAPTER FIFTY-THREE
A MESSAGE

The women ran down the stairs and stood in the doorway. The Bird alighted, and they could see that it was holding something in its beak. It was no bird they knew, although it most closely resembled a flamingo, but with a distinct bluish color. Alice gave an involuntary shudder.

The Bird cocked its head and looked at them inquisitively. Then it shook its beak in a significant manner, as if to say, "Come on, now, I haven't got all day."

The squabbles over lunch forgotten, each woman reached for the other's hand. They felt that they were on the edge of something. Together, they stepped towards the Bird, which trotted forward to meet them, prancing in the most comical manner, although neither was in the mood for amusement at that moment.

Dorothy held out her hand, and the Bird dropped the object onto her upturned palm. Then, with a joyful crow, it turned around, leapt into the air, and flew off.

Dorothy and Alice looked down at the Bird's delivery. It was a large leaf, tied up with grass into a sort of package. Dorothy fumbled for a few minutes to untie the package without damaging the leaf. At last, the package opened, and inside were Peter's thimble and the acorn Wendy had worn around her neck. The leaf was thick and fleshy, and someone had scratched a note upon its surface.

"Dear, dear friends" it read. "I cannot thank you both enough for all your help. Peter and I are so grateful that we each send you a kiss. Peter, Margaret, and I are safe and happy. I won't be going back with you, for our paths lead elsewhere. Go home, be well and happy, and know that I will always think of you. Margaret and I, and Peter too, are in your debt, for at last we have been able to complete what we started. Do not look for us. I love you both, Wendy."

They both stood, silent and wondering. "Are we to leave now?" asked Alice.

Dorothy replied, "No, we should stay. We should still wait."

As they spoke, the sky had begun to darken with clouds. The wind had picked up speed, and the two of them felt suddenly exposed. A shaft of lightning appeared and struck the ground uncomfortably near them.

They turned back to the lighthouse, intending to seek shelter there. But in the few moments they had been with the Bird, the lighthouse had undergone a transformation like the rest of the island. It had been a bit shabby, but still a habitable and cozy place when they first arrived. Now, it looked ruined, stones crumbling off the walls, and more alarming, a spectral seaman, pale and ghostly, now blocked the entrance.

"The lighthouse has become haunted!" Alice cried. "It's another adventure coming to life for the island."

The Neverland had indeed awakened and readied itself for another round of adventures. Dorothy and Alice had no business in those adventures, so the island was rather forcefully encouraging them to leave before the excitement began. The downpour began with all the fury of a tropical storm.

Dorothy threw her arms around Alice and clicked her heels together. "Oz, Oz, Oz!" she cried over the roar of thunder.

CHAPTER FIFTY-FOUR

THERE'S NO PLACE LIKE HOME

They arrived in Oz, wet and cold, but none the worse for the journey. Ozma was there, as was Glinda, once again in her radiant white sorceress's gown. Glinda's red-gold hair curled around her face and lay in ringlets across her shoulders, almost unrecognizable from when they last saw her as the Gnome King's mother. She was holding the Magic Picture with a worried frown on her wise and beautiful face.

Ozma rushed forward and embraced Dorothy, not caring that Dorothy's damp and dirty clothes would spoil her royal garments. "We had just checked the Picture and saw you in the fiercest storm!" she exclaimed. "I am so relieved you made it back safely! But where is Wendy?"

Glinda arose, holding the Magic Picture. "Welcome back, my children," she said to them, kissing them each on the forehead. "We have been keeping our eyes on you through the Magic Picture, as we promised. However, for almost two days now I have not been able to see your friend. I've tried every enchantment I can think of, but she remains hidden to me, as does her granddaughter and the boy Peter. I am at a loss."

Alice removed from her lab coat pocket the note the Bird had delivered to them, along with the acorn and thimble. The note had been dusted lightly with a few mushroom spores, which had remained in Alice's pocket. "This is our last communication from Wendy," she said.

Dorothy started to tell Glinda all that had happened between Peter and Wendy, but Glinda gently placed a finger across her lips to quiet her. "No need to recount your tale", she said. "These will tell me."

Glinda took the objects and examined them gravely. When she saw the mushroom dust, she cocked her head, gave Alice a sidelong glance, arched an eyebrow, but said nothing.

She walked over to the great fireplace in the easternmost corner of the throne room and placed a green silk cloth over the hearth. Glinda then laid the objects out before her on the cloth, closed her eyes, and passed her hands over them three times. The letter, acorn, and thimble rose in the air and hovered before her face. She opened her eyes and watched as they danced slowly before her. Finally, they returned to rest on the green silk, and Glinda folded them up into the cloth and handed it back to Alice.

Glinda reached out, and with each hand touched the cheek of each woman. "You have done well," she told them. "You have been on a perilous and beautiful journey and were brave, resourceful, and kind. You have succeeded! Wendy is reunited with her granddaughter Margaret, and they are safe and well and happy. You are not meant to know any more, and you shall not, at least for now." Again, she kissed each on her forehead.

Ozma stepped forward. "And Dorothy, you and your friends have cured the Scarecrow and saved all of Oz once more! Won't you stay now, and live with us forever?" Ozma turned to Alice. "Invitations to settle in Oz are exceedingly rare, but this is a rare occasion. Should you choose, you would also be welcome to stay with us here. You are both Heroines of Oz!"

Alice replied first. "Thank you, I am honored. But I think I should return to my work. I know that I shall do a better job because of this experience. However, if I may, I would like to remain here for a few weeks and do Oz a service that I believe I am particularly qualified to do."

"Of course," Ozma replied. She turned to Dorothy. "Oh please, do stay! You are like a sister to me, and it is clear, Oz will always need its Heroines."

Dorothy hesitated, tears beginning to creep out of the corners of her eyes. "Oh, I love you all so much! But I have lived elsewhere for twenty years, although it doesn't seems like that for you. I don't know what to do. As Alice, I mean Dr. Liddell, has said, we have valuable work to do there. Must I decide immediately?"

"Of course not," Ozma replied. "You may stay for as long or as short as you like. But since Dr. Liddell is staying a few weeks, perhaps you would like to stay and visit all your old friends? Glinda and I shall be taking a tour through all the Counties…Gillikin, Winkie, Munchkin, and Quadling, to make sure that there are no remaining threats from the Gnome King and to undo any mischief he has done."

Dorothy readily agreed to this plan, for she was longing to see all her old friends, and to visit with her Uncle Henry and Aunt Em. "They always used to say I grew like a weed. Won't they be surprised now to see how I've grown?"

On her grand tour of Oz, Dorothy was reunited with many old friends, including Jack Pumpkinhead, the Patchwork Girl, and Rinkitink. She also helped Glinda and Ozma to undo all of Ruggedo's evils.

Meanwhile, back in the Emerald City, Alice took on the therapy and rehabilitation of the evil Gnome King. He had refused all offers of help and thwarted all the tricks to get him to drink the Water of Forgetfulness again, which actually suited Alice's purposes.

She spent weeks doing what she did best, helping Ruggedo understand the root causes of his evil impulses and how to think and behave differently. By the time Dorothy returned from her travels, he was a changed Gnome.

Dorothy and Alice were both still troubled that they did not know what had happened between Peter and Wendy. Dorothy had decided to split her time between Oz and our world, and Alice promised to make a return visit every now and again to make sure the Gnome was not slipping back into his old ways, and to visit with Ruby the kitten, who had become so fond of talking that she did not want to return to a place where she could only mew.

The time had come for them to go home once more. They did not use the silver shoes, but instead Glinda transported them to Wendy's room, just a few moments after they had first been pulled through the mirror.

CHAPTER FIFTY-FIVE

ENDINGS

The two women looked around the plain hospital room. The mirror was clouded, and through the cloudy glass they saw the fading images of their own selves, walking into the garden. The mirror cleared rapidly, leaving them alone.

Alice suggested that they leave the room immediately and allow Wendy's disappearance to be discovered later. They would both be questioned, but it seemed likely that it would be considered an escape. And perhaps in a few days or weeks, Wendy might return, either as her old self or perhaps as her young self with Peter. They quietly slipped out of the room and walked to Alice's office to work on their story together.

When they came to Alice's office, Michael Darling was still there. After a quick and understanding exchange of glances, they related all that had happened. He listened solemnly, nodding from time to time, his eyes watering at times. Then Alice gave him the note, the acorn, and the thimble.

"Thank you," he said. "I hope that I will hear from my sister soon, but even if I do not, I am so glad to know that she and Margaret are safe and happy. And I will ensure that neither you nor this institution will suffer either financially or by reputation as a result of my sister's disappearance." He hugged them both, a great bear hug with one arm encircling Alice and the other Dorothy. Finally, he broke off the embrace and murmured, "This may be a bit difficult to explain to John," as he left the office.

EPILOGUE

What did Peter and Wendy decide to do? Alice and Dorothy never found out for certain, although conflicting clues crossed their paths in the ensuing months.

Michael was true to his word and kept to the story that his sister had most likely left the hospital of her own accord, and as she had been past the crisis, the family was sure she would turn up soon.

Shortly afterwards, he let it be known that his sister, and his niece were staying with him at an undisclosed location, and were doing well, but wished to be left to their privacy, as Mrs. Winthrop was retiring from her public and charity work. Michael Darling assumed leadership of the Foundation in his sister's stead.

Alice and Dorothy immediately contacted Michael Darling to find out whether it was true or was just a cover to explain Wendy and Margaret's disappearance. They were less than satisfied with his answer.

"I can't say it is true," he had replied to their inquiries. Dorothy and Alice debated between themselves. "Does this mean it isn't true, or does it mean that he can't say it's true?" Dorothy asked.

"I don't know," Alice replied. "But did you notice that he didn't ask us whether we had heard from her? Because if it's true, or if he has heard from her, he wouldn't need to ask us."

Mr. Darling gave them no other clues. As the weeks passed, Dorothy thought she spotted a young couple with a small girl walking far ahead of her on a path in the park. The little girl threw back her head and gave forth a loud crowing noise. As the man and woman turned to each other and laughed, she thought their profiles looked like Peter and Wendy and she ran to catch up, but they turned round a corner and by the time she got there, they were nowhere in sight.

Talking to Alice afterwards, Dorothy said, "It might have been them, but I can't be sure."

Alice replied, "No, you can't. We want to see them everywhere. Just last week, I went to see Michael Darling again, and while I was waiting outside his office, I was sure I could hear him talking to someone. It sounded like an older woman, and I am sure I heard a child laugh. But no one came out, and when I was allowed in, he was alone. I asked him again if he had heard from his sister, and he replied, 'I can't say that I have, honestly.' I mean, that could just be his way of talking, or it could be his way of being as honest as he can."

Later that month, Alice had a new patient, a little girl who claimed that a boy flew into her room each night and hid behind the curtains to hear her mother's stories. The description of the boy was too vague to confirm that it was Peter. It might just as easily have been one of the Lost Boys. Alice was sure that if Peter had left the Neverland, the one called Rascal would soon take the lead.

I wish I could say that after their adventures, Alice and Dorothy became the best of friends, but they did not. They were, after all, so very different. Their bond was deeper than friendship. They had developed a deep respect and love for each other, having learned to appreciate their differences during their adventures, and they were bonded in their ongoing love and concern for Wendy.

One day, some months after their adventure, they were lunching together at an outdoor café at the edge of the park.

"I don't think we will ever know," said Alice.

Dorothy nodded and sipped her tea. Suddenly she looked across the park and spotted what might be the couple and child she had seen months before. She leapt up and pointed at them, preparing to run.

Alice pulled her down. "It might be them, or it might not. That might have been Peter in my patient's room, or it might not. Michael Darling might be telling the truth, or he might not. It doesn't matter. Peter and Wendy were given a second chance, to be together however they wanted to be, or not to be together, but to be whoever they wanted to be. I have faith that they chose well and are now at peace with their choices. It was clear that neither had been content with their decisions made long ago. We must let it go and believe."

Dorothy sat down and smiled, "Dr. Liddell," she said. "This is so uncharacteristic of you, or at least the 'you' I knew before our adventure."

"Yes," Alice replied with a Cheshire cat smile, reaching into her lab coat to stroke the small grey kitten nestled inside, "I suppose it is."

THE END